Praise for the Noble Dead Saga
by Barb and J. C. Hendee

"A mix of *The Lord of the Rings* [...]
—*New York Times* bestselling author Kevin J. Anderson

Child of a Dead God

"Readers who love vampire novels will appreciate the full works of Barb and J. C. Hendee as they consistently provide some of the genre's best. . . . The audience will want to read this novel in one sitting."   —*Midwest Book Review*

"An adventure-type fantasy, of epic nature, with lots of bloody scenes and characters full of personality and imagination . . . much like *The Lord of the Rings*. . . . A great adult-look at the world of dhampirs, and the always constant battle, in any world, between good and evil."   —*MyShelf.com*

"The Hendees have become true masters of character and world building. This is a fast-paced, action- and adventure-filled dark fantasy . . . fabulous dark fantasy world."   —*SciFiChick.com*

"Complex and bloody. . . . Interspecies distrust, grand ambitions, and the lure of dangerous secrets protected by the undead drive the action in this neat mix of horror with more traditional fantasy elements."   —*Publishers Weekly*

"Fantasy and magic blend with vampire lore in another spellbinding story in the Noble Dead series. This may be book six, but new readers will get caught up quickly. Brilliantly conceived characters face danger and inner conflict in a vividly imagined world that's full of violence and gore. Readers will be on the edge of their seats."   —*Romantic Times*

Rebel Fay

"A tale of ancient enmities, long-standing treacheries, and a hidden evil . . . peopled . . . with fascinatingly complex characters."
—*Library Journal*

"Entertaining . . . a hybrid crossing Tolkienesque fantasy with vampire-infused horror . . . intriguing."   —*Publishers Weekly*

"A real page-turner."   —*Booklist*

continued . . .

Traitor to the Blood

"A rousing and sometimes creepy fantasy adventure . . . this is one of those books for which the term 'dark fantasy' was definitely intended." —*Chronicle*

"There is a lot of intrigue in *Traitor to the Blood,* which is one of the reasons it is so hard to put down. . . . Readers will eagerly await the next book in this terrific series."

—The Best Reviews

"Winning. . . . Fans of the series are sure to be pleased, while the novel stands well enough on its own to attract new readers." —*Publishers Weekly*

"A unique tale of vampires and half-vampire undead hunters set against a dark fantasy world ruled by tyrants. The personal conflicts of the heroes mirror the larger struggles in their world and provide a solid foundation for this tale of love and loyalty in a world of betrayal." —*Library Journal*

Sister of the Dead

"A spellbinding work that is creative and addicting."
—*Midwest Book Review*

"A treat." —*SFRevu*

"[A] wonderful addition to the Noble Dead series. . . . *Sister of the Dead* leads us on an amazing adventure that will keep you engrossed until the final chapter. . . . This is a series that will appeal to both horror and fantasy fans." —*SF Site*

"The Hendees continue their intelligent dark fantasy series by cleverly interweaving the sagas and personal demons of their heroes with rousing physical battles against the forces of evil. Much more than a medieval 'Buffy does the Dark Ages,' *Sister of the Dead* and its predecessors involve readers on a visceral, highly emotional level and fulfill a craving for nifty magic, exciting action scenes, and a strong heroine who defies genre clichés."
—*Romantic Times* (4 stars)

Thief of Lives

"Readers will turn the pages of this satisfying medieval thriller with gusto." —*Booklist*

"Fans of Anita Blake will enjoy this novel. The characters are cleverly drawn so that the several supernatural species that play key roles in the plot seem natural and real. Supernatural fantasy readers will enjoy this action-packed strong tale because vampires, sorcerers, dhampirs, elves, fey-canines, and other ilk seem real." —*Midwest Book Review*

"*Thief of Lives* takes the whole vampire-slayer mythos and moves it into an entirely new setting. The world the Hendees create is . . . a mixture of pre-Victorian with a small slice of eastern Europe flavor. . . . Magiere and Leesil are a really captivating pair. . . . [The Hendees] handle the ideas and conventions inherent in vampires really well. While, thanks to the clever setting and characters, they make it feel like a very different twist on the subject." —*SF Site*

"The Hendees unveil new details economically and with excellent timing, while maintaining a taut sexual tension between Magiere and Leesil. The multifaceted personalities of these two are what make this series so enjoyable. The mysteries . . . add texture and depth." —*SFX Magazine*

Dhampir

"*Dhampir* maintains a high level of excitement through interesting characters, both heroes and villains, colliding in well-written action scenes. Instead of overloading us with their world building and the maps and glossaries typical of so much fantasy, the Hendees provide well-rounded characters that go a lot further than maps in making a lively fantasy world." —*The Denver Post*

"An engaging adventure that is both humorous and exciting." —*New York Times* bestselling author Kevin J. Anderson

"Take Anita Blake, vampire hunter, and drop her into a standard fantasy world and you might end up with something like this exciting first novel. . . . A well-conceived imagined world, some nasty villains, and a very engaging hero move this one into the winner's column." —*Chronicle*

"An altogether compelling and moving work. . . . These are characters and a world worthy of exploration." —*Hellnotes*

By Barb and J. C. Hendee

The Noble Dead Saga—Series One

Dhampir
Thief of Lives
Sister of the Dead
Traitor to the Blood
Rebel Fay
Child of a Dead God

The Noble Dead Saga—Series Two

In Shade and Shadow

BLOOD MEMORIES

A VAMPIRE MEMORIES NOVEL

BARB HENDEE

A ROC BOOK

ROC

Published by New American Library, a division of
Penguin Group (USA) Inc., 375 Hudson Street,
New York, New York 10014, USA
Penguin Group (Canada), 90 Eglinton Avenue East, Suite 700, Toronto,
Ontario M4P 2Y3, Canada (a division of Pearson Penguin Canada Inc.)
Penguin Books Ltd., 80 Strand, London WC2R 0RL, England
Penguin Ireland, 25 St. Stephen's Green, Dublin 2,
Ireland (a division of Penguin Books Ltd.)
Penguin Group (Australia), 250 Camberwell Road, Camberwell, Victoria 3124,
Australia (a division of Pearson Australia Group Pty. Ltd.)
Penguin Books India Pvt. Ltd., 11 Community Centre, Panchsheel Park,
New Delhi - 110 017, India
Penguin Group (NZ), 67 Apollo Drive, Rosedale, North Shore 0632,
New Zealand (a division of Pearson New Zealand Ltd.)
Penguin Books (South Africa) (Pty.) Ltd., 24 Sturdee Avenue,
Rosebank, Johannesburg 2196, South Africa

Penguin Books Ltd., Registered Offices:
80 Strand, London WC2R 0RL, England

Published by Roc, an imprint of New American Library, a division of Penguin
Group (USA) Inc. Previously published in a Roc trade paperback edition.

First Roc Mass Market Printing, October 2009
10 9 8 7 6 5 4 3 2 1

Copyright © Barb Hendee, 1998, 2008
All rights reserved

Roc REGISTERED TRADEMARK—MARCA REGISTRADA

Printed in the United States of America

Without limiting the rights under copyright reserved above, no part of this
publication may be reproduced, stored in or introduced into a retrieval system,
or transmitted, in any form, or by any means (electronic, mechanical, photo-
copying, recording, or otherwise), without the prior written permission of both
the copyright owner and the above publisher of this book.

PUBLISHER'S NOTE
This is a work of fiction. Names, characters, places, and incidents either are the
product of the author's imagination or are used fictitiously, and any resemblance to actual persons, living or dead, business establishments, events, or lo-
cales is entirely coincidental.
    The publisher does not have any control over and does not assume any re-
sponsibility for author or third-party Web sites or their content.

If you purchased this book without a cover you should be aware that this book
is stolen property. It was reported as "unsold and destroyed" to the publisher
and neither the author nor the publisher has received any payment for this
"stripped book."

The scanning, uploading, and distribution of this book via the Internet or via
any other means without the permission of the publisher is illegal and punish-
able by law. Please purchase only authorized electronic editions, and do not
participate in or encourage electronic piracy of copyrighted materials. Your
support of the author's rights is appreciated.

For J. C. and Elaine, who never quite got the hang of people, but always save lost kittens from the rain.

chapter 1

I was with Edward the day he killed himself.

It happens to us sometimes, especially the old, the ones who've lost the joy of then and can't quite grasp the now. I don't know why. But I'd never seen it until that morning Edward jumped off his own front porch and exploded in the sun like a gas fire.

We'd been friends for a long time. I know everyone else thought we were mad for living in the same city. But he stayed out of my hunting territory, and I stayed out of his. Besides, sometimes it was nice to talk to someone without lying.

I was on my way out at about two o'clock that morning when the phone rang.

"Hello."

"Eleisha, it's me. I wanted to tell you good-bye."

He'd never called me before, but Edward's accent combined traces of a British accent with a New York pace. I'd have known it anywhere.

"What do you mean, good-bye?"

"This house is bright and loud," he whispered. "I don't think I can live here anymore."

That didn't make sense. He'd been in the same house since 1937.

"Did you buy a new place? Do you need me to help you move?"

"No. That wouldn't help. One place is the same as another. I don't belong now, Eleisha. A new house would be worse."

Something in his calm whisper frightened me, like tiny invisible fingers digging under my skin.

"Edward, stay there. I'm coming over."

"Do you think that will help? I don't think so."

"Just stay there."

Money isn't really a problem for me, so neither are traffic tickets . . . although attracting police under any condition is a bad idea. But not caring who pulled me over, I hit ninety on the freeway that night driving to Edward's. I just couldn't see him freaking out. He wasn't the type. We'd both been warned about time adjustments, but he did all the right things: read contemporary magazines, updated his wardrobe, and saved a collection of personal items from the past to keep his history intact.

Everything.

I tended to interact a lot more with the general populace than he did. He might have been a bit of a recluse, but not to the point of being unusual. He even took occasional trips back to Manhattan or London just to unwind.

When I pulled up to the house, the music of his Tchaikovsky album was pouring out the windows at max volume, loud enough to wake the neighbors. Thinking about his albums made me remember I'd been buying him CDs for the past five years and he never played them.

"Turn it down," I said, slipping through his front door, "before some pissed-off housewife calls the cops."

"Eleisha," he said, smiling. "What are you doing here?"

I almost backed up when he stepped onto the soft carpet of the front hallway. Dressed in an old pair of sweatpants—and nothing else—he looked half starved, with blue-black circles under both eyes.

"Edward, what are . . . ? What's wrong with you?"

"Wrong? Nothing. I've been cooking. Do you remember cooking? I went shopping last night and found a leg of mutton in the meat department at Safeway. Can you believe it? In this cultural wasteland? A leg of mutton?"

I felt cold. "Jesus, have you been trying to eat?"

"Cooking. Cooking is a lost art."

He looked about thirty-three, with mink-brown hair and dark green, bloodshot eyes. I'd never seen the whites of his eyes completely clear. He loved simple pleasures and elitist luxuries like imported tobacco and suits from Savile Row. People were attracted to him because he played the perfect, sweet, vogue, vague snob. He was the sanest vampire I'd ever known.

"What did you eat?" No wonder he was sick.

"Come and see."

"Turn the stereo down first."

The smell from the kitchen nauseated me. Looking through the bar-styled doors, I saw what he'd been doing, and I'd never felt so lost.

A dead Doberman lay on the table, dried blood crusted on its black and brown muzzle. Three decomposing cats had been thrown into a heap of rotting vegetables on the counter. He'd also been shopping. There were brown Safeway bags strewn all over the floor. I couldn't take it all in at once: cartons of spoiled milk, broken lightbulbs, whole fryer chickens, mashed potatoes, and dirty dishes. Streaks of dried blood smeared the walls.

He pushed past me and picked up a grocery bag.

"Paper or plastic?" He smiled.

I grabbed it out of his hand. "We've got to clean this up. What if somebody comes in here when you're asleep? Are you listening to me? What do you think will happen if someone sees this? They'll think you've lost it."

"I have lost it, baby." He fell into his uptown cool routine. "So have you. Just two little productive members of society, aren't we? Keeping the population down. You know, I've been thinking we might move to China. They could certainly use us there."

"Stop it. You're scaring me."

"Really? We can't have that, now can we?"

My kind has no doctors or lawyers or psychologists to help us. We don't have group therapy for undeads who slip out of reality. I remember feeling angry at myself because I didn't know what to do. How bad off was he? Would he get better?

I handed back his grocery bag and pushed the hair out of his eyes. "Don't take this out on me. Let's just clean up this mess and go hunting. We haven't been hunting together since that New Year's Eve party at the Red Lion in 'seventy-eight."

That was a great party. Edward always looked hot in a black tux.

"Can't," he whispered.

"What do you mean, you can't? You have to feed."

"I can't. I don't want to."

"Okay, then come and stay with me and William for a few months. Maybe you're spending too much time alone."

William is an old man who lives with me. I'll talk more about him later.

"And then what?" He dropped the bag and looked straight at me through his cold, green, bloodshot eyes. "A few months? Hardly worth noticing to someone like you, is it? Nothing would change in the world around us besides the skirt length in Paris and Tom Cruise finding his next wife. What happens in ten years? Twenty? I see the same face every day when I look in the mirror. It never changes."

"I know. You just have to deal with it."

"Don't you get tired of seeing the same face every day?"

"Sometimes."

He smiled again and picked up a butcher knife lying by the dead cats. "I could change it for you. But that wouldn't matter either, would it? You'd look the same in a week, so it wouldn't do you any good, unless I cut your head off."

I backed up. "Do you want me to leave?"

"I don't care what you do."

"Fine. You stay here in this pig pit and talk to yourself. But you'd better get it together and clean this mess up by morning, or it's going to stink and get some nosy neighbor poking around in your stuff."

"By morning it won't matter," he whispered.

I turned back to him in frustration. "Edward, what's wrong? Let's just get out of here. Let's go to my place."

"No, it's too late . . . I'm sick of it all, Lady Leisha."

He hadn't called me that in over a hundred years. It was a nickname he'd picked for me when I first stepped off the boat from Wales in 1839, looking like a frightened, half-drowned mouse. He'd been so nice to me back then.

Softly grasping his wrist, I pulled him down to a crouched position on the floor. "Talk to me."

"Do you remember church? I don't mean the religion itself, but how we used to wonder about death?"

"I remember, but I don't think about it very often. Should we?"

He pushed me back against the bloody kitchen wall, and then he lay down on the floor with his head in my lap. I wrapped my arms around him, and his butcher knife clattered harmlessly onto the checkerboard linoleum.

"You're going to kill yourself, aren't you?"

"I'm tired," he whispered.

"Don't do it."

He didn't answer, and we just sat there like that, not saying anything until five thirty, when I saw streaks of light peeping through the eastern sky.

I tried lifting him. "We've got to get underground."

He crawled to his feet but didn't head toward the cellar door. Instead he walked into the living room and restarted the Tchaikovsky album at max volume. *Francesca da Rimini* screamed out the front windows.

I panicked.

"Stop it! Turn it off. We've got to get below."

Looking back now, I think he wanted the neighbors to complain. He wanted someone to find what he'd been doing in the house. He wanted the police to show up, and I never did understand why.

But my stomach lurched when the blue and red flashing lights pulled up in front of his house.

Grabbing his shoulder, I tried pulling him toward the cellar door. He threw me off easily and looked at me with something close to contempt. "We don't really live forever, baby. We just cheat for a while."

Rays from the morning sun filtered in through the living room window and touched the carpet. Two policemen and a tall, blond guy in faded Levi's were walking up Edward's front lawn. The whole world shifted into slow motion as he kissed my forehead and started running toward the door.

Nothing could have stopped him. As his half-naked form burst out onto the front porch, screaming like an animal in pain, one of the cops pulled a gun. I just stood there.

He loved imported tobacco and Savile Row suits. He loved sitting by the hearth and playing chess. He loved dancing at midnight and watching Monty Python films. He loved Sir Arthur Conan Doyle novels. He looked hot in a black tux. The sanest vampire I'd ever known.

He was on fire before his feet hit the grass. Both uniformed cops jumped back, and the guy in Levi's just stood his ground, staring—like me. I had to go, to run before somebody spotted me, but I stayed frozen by the window watching as Edward sank down in a burning heap on the lawn. He had once told me what happens when we die. At the time I hadn't believed him.

It hit me like a wall falling down, almost visible. The psychic energy of a thousand lives burst from Edward's mind like prisoners fleeing their cage. I saw a thousand deaths, a thousand lives lost. The terror and anger and pain cut through me in an unstoppable flow. The carpet rushed up, and I lay there writhing until the pain faded. Edward had told me that only others of our kind would feel this agony . . . this release, and would know that one of us had passed over.

Poor Edward.

Fear and instinct pushed me up onto all fours.

The police would be calling for backup or entering the house on their own any second. But while crawling toward the cellar, I heard someone else screaming, and I forced myself to look back outside. The light hurt my eyes. The guy in jeans was rolling on the ground, holding his head.

Something touched my mind, something alien—not Edward. It was the blond man on the ground, frightened and suffering. I could feel him, see the scattered, disoriented terror running through him. But he was mortal. He shouldn't have felt anything.

The house. What would they learn when they searched the house? I looked about wildly for anything to take with me. I'd never been awake this late. My eyes burned, and my legs were weak. Edward's personal address book lay under the phone. I grabbed it and stumbled for the cellar door, looking back only once at the large, framed photograph of myself hanging over his fireplace.

chapter 2

My eyes opened to darkness. Like an infallible clock, my internal second hand woke me precisely at twelve minutes past sundown. In our inverted world, this almost physical connection to time was a blessing and a curse—or that's what Edward once told me. He never liked his world to be too regulated.

Edward.

I lay on his mattress.

He had divided his cellar into four dingy storage rooms, with no soft carpets or velvet furniture, not even linoleum—just aging floorboards. Most of us keep mementos of past time periods, reminding us to flow and change and evolve with each new generation. Edward had never purchased a bed, though, and he had been sleeping on a sheetless Posturepedic mattress for years. That old folktale about coffins is a lie. I'd get claustrophobic.

Like projections against a blank wall, images from that morning flashed before me: his face, hair, and fingers bursting into flames. Had it hurt? Did death hurt us? I couldn't mourn him yet, or I'd get lost inside myself, and survival always outranks emotion.

What had happened while I slept?

The police had probably searched the house from floor to ceiling. The tiny space I now occupied was hidden behind an invisible door in the west wall. At least they hadn't found me.

Listening for a full minute, I heard nothing. I pushed on the sliding panel once to release it.

Empty room.

Odd smell, sweet and musty.

Was it floating down from the mess in his kitchen? God, what had the cops thought of that? Slipping Edward's address book inside my jacket, I stepped out to find the stench growing stronger, and to see a pile of torn-up floorboards. They'd torn the floor up? Why? Rotting shards of wood and fresh, uneven piles of dirt lay all around me.

Then I noticed a small, gray-white spot in the dirt and leaned down to look closer. It was a bone, part of an index finger.

"No."

My mind couldn't accept the implication. We disposed of bodies, dumped off or disguised, as far from ourselves as possible—meaningless dried husks no longer connected to us. Had he been carrying corpses home or luring live victims into his house and draining them here? A madman. Two facts shone brightly through this haze. First, he'd been sliding in and out of reality long before last night, and second . . . this situation was far from over.

How many bodies had they found? The authorities

would probably consider Edward a psycho killer who'd finally lost it and committed suicide.

Maybe they were right.

It was all a matter of perspective. But right now, the whole sordid story was being aired on the evening news.

I had to get out of the house.

Apparently, the police had removed the bodies. In fact, they'd gutted the entire basement. I kicked up cold, loose dirt running for the stairs. The upper floor was a shambles, but nothing seemed to have been removed yet. However, I didn't stop for inventory and moved straight for the front door.

And there, parked right in front of the house, in all its bright red glory, was my main concern. Since I'd been trapped inside all day, my little Mazda had been just sitting there for the police to go over with a fine-tooth comb.

I looked up and down the street. Well . . . other cars were parked nearby, so perhaps they'd run a check on all of them.

In any event, it was likely the authorities had done a search on my license plate by now and located my name and address. Bastards.

Managing to keep the needle under sixty all the way home was difficult, but getting pulled over could have been a tragedy.

William had been home alone all this time. Fear and anger surfaced slowly through my numb layers of skin. The house we lived in was perfect: back in the trees, high fence, deep basement, few neighbors—and private ones at that. Now we were going to have to move.

Where? There wouldn't be time to find us someplace secure or permanent. Whatever I came up with would have to be fast and temporary.

Not bothering to put my car in the garage, I ran up the outdoor steps and through our back door.

"William?"

The interior wasn't exactly gothic. Our kitchen was actually quite cheery in spite of the fact that we didn't use it for much, decorated in soft yellow tones. I'd bought the house new back in 1912, but it had undergone several major renovations since then. Keeping up normal appearances was an art that Edward had drilled into my head nearly a hundred and seventy years ago.

A tall, wrinkled old man shuffled in, wearing brown trousers and a faded burgundy smoking jacket. Silver hair hung past his shoulders with tiny dry wisps floating now and then across his narrow face. Veins in his hands, once blue, lay flat and purple beneath flesh so dry it crackled at contact with anything else. Milky white eyes gazed out at me in hurt confusion.

"You weren't here for dinner last night. Left me hungry," he said.

"I'm sorry, William. We have to move again. Edward Claymore killed himself this morning, and the police found bodies in his cellar. They'll be looking for people to question."

"Have you called Julian?"

Sometimes William surprised me with a flash of memory or clarity of thought.

"No," I answered. "We have enough money to relocate. I'll call him once we're settled." Explaining all this to Julian was going to be a nightmare. I'd put it off as long as possible.

William's momentary comprehension faded. His eyebrows knitted slightly. "What about dinner?"

"Of course." I pulled a kitchen chair out for him. "Just sit down, and we'll fix you up."

Rows of rabbit hutches lined the back of our house. A large part of my job was caring for these small creatures that nourished William. He'd always been too weak to absorb human life force.

When I came back in, he was sitting in his chair, waiting. After covering his clothes with a large tablecloth, I held a struggling brown rabbit up to his mouth. He bit down through soft fur and drained the animal until it stopped kicking and fell limp in my hands. He smiled slightly with blood smeared all over his mouth and began pulling at the tablecloth.

"Hang on," I said. "Let me wipe your face first."

He was surprisingly careful about his appearance, in spite of the fact that no one ever saw him except me.

Most other vampires are obsessed with beauty and perfection, and so William made them uneasy. Edward couldn't stand the sight of him and often remarked about what a horrible lot I had. "Julian is a pig, pushing his responsibility off on you," he used to say. Of course, he never said it to Julian's face. Edward may have been cynical, but he wasn't stupid.

My old charge was one of a kind. He couldn't hunt or protect himself. Edward had been wrong about my lot, though. I loved William's sweet, wrinkled face and honestly didn't mind taking care of him. It gave me something to do.

After cleaning him up, I took him into the study and built a fire. Then I brought him some small blocks of wood, a knife, sandpaper, and paint.

"Could you make us a new set of checkers? I've got to go out and find us a place to stay for a few days. If you make us a new set, we'll have something to do when we get there."

"Will you play with me?" he asked.

"Even let you win."

He smiled and picked up one of the small wood blocks. We had nineteen sets of checkers and two half-finished sets of chess pieces upstairs, but he loved to work with his hands, and I needed something to keep him busy for a few hours.

Hurrying into the bathroom, I looked in the mirror and grimaced.

My face was smeared with dirt, my clothes smelled like dead cats, and my hair was dotted with dried blood flakes from leaning against Edward's kitchen wall. Oh, that story about us not being able to see our own reflection is absurd, too. We're solid. Of course we can see our reflection.

I took a shower, blow-dried my hair, and put on a peach, ankle-length sundress. That's kind of funny, isn't it? A sundress?

William was already settled in the study, so I didn't bother popping back in on him before leaving. Too many intrusions would only confuse him.

I put my car in the garage, as driving it seemed risky. I could just picture some overzealous rookie spotting it and picking me up for questioning. I really don't like cops. Besides, the walk toward downtown Portland is nice.

Portland was a great place for us. Old, but not too old. Vogue, but not too vogue. Decent crime rate, but nothing like New York or Chicago. Plus . . . besides Edward, none of my kind had ever been drawn to set up a home here, which was a good thing. Stepping on someone else's territory could be a real problem for me. I'd get my head ripped off. We all have certain gifts that make survival possible—except for William, of course—but physical strength wasn't one of mine. We don't choose our gifts.

My particular gift has so many advantages that I'm not sure I'd trade it in if I could. As the smell of Portland's downtown air blew gently into my nostrils, I put my talent into motion. Too easy.

The dim light of Mickey's, my favorite bar, glowed off my dress as I walked in the door. I drew my shoulders forward slightly. My wispy blond hair fell down to cover half my face as I assumed a long-accustomed role: fragile and helpless. It never failed.

The dance floor was crowded. Unrecognizable bodies clutched at each other, moving slowly to the sappy lyrics of Journey's "Faithfully." This place was one of my ideal hangouts.

"Eleisha."

A familiar face called to me from the bar, but not the face I'd come looking for. I shifted my features to a frightened, hesitant expression.

"Hi, Derek." I moved up to the bar and to the inside of his stool, as though intimidated by the crowd and the noise. He knew me pretty well—at least in this persona—and put his hand on my waist in a protective gesture.

"Where you been?" he asked. "You ain't been here in weeks."

Derek was okay. I actually thought of him as sort of a friend, as much as he could be. Irish American, with red hair and a short-trimmed beard. Nice guy.

"I came to see Brian. Is he here?"

Derek looked surprised. "Yeah, he's around somewhere. Doesn't strike me as your type."

I flashed him an embarrassed smile. "It's nothing like that. I just need a favor."

"Why didn't you tell me?" He pulled out his wallet. "How much do you need?"

"No, that's not it either."

Lightly, I touched his wrist with the tips of my fingers. The tiny hairs on his arm stood up and his breathing quickened.

"Then what?" he asked. "You never let me do anything for you. You come in here and talk to me and then either leave by yourself or with some loser. I thought we were friends."

"That's why you never leave with me. I need to keep my friends. Find Brian, please."

If this had been anyone but me, he would have spat, "Get lost," and turned back to his beer. But he didn't. His eyes were hurt and confused and bright green like Edward's. Sometimes he actually got to me.

"Okay," he muttered. "Stay here."

I watched him work his way through the crowd, and then I turned to Christopher, the bartender, a pseudointellectual with a master's degree in anthropology.

"What does Brian usually drink?"

"Rum and Coke."

"Get me one of those and a red wine."

He grunted something unintelligible and reached toward the glasses. People here were an odd mix of lower-middle-class folks looking for company and a good time. I hung out here because that particular social level of men is especially susceptible to a pretty, young girl who needs someone to "take care of her." I think it's because they work so hard, and they sometimes just look at their lives and think, "Why am I doing this?" Then they meet some tiny, helpless creature who looks up to them, and they don't stand a chance. It's not really fair, but that's my gift. That's what I was given. I don't like killing. I hate it. There just isn't any other way.

Derek worked his way across the dance floor, followed by a stocky Italian. Relief washed up into my throat. Brian was a perfect mark—an egotistical pig who owned a cheap basement condo on the south side.

I pulled my small body back up against the bar and looked desperate. "Hi, Brian. I ordered you a drink."

He seemed amazed and excited but was trying to play it cool. He'd been hitting on me for months. Pathetic.

"Derek says you want to talk to me?"

"Yeah," I answered quietly, "but it's private."

Christopher, the anthropologist bartender, slammed our glasses down on the bar. Derek looked miserable. Brian paid for the drinks and motioned with his head toward an empty table.

"Over there."

With the sounds of Journey still rolling through my ears, I made a point of following, not leading, Brian to the table.

"What's up?" He was still playing the unshakable uptown boy. Poor thing.

"I'm in some trouble. I need a place to stay for a few days."

His eyes lit up like candles in a dark room. If I had said "weeks" he might have balked. Taking advantage of some frightened girl's situation and letting her sleep in his bed for a few nights was his style. Any longer than that and he'd get bored. Of course, as soon as he unlocked the condo door, I was going to kill him, steal his keys, dump his body, and go get William.

"What kind of trouble?" Brian asked.

Maybe he wasn't so gullible. I crossed my arms as though shivering and stared at a knot in the wooden table.

"I moved in with this guy a few months ago . . . and then he got mean. I just need someplace to stay. Please."

He was almost hooked. "Why not stay with Derek?"

"Because he can't take care of himself like you."

That did it. Catering to the male ego is so easy it sometimes scares me. They lap that shit up like a cat turned loose on a dairy farm.

"Okay." He nodded, and I could see a lecherous-father speech coming on.

I look about seventeen years old, and he looked about twenty-eight, but he was going to warn me about the evils of the world anyway. I had phony ID under six different names. Nobody believed I was twenty-one, not even Christopher, but nobody really cared as long as the ID looked real.

"Listen, Eleisha," Brian began. "You got to watch out for people. Most of the crowd here would eat someone like you for breakfast. You don't just 'move in' with some guy you just met."

I nodded, still staring at the table. Of course, his gallant words wouldn't stop him from coming on to me the minute we were alone.

"Stay here," he said. "Let me get my coat and take you home. Don't worry about anything."

Yeah, right. For about a week.

God, he was a pig. I almost didn't feel sorry for him.

Watching his broad back move through the crowd, I wondered how long it would take me to move William in and get him settled. Since his memory was so short, he had probably already forgotten that Edward was dead and we were in danger. I glanced at my watch: ten forty-five p.m. I'd have to hurry.

What happened next is hard to describe. My mind was drifting in several directions when something touched it. The invasion was not subtle or gradual. It hit me like icy water in a sharp, sudden splash. I lost sight of the table and saw through someone else's eyes. It was definitely a man. I felt the random movements of his thoughts.

Shock.

Confusion.

His name was Wade.

I tried to tear away, but I couldn't get him out of my head. The tabletop shifted into focus, and I looked up. Two men were moving across the room toward me. In stunned fear, I recognized both of them—they had been out on the lawn at Edward's. The tall, blond man leading was the one who'd collapsed from the impact of Edward's psychic life force pouring out. He was Wade.

The stocky man following was a cop. No one here could help me. Not even Derek would get between me and the police.

I bolted for a back door.

Fear kicked my instincts into motion. I slipped through bodies without touching them and ran down the back alley so fast that Wade's thought waves grew faint.

He was running. He had seen me. His partner's name was Dominick. Pictures passed through his head for me to see: bodies in Edward's cellar, the framed photograph of me over the fireplace, and an oil painting of me he'd found in the storage room. The portrait perfectly matched the photograph, but it had been painted in 1872.

How could I have forgotten the painting?

Even knowing I could outrun both of them, I was so panicked I didn't slow down until Wade was gone, until he had completely lost me, and I was no longer tangled in his thoughts.

What was he? How could he push into my head like that? How much had he seen? It couldn't have been much. He'd felt almost as startled as me, his thoughts rapid and scattered.

Now what? Staying at Brian's was out. If Wade had actually tracked me down telepathically . . . How could he?

"We've got to get out of here," I whispered to myself all the way up the back stairs of our house. Simply relocating to another part of Portland wouldn't help us. We'd have to go much farther.

chapter 3

Ten minutes later, I was sitting in a chair by the fire, wondering what to do. William was absorbed in painting the red checkers that he'd carved out but not sanded properly. For the first time in my memory, I wanted him to talk to me, to offer me some sort of advice.

"What are we going to do, William?" I whispered absently, voicing my wish.

"You should call Julian."

His answer surprised me. Not because of the suggestion itself—he always wanted to solve problems by calling Julian—but because he was vaguely aware that we had a situation to deal with.

"We can't call him. If he finds out the police are involved, he'll kill me."

"Then call someone else."

Call someone else? Who? I'm sure that I would have remembered Edward's address book sooner or later, but William's suggestion jolted it to the front of my thoughts. Why had Edward kept an address book?

"Stay here, William. I'll be right back."

My clothes were still lying on the bathroom floor. Kneeling by the bathtub, I reached into my soiled jean jacket. The book itself was quite lovely, decorated in blue and black quilted Chinese letters. I'd never seen it before last night.

The first name my eyes hit upon, when opening the cover, was my own: Eleisha Clevon, 2017 Freemont Drive, Portland, OR 97228. I didn't want to believe it. For a minute I didn't. My full name and correct address. It was impossible that Edward could have done this. I started flipping pages.

The list wasn't alphabetical. The next name was Marquis Philip Branté, with his address in France. I felt numb, but kept reading. My stomach lurched when I turned the page and read its red-penned entry: Lord Julian Ashton, 6 Chadstone Road, Milesfield, Huddersmith, HD7 5UQ, Yorkshire.

"Oh, Edward."

They would have murdered him for this. Of all the unwritten, unspoken rules we followed, protecting each other's identity was the most important. I mean . . . I *knew* several phone numbers and addresses, but I would never write one of them down. Edward must have been mad. Why would he do this? I had to burn it quickly.

Then the name on the final page caused me to stop: Margaritte Latour, 1412 Queen Anne Drive, Seattle, WA 98102, (206) 555-8401. Maggie. How long since I'd seen Maggie? She lived as a vague image in my past. I remembered the sight of her in a dark red dress, holding on to Philip Branté's arm shortly before I left Wales with William in 1839. Would she help us? Could she?

I carried the book back into the study and picked up the phone. For all I knew, she might have moved seven times since Edward had written this phone number down.

"Are you calling Julian?" William asked from his little worktable.

"No."

"Ask him to send me a new smoking jacket. This one is wrinkled and chewed by moths. We have moths, you know. And mice. I keep telling you to get a cat, but you don't."

Cradling the phone between my shoulder and ear, I read Maggie's number again and murmured to William, "I'll get you a new smoking jacket, and we don't need a cat."

The line rang twice. I tried to keep calm.

"Hello," a deep female voice answered. Even in that one word, I could hear a hint of her French accent.

"Maggie?"

The line was silent for a moment, and then, "Who is this?"

"It's Eleisha. I need help. William has to be moved."

She hung up.

I should have known better. We don't make a practice of calling each other. We don't visit each other. Everyone who knew that William and Edward and I actually lived in the same city thought we were twisted aberrations.

"What happened?" William asked.

"Nothing for you to worry about. Just be quiet for a few minutes."

I dialed the number again and let it ring nine times.

I heard a click when she picked up, but I jumped in before she could say anything.

"Listen to me. I'm in the middle of something here, and William's got to be moved. If you don't help, I'll have to call Julian, and I'll tell him you left us to rot. That should put him in a good mood."

She didn't speak for almost thirty seconds, and then asked, "Where did you get this number?"

What should I have told her? And how much? It would be foolish to make her more afraid of the police than of Julian.

"I've got to get William out tonight."

"Is it that bad?"

"It's worse." I paused. "Edward's dead. He killed himself."

Had she felt him die? Could she, from almost two hundred miles away? I didn't know how that worked.

The line was silent for another long moment. "Do you have my address, too?"

"Yes, on Queen Anne Hill?"

Her voice changed. It had always been deep and smooth, but now an undertone of hatred dropped it lower. "Get on a plane and bring him here. You've got about five hours till dawn. But don't drag any of this down on my head, or I'll cut yours off and burn it."

Click.

Two minutes later, I was on the phone with a travel agent. Notice may have been short, but she managed to book us on a 1:30 A.M. United Airlines flight to Seattle. I called a taxi, not bothering to pack much—just a few changes of clothes.

Before we left, I tore out the page with Maggie's address on it, and then threw the book on the fire, making sure it burned completely. After that, things seemed a little safer. Then I ran outside and let all the rabbits go.

The whole ordeal was hard on William. He hadn't been out of the house in ninety-six years. I covered him with a hooded cloak and led him to the cab.

"I'm sorry, William, but you've got to hurry. We have a plane to catch."

He wouldn't know what a plane was, but my words moved him a bit quicker. Poor thing. A cab ride was only the beginning. The lights at the airport and all the noise might throw him into shock.

A middle-aged Asian sat behind the wheel.

"Take us to the airport, please," I whispered. "We're late."

"We'll miss dinner," William rattled through rapid, nervous breaths. "If we don't get home soon, we'll miss our dinner."

"We already had dinner. Don't you remember? I brought you the rabbit myself. You almost got blood on your smoking jacket."

The cabbie glanced up, but I ignored him. At that point, it didn't matter what he thought.

"It's late. Very late," William insisted. "We must get back home."

What was I supposed to say? That we weren't going home? That we no longer had a home? That Edward had ignited himself on purpose and the police watched it happen and now we were paying the price?

"We're going visiting. Do you remember Maggie Latour? Philip's mistress? The dark-haired one? She always wore red dresses and held on to his arm."

His face twisted. He tried to think back, to remember. "Katherine didn't like her."

He did remember. Lady Katherine had been William's wife all those years ago.

"Yes." I smiled, sitting close to him. "Katherine didn't like her because she was so beautiful and her family was poor and Philip used to talk about marrying her. Do you remember?"

His face grew animated at my words. These people I spoke of were links between ourselves and the past, a distant past no longer connected to us except by such sweet champagne memories. Maybe that's why I loved William. He was my chain to reality, my line to what once had been.

"Yes," he whispered. "I remember."

I reached over and grasped his wrinkled old hand. "Nothing is going to hurt you. We're going to get inside a large steel bird and fly to a different city. We'll be safe before morning, and we'll live with Maggie for a while. Understand?"

He stared out through misty, milk-white eyes in confusion but nodded just enough for recognition. "Is Maggie expecting us?"

"Yes."

He relaxed but held on to my hand tightly. When we stopped at the airport terminal, his fingers tensed.

"It's all right," I whispered and handed our fare—plus a twenty-dollar tip—to the cabdriver.

The trip might have been easier if we hadn't been so pressed by the clock. Passing time never stopped haunting me. We couldn't miss our flight, and we had to get to Maggie's before dawn.

Bright lights in the airport's wide corridors hurt William's eyes, but he held my hand and followed me. I kept his cloak pulled low over his face and tried to avoid attention. A few perfectly curled check-in girls stared at us curiously, but I dropped the helpless routine and glared at one of them. She didn't give me any trouble and handed over our boarding passes.

Getting through security wasn't as bad as I expected because the line was short at that hour. I'd kept several IDs for William updated, and he stayed quiet, just following my lead.

After that, the rest of the flight involved waiting. Once William was down the covered on-ramp and settled inside the plane, he fell asleep. Severe stress put him into a state of exhaustion. That's why I protected him from it as much as possible. Sitting strapped in my aisle seat from Portland to Seattle, I allowed myself the luxury of seething in hatred and blame toward that psychic cop—if he was a cop. He ran with cops, so he must be one.

It's funny how I never once blamed Edward. Maybe because he was dead. I only blamed the man named Wade, who'd tracked me into Mickey's Bar. All of this fear and flight was his fault. I'd never really wanted to kill anyone in my life, but all the way to Seattle, I mulled over fantasies of ripping his throat open after listening to him scream for a while.

Pity for William filled me again when the plane landed at Sea-Tac. He'd been through enough.

"Wake up. Just a little farther now."

He was too heavy for me to carry, and that would have attracted undue attention. But I had to half drag him anyway. Thank God a lot of really weird people hang out at airports. Nobody more than glanced at us on the way out.

I hailed another taxi and almost melted in relief when the driver stopped for us. By that time, I was so exhausted that I couldn't do more than hand him Maggie's address and whisper, "Here. Take us here."

William fell asleep again. The driver was a young guy wearing three days' growth and a Seattle Mariners baseball cap. He glanced at me with something akin to concern on his face, and then changed his mind and pulled out onto the street. We must have looked pretty wiped out.

Streaks of pale yellowish white were running through the sky when the cab pulled up to a large brick house covered in dark green ivy and built way back behind a chain-link fence.

"Here you go," the driver said. "That'll be thirty dollars."

I handed him two twenties and tried to wake the comatose William.

The driver's face wrinkled as if he was wondering what to do. "Do you need some help with him? I can get him up to the house for you."

"No . . . thanks. I've got him."

With all the strength left in my body, I wrapped William's arm around my neck and dragged him from the cab. Without looking back, I held on and half carried him up to the house.

"Almost there," I told him over and over. "We're almost there."

The place looked old but well kept. The brick stairs

to the front door seemed like an endless flight upward. Only the light from the east kept me from collapsing into sleep like William. How lucky he was, just to sleep. I blinked once and pictured the comfort of relaxing all my muscles and drifting away into oblivion, not caring about anything.

Reaching the top, I dragged William across the porch. Before my finger touched the bell, the door opened, and a pale, angry, perfect face stared out at me. Even in my state of fatigue, I couldn't help being jolted by Maggie's ivory face. She wasn't just beautiful. She was different. Even in mortal life, I'd never seen any woman who looked quite like her.

"Get inside," she hissed. "And get him below."

When she turned around, a mass of brown-black curls shifted with her and bounced softly all the way down to the small of her back. She withdrew, and I followed her curls blindly down into some sort of basement. I don't remember what anything looked like except for her hair and her small, curving shoulders.

She opened a door and pointed to a bed in a windowless room. "Go to sleep. You'd better have a very special story to tell me tonight, or I may just call Julian myself."

I nodded, beyond caring, and dragged William to the bed. I don't remember falling onto it or even hearing the door close.

chapter 4

My internal clock woke me up that night. It seemed as though I'd barely closed my eyes. For the second night in a row, I found myself in a strange place, not my home. At least William was with me. He'd never developed any connection to dusk or time, so he lay dormant. I watched him sleep for a little while and then got up to find Maggie. She would be awake and waiting for me by now.

The door was unlocked, and I walked out into a basement storage room that was remarkably empty and clean. Obviously Maggie didn't save things as Edward had. She did appear to keep a "guest room" in the basement, though. Who else had slept there in the past hundred years or so?

Finding the stairs, I came up from the basement onto a main level of polished hardwood floors.

"Maggie?"

"Up here," her deep voice answered from what sounded like far away.

Following the sound of her voice, I walked up a curved stairway with cream carpeting, Impressionist paintings lining the wall, proving to me once again that it was possible to be born outside of nobility and still have excellent taste.

My hands clenched and unclenched as I wondered what to say. I'd have to make this good.

Once upstairs, I entered the first bedroom. My breath caught slightly. Julian had sparse taste. His estate house in Wales, called Cliffbracken, had always been cold and bare. That was once my concept of the rich and noble. Not until after coming to America did a slightly different picture take shape. Here, money meant extreme comfort.

But Maggie's bedroom went beyond comfort. It was decadent in an almost surreal way—like Maggie herself. Every square inch of the floor and walls was covered by something cream or deep brown. Satin drapes, giant antique fans, dried flowers, and long, lace wall covers. Above her cherrywood bed stretched a lace canopy with countless yards of cream satin pouring down around it. Resting perfectly on the polished dressers and wardrobe and end tables sat antique toiletry sets, fragile perfume bottles, and silver hand mirrors.

"Stop staring and sit down."

She sat at a dressing table. Chocolate and sleek and ivory, her hair and the perfect pale lines of her face set off her dark eyes. She wore a faded Armani dress and torn, black nylon stockings. While making her look like a lady of means down on her luck, the dress accented her tiny waist, curved hips, and high-set breasts.

Her stark, sexual visage in the center of all that lace made me wonder if she were real.

"Did you hear me?"

Her voice cut through my haze like a hatchet.

"Yes, I'm sorry."

"I doubt you're sorry enough."

She was real, all right, in full color, exuding the power of her gift. When we are turned by our makers, the strongest trait of our personality intensifies to an alluring, alarming degree. That's how we either draw or paralyze our prey. Maggie's gift of sexual attraction made her nightly hunting easy. Victims literally fell into her lap. But in this situation, I had the advantage—nearly immune to her gift, while she was not immune to mine.

"I am sorry, Maggie. Where else could we go?"

After walking in, I crouched to my knees on the floor, so she would be forced to look down at me.

"What happened?" The cutting edge of her voice faded slightly.

"Edward just . . . he just lost it. He seemed fine, and then he called me the night before last and started talking crazy. He'd been going to Safeway and buying mutton . . . bringing dead animals into his kitchen. He wouldn't hunt. I didn't know what was wrong with him."

"You shouldn't have been living so close to him in the first place."

"It all happened too fast. He waited until morning and then turned the stereo up so loud the neighbors called the police. When they pulled up, he jumped off his front porch . . . They watched him burn. I got trapped inside."

For a second, her expression shifted into something

vaguely resembling pity and then hardened again. "That doesn't explain what you're doing here."

What should I have said about the next part? I barely believed it myself. "One of the cops—at least he might be a cop—felt Edward die."

"That's impossible."

"No. It's not a lie. He felt it, and then I ran downstairs. When I woke up that night, Edward's basement had been all torn up, and I found a human bone."

"Oh, no." Her face became even paler, and she seemed to grow less accusing of me and more caught up in my nightmare story. I decided not to tell her everything about Wade, that he had pushed inside my head and shown me visions of his own thoughts.

"It gets worse," I went on. "My car was parked outside his house all day, so they have one of the names I use and my home address. Edward had a photograph of me over his fireplace . . . that he shot ten years ago, and an oil painting in the cellar from 1872."

She gasped and then snapped, "How stupid can you be? Why did I even let you in here? Julian wouldn't blame me for pitching you out right now."

"I didn't think—"

"That's pretty obvious, Eleisha. Your job is to take care of that old senile abortion. That's why Julian made you. None of this has anything to do with me."

Staring at the carpet, I let my shoulders turn in. "Please, just for a week or so, until I can find us someplace else. Maybe living so close to Edward was a mistake, but he helped me. No one else taught me anything. I've never been without him, Maggie. Don't make me leave."

She was silent for a moment. I knew her dilemma had more complications than the surface details we were discussing. Maggie and I had different makers. The children of different makers avoid each other in the name of survival. If Julian came looking for me, he wouldn't have a second thought about killing Maggie.

"Please," I whispered. "We'll be out in a week."

"Oh, Leisha."

I knew she was looking down at the top of my silky head. Every dormant mothering instinct inside of her was fighting against reason, the helpless, little-girl emanation of my gift rushing through her psyche like a white wind.

"You'll keep the old man out of my sight?"

"Promise."

She sighed. "You can stay a week as long as Julian never finds out you were here. He can't find out I had anything to do with this."

"He won't. It'll be at least a month before he figures out we're not in Portland anymore. By then we'll be settled someplace else. We'll probably rent for a while, and I'll tell Julian . . . I'll tell him something."

Maggie nodded. "But I want you to know that I don't like this, and it isn't fair of you to ask this of me."

The room suddenly felt too soft. "I'm hungry. We need to hunt."

Instead of telling me to go hunt by myself, she reached down and picked up a lock of my hair. "You can't go anywhere looking like this. Did you bring any other clothes?"

"Not much. We left in a hurry."

"Come look in my closet. You're small, but I might have something that works."

Her abrupt change in attitude caught me off guard. I looked up at her beautiful face, but saw no malice or guile. Now that she had given in, she was letting her emotions take over. Good.

"What do you usually do with your hair?" she asked.

The question threw me. "Brush it."

Raising her eyebrows, she said, "Stay here."

She left and came back with a set of hot rollers. Then she opened the door of a walk-in closet at least the size of her bedroom. She disappeared inside and came out holding a small, red minidress with a rip in one side.

"Try this on."

I undressed immodestly in front of her. She watched me with a detached interest.

"You have a pretty body," she said. "Too fragile maybe, but some people like that."

I listened to her comments, surprised by how enjoyable I found this entire conversation, different than my talks with Edward—more personal.

"How long have you lived alone?" I asked.

She moved up to help me zip the dress. "How long? I left Philip in 1841 and sailed from France to Boston. Sometimes it feels like yesterday and sometimes it feels like forever."

Philip was her maker. I wanted to ask Maggie why she left him in the first place, but thought better of it and looked in the mirror, quite startled.

The dress fit tightly, snug all the way from my shoulders down over my hips just to the tops of my thighs. I looked different.

"Good." Maggie smiled. "Now sit down and let me do your hair."

This felt strange, like missing something I'd never had. She seemed pleased to be fussing over me. It started to make me nervous. Using her was one thing, allowing myself to become involved was another. But I didn't move, just sat there letting her touch me and put curlers in my hair.

"You might find this look easier," she said. "We can change our gifts for the moment, baby. You don't always have to stay with the same routine."

I assimilated two important facts from her words. One, the fact that she'd called me baby meant that she was completely seduced, and two, I could learn a great deal from this woman.

"You can alter your gift?"

"Sometimes," she answered. "It depends on the situation. What you do should always depend on who you're with."

"Like how?"

"I'll show you when we get downtown. I haven't seen your own routine yet, but I can guess what it is."

Odd how she was smart enough to see me for what I was and still allow herself to be influenced. Maybe she had been alone too long.

"What are you doing to my hair?"

"Hang on, and you'll see."

While the rollers rested in uncomfortable heat against my head, she tilted my chin back and put black liner under my eyes and a russet-brown lip gloss on my mouth. Then she took the rollers out.

"Shake your head, Eleisha. Then look in the mirror."

I did what she asked . . . and stood staring. I hardly recognized myself. Wheat gold hair spread out in a mass across my shoulders. My hazel eyes looked huge, and my mouth stood out like a dark heart in my small face. "What did you do?"

"Didn't take long, did it? Don't worry. In a couple of days you'll be doing it by yourself."

Yeah, right.

A voice from the hallway startled me into reality. "Eleisha! Where are we?"

Maggie's face clouded. I bolted away from the mirror and out into the hallway in my bare feet.

"William, it's okay. Don't you remember? We're at Maggie's. We came on that big silver bird last night."

He looked frightened and lost, starting at the sight of me. "Eleisha?"

"It's me. I've been playing with Maggie. Remember Maggie?"

Sad sweet thing, my William. Maggie appeared in the bedroom doorway, none too pleased. I'd promised to keep him out of sight.

"Maggie," he whispered, "always wore red dresses and held Philip's arm. Katherine hated her because she was pretty and poor. Philip used to talk about marrying her."

Something clicked across her features, something like pain. I jumped forward and took his arm. "Let's go back down to the basement. We'll talk there."

"What about dinner?"

"I have to catch your dinner. We're not at home anymore, are we? That will make quite a story. I'll catch you a wild alley cat in downtown Seattle and tell you about the hunt."

"No," Maggie said suddenly. "He's all right. There's a leather chair in the living room by the fire. Go settle him there."

"You sure?"

She nodded and turned away. What changed her mind? I made William comfortable and went back to the bedroom. She sat, looking into the mirror.

"I thought you didn't want to see him?"

"You make me remember things," she whispered. "Both of you. Things I haven't thought about for a long time."

"Do the memories hurt?"

"A little. Maybe sometime I might ask you what really happened to William. You and Julian are the only ones who seem to know."

Maybe mortals die so quickly because none of us were meant to live forever. William and I had been comforted in the cab talking about the distant past, when we lived in a world where we belonged. Maggie must have experienced the same thing. Only she had a lot more to miss than I did. I had just been Lord Julian's serving girl. Philip had turned her undead out of love.

"Do you miss him?" I asked.

She knew who I meant. "Sometimes, but not the way you think."

"Then why'd you leave? I'd never have left Wales if Julian hadn't forced me."

"I know." She turned from the mirror and looked at me. "I felt sorry for you. But . . . maybe you'll understand someday. Not now. You've lived a long time without really learning anything because you're so tied to William."

"I take good care of him."

"Yes, and that's all you do. That's all you've ever done."

Her words amused me. What did she know? I'd learned quite a bit since coming to America. I wielded my gift as well as anyone, including her.

"So why don't you show me a new side of life?" I smiled. "Why don't you show me this city?"

This room made me feel reckless. I wanted to roll in satin bed drapings and run my hands through thick carpets. Maggie almost smiled back. Then she got up and walked into the closet.

She came out, handing me a pair of black pumps. "You are interesting, little one. Just don't make me regret any of this."

"We should hunt," I said. Then I looked at the shoes and shook my head. "Something flat."

"Flat? With that dress? You need a heel."

Upon this point, I would not budge. "No. I won't wear anything I can't run in. Find me something flat."

She frowned and dug out a pair of lightweight, flat sandals.

"Good," I said, putting them on. "Where's your car?"

She seemed slightly put off by the question and said, "I called a cab."

"You don't have a car?"

"I don't drive."

Really? And she'd accused me of not learning enough. I let it go.

William sat by the fire in his leather chair when we walked past him toward the front door. Maggie touched his sleeve and said, "We won't be long."

Rejoicing inwardly, I knew that somehow, in some way, a very quiet little battle had been won with me as the victor. An hour ago this woman would have gladly dropped us into a pit. Now she seemed concerned for William's feelings and was letting us live in her home.

I watched her open the door and followed her out into the cold night air. Everything around us glowed with life. Looking at her, I felt careless and wild. We both wanted to watch each other and learn, to get lost in the hunt.

chapter 5

Maggie and I stepped out of a taxi on Madison. Downtown Seattle struck me as a cultural smorgasbord. Portland isn't exactly conservative, but the Seattle waterfront was like nothing I'd ever seen. The two of us fit in so well I felt at home immediately—not because we looked like everyone else, but because no one looked quite the same.

During the day, these shining glass skyscrapers housed brain-dead executives who wore twelve-hundred-dollar suits, but at night the doorways were crowded with starving bums hoping some heat would leak through the cracks. On every street corner stood some guy playing a guitar or trumpet, his case left open on the concrete sidewalk for donations. Prostitutes, drug dealers, and cross-dressers lived and breathed right in the midst of yuppie corporate sharks who earned four hundred thousand a year and wouldn't throw a quarter to a bag lady.

In a city like this, no one would even blink at a dead body. I'd never want to leave.

"Has it always been like this?"

"No." Maggie smiled. "Of course not. Places grow and change, like people. It started out as a logging town."

"Why did you come here?"

"New territory. None of us ever lived this far north. I wanted to be alone."

That made sense. This must have been a wonderful place to run away to. "What year?"

"What year?" Her dark eyebrows knitted. "In 1932, I think. Middle of the Depression."

"Where were you during the Civil War?" I asked, finding the tale of her past intriguing—as Edward's and mine had been so intertwined.

"New Hampshire," she answered. "You?"

"Manhattan."

None of this century's wars had affected us much, but in 1861 the Civil War hit America so hard even we couldn't help feeling its backlash.

I suddenly realized we'd walked quite a ways, and the buildings were looking dingy. "Hey, where are we going?"

"My favorite bar," she said. "Just watch me for a little while. I usually pose as a hooker from a wealthy but sordid past."

"Is that what you tell them?"

"Not really. I just drop hints. My clothes and accent do the rest."

"Doesn't anyone get suspicious when all of your customers turn up on the back of a milk carton?"

"Don't be dense. Of course they don't all turn up missing. I have to keep up appearances."

For a moment that confused me and then I stopped walking. "You mean you . . . ?"

"I what?"

"You actually have sex with some of them?"

Her low laughter echoed down a dark alley. "For God's sake, Leisha. What did you think? If no one recommended me and all the men who employed me turned up dead, I wouldn't be in business very long, now would I?"

She thought me naïve, and I found it humiliating. "No, that makes sense. I just never touch them unless I'm feeding."

"Really? I told you that you've been too wrapped up in William. I once lived with a professional baseball player for eight months."

Maybe I *was* naïve, because that did stun me. "You lived with him? Did he know what you are?"

"Yes, but it didn't matter. He was in love with me, and he made me feel alive."

"Where is he now?"

"Dead. Things went sour after a while, and I had to kill him."

She related the last statement with all the passion of someone discussing the rising price of tomatoes. That was one basic difference between many of my kind. We all viewed death differently. Julian liked killing, Maggie didn't give it much thought, and I hated it.

"Here we are."

She stopped in front of a small, barely noticeable wooden door. The building was sandwiched between a run-down Chinese restaurant called Yan's and an

H&R Block tax office. A sign above the blacked-out window read "Blue Jack's."

"Why here?" I asked. "It looks like a dive."

"You'll see."

For the first moment after she opened the door, all I could see was blue smoke and black leather. It hardly seemed like a place where Maggie would hang out. I had some expensive cocktail lounge in mind, like the Red Lion, or at least someplace popular like Neumo's or even Chop Suey, where she would look sad and down on her luck, someplace where she could make people feel superior and let them believe they were taking advantage of her.

The smoke cleared slightly, and we walked in. A guy with spiked hair and a pewter cross in his ear smiled at me. I didn't smile back.

"Maggie, I don't like this."

"You will."

The bar itself seemed bigger on the inside than on the outside. Large neon Budweiser signs glowed off the walls, and overworked waitresses in short skirts hurried from table to table as they laughed with one customer and then listened to the next one complain.

"Hey, Maggie! Where you been?" a deep voice called.

A huge man in a black T-shirt with a tattoo of a palm tree on his arm put down his pool cue and started walking toward us.

"Ben." She smiled. Her white teeth glittered through the blue smoke haze and a thick mass of wavy hair fell forward over one eye. "I've missed you."

"Bullshit. You never missed anyone in your . . ." He stopped at the sight of me. "Who's your friend?"

"Just a friend."

He shrugged and pointed to the pool table. "Hey, I got a game going. Come watch for a while?"

The idea of watching two unwashed bikers play pool didn't exactly strike me as appealing. What were we doing in this place?

Maggie pulled me along while following him, but she whispered, "Not that one. He's here too often."

Something in her statement made sense to me. This must be a transient place, a lot of people coming and going. And for all his rough manners, I did notice that Ben revered Maggie. He didn't treat her like a prostitute. He actually pulled a chair out for her, then went to the bar and bought us each a glass of cheap red wine before resuming his pool game.

"He's nice," I whispered.

She gave me an inquisitive look and then motioned slightly toward Ben's opponent. "I don't know that one. When they take a break, find out where he's from."

"Okay."

I took a long look at him. He was tall—no visible tattoos—wearing a black T-shirt like Ben's. His hair was long and kind of stringy, and his nose looked as if it had been broken about six times since childhood. He glanced over at me, and I smiled.

A lot of people in the place seemed to notice us. My usual game was to stay unnoticed until I chose a mark. This whole routine was uncomfortable and alien. It felt weird to have so many people looking at me.

"Does your bartender have a degree?" I asked Maggie while watching him draw beer as fast as his hands could move.

"Doctorate," she said, nodding. "Classical mythology."

Ben won the pool game. His opponent followed him to our table, and they both sat down. There weren't really any formal introductions. Ben laughed a lot and always kept the conversation going. His face glowed whenever he looked at Maggie. Somewhere, somebody mentioned that his friend's name was Gunner—I didn't ask what it meant.

Soon, Maggie and Ben drifted off toward the bar. The night seemed to be moving along quickly.

"You been in Seattle long?" Gunner asked.

So far I hadn't said much of anything, but instinct told me to drop back into my usual frightened, hesitant act. "No, just a few days. I didn't have anywhere else to . . . Maggie's been helping me out."

He glanced over at her dress. "Has she shown you around much?"

"No, this is the first time we've gone out."

"Really?"

That got his attention. I wondered what he was thinking. This actually wasn't all that different from my own routine, just a little more glitz and a little more dirt.

"I pulled in yesterday," he went on. "Came up from California. Got a buddy in Canada I haven't seen for a while."

"Passing through?"

"Yeah, don't know anyone in town."

"You just met Ben?"

"Uh-huh."

I made a point of not looking at him and kept running my finger around the top of my glass as if I was nervous. He reached out and stopped my hand.

"You don't like it very much in here, do you?" he whispered.

"No."

"I've got a room a few blocks away. You want to just go there and talk?"

"I don't know . . . What about Maggie?"

"She looks pretty busy."

I didn't say anything. He stood up and held out his hand. "Let's just get out of here."

My own hands are so little that when I reached up he suddenly seemed afraid to grasp one. "Okay," I said, "but I've got to tell Maggie where I'll be. What motel are you in?"

"Green Clover Inn, room eight."

"Wait here."

Maggie was sitting at the bar, laughing with Ben. The buzz in the place drowned out my words as I leaned over to her ear.

"Just a drifter. Green Clover Inn. Room eight. Ten minutes."

She nodded very slightly without breaking her smile and turned back to Ben.

Gunner came up behind me and put his hand on my back. He talked to Ben for a few seconds, and then steered me toward the door. "You'll feel better once we're outside," he said. "It's pretty smoky in here."

That was kind of funny since he was holding a lit Marlboro between his teeth.

The streets were busy outside. I stopped to put a few dollars in an open guitar case but didn't talk much to Gunner—what a stupid name. At that point I didn't want to talk.

"Is your friend back there trying to get you into her line of work?" he asked suddenly.

"I'm already in her line of work."

"You don't act like it."

"How should I act?"

That made him uncomfortable, and he shut up for a few seconds, then spat out, "How much?"

How much? Oh, great. Maggie didn't tell me anything about that. I had no idea what to say. "Don't worry about it."

He glanced at me sideways. Yeah, that was the ticket, just convince him he was such a stud I'd get him off for free. Maybe he'd believe it. I hoped so. Maggie had a lot of questions to answer later.

"This is it."

He stopped in front of a run-down motel sans any porch lights. Pulling a key from his pocket, he opened the door to room 8 and motioned me in.

"You hungry?" he asked. "We could order a pizza or something."

I wondered if most guys offered to buy pizza for hookers, but that seemed unlikely. It bothered me that he was being so nice.

"No, I'm okay. But go ahead if you want one."

He sat down on the bed. There were dead cockroaches in the air vent over his head, and the bedspread sported two gaping cigarette burns.

"I don't think I ever caught your name," he said.

"Eleisha."

"Hey, listen . . ."

A knock sounded on the door. His eyebrows wrinkled. "Someone's probably got the wrong room." He opened the door and Maggie walked in.

"Just thought I'd check on you." She smiled with an odd light in her dark eyes.

"What about Ben?" Gunner asked.

"I told him I wanted to show Eleisha a few things. He understood."

Every time I looked at her it took me by surprise. It was hard to believe anything so perfect could be walking around. She obviously had the same effect on Gunner, but he'd been caught off guard by her sudden appearance. Before he could move, she ran her hands up his chest. I stood staring in rapt interest. The whole scene took on the same unreal quality as Maggie's bedroom.

His expression went blank. Then something close to pain, but not quite, flickered through his eyes. Staring down into her beautiful face, he seemed to forget my existence. Maybe he even forgot his own. With one hand he grasped the back of her thick mane and pulled her mouth up to his. I couldn't take my eyes off them. She'd achieved absolute control in a matter of seconds.

But she didn't waste any time.

I'd killed hundreds of people since the nineteenth

century, but until that night, I'd never actually watched one of my own kind feed. With the exception of Edward, I'd never seen one of them kill. He operated hard and fast, like a machine. I used to go to horror movies and grimace every time some supposed vampire's face distorted into a grotesque demonic mask and his fangs grew to epic proportions. It isn't like that. Our fangs don't grow. Our eyes don't turn red. We don't hiss or spit or turn into slaughter-crazed animals.

Maggie didn't do any of those things. She just moved her mouth down to his neck, pinned him back against the wall, and bit down until she punctured his jugular. He didn't scream. He didn't struggle—much. I'm not even sure he knew what was happening to him. Quiet and simple.

I just stood there, watching.

She let his body slide to the floor and knelt there, drinking for a while. Then she looked up at me. "Hurry up. His heart's still beating."

It's not just blood that we take in. It's life force. Both Maggie and I would feed on energy through his blood. Without letting myself think, I walked over and crouched down, putting my mouth on his neck. Of course none of us could drink all the blood in a grown man's body. All those stories about us draining bodies are lies. We don't leave neat little snake-eye puncture wounds either. No one could feed like that. Most victims die from blood loss, but more than half of it ends up on the floor. This guy's throat was a mess. Even if we didn't drink from him, he'd bleed to death in a matter of minutes.

I sank my teeth in and drew down . . . and then as

always, while feeding, images of his life passed through my mind. This was a side effect of absorbing his life force. I'd grown accustomed to it many, many years ago.

This time, I saw a small, decaying house on a run-down street, an unshaven man—Gunner's father—drinking from a bottle. I saw a thin woman with a sad face, and then flashing visions of different motorcycles . . . a pretty girl with long black hair, laughing in one moment and slapping him in the next. I saw a long string of bars and pool tables . . .

Maggie must have taken a lot because I held his head with one hand and drew fluid out of his throat until his heart stopped beating. It's a cold experience to feel someone's heart just stop like that.

"He's dead," I said woodenly, pulling back.

"Good," she said from the bathroom, cleaning up. "Get his wallet, wash up, and let's go."

"What about the body?"

"Leave it. Nobody cares. Without his ID, he's just another John Doe."

"He must have given his name to the clerk."

"I doubt it. Cash-and-carry business around here."

Hiding or disguising or dumping bodies was a natural part of hunting for me. Leaving him made me nervous, but Maggie was already outside. I washed up and followed.

I didn't feel so reckless anymore. We walked more than a mile before she said, "You did good back there. Better than I'd expected."

"What do you mean?"

"I mean you pegged that guy in a hurry. I was watching you from the bar and you had him in less than ten minutes. Surprised me."

Her praise had an odd, soothing effect. I hunted to survive, so that I could go on living and taking care of William. No one had ever judged my technique and said "Good job" like that before. The opinions of others didn't really matter much to me, but for some reason I liked hearing how pleased she was.

"Can we go to a higher-class place next time?"

"Oooooooh." She laughed. "Getting snooty already? People in the higher-class places get missed. Better get used to smoke and tattoos."

"Fabulous."

Warmth glowed from her pale face in a way that made me feel welcome. She'd been alone too long. It's funny how she thought herself so worldly and couldn't recognize the scars of loneliness.

She broke into a run down an alley—still wearing those heels. I watched her hair blow back like a cloud and then followed her into the darkness. I felt right somehow. Happy.

Maybe I'd been lonely, too.

chapter 6

C ool, salt-laden wind from Puget Sound felt good blowing through my hair, a tiny breeze compared to the great gusts I'd grown up with in Wales. Exactly a week to the day after our experience together at Blue Jack's, Maggie dressed us both up to go hunting again, only this time we hit the waterfront.

Maybe it was my newfound companion, or maybe the wide assortment of people who lived here, but Seattle appealed to me more and more each night. A haven. A paradise. Even though we hadn't made another kill together yet, Maggie showed me the city and even insisted once that we take William for a walk on the street outside her house. He objected, shaking in agitation, but then calmed down when we both stayed right beside him and chatted of silly topics like trees and squirrels. I think he even enjoyed himself.

But tonight was different. I could feel it in the clothes she chose, the time she took with her hair and makeup, the pale cast of her face, the hard look in her eyes.

Now she leaned on the pier railing in her black Lycra tank dress and fishnet stockings, her hot-chocolate hair wisping across her cheek. She looked like a cartoon cut-out from some teenage boy's fantasy magazine. That should have tipped me off. Maggie never did anything by accident.

She didn't look excited or anticipatory, not as I had expected. Edward hadn't exactly enjoyed breaking somebody's neck, but the actual prospect of hunting had sometimes filled him with glittering energy that made me turn away in disgust.

Don't get me wrong. I knew the game and the score, but simply having the facts didn't fill me with blood-lust. I took no pleasure in the fact that some mortal had to die so I could go on living. Still, I obeyed the cardinal rule we all followed: never leave a witness. Our existence depended on absolute silence. Blackness. Anyone who knew our secret had to die. The body dumped. The life erased.

No one knew the score better than me.

But Maggie viewed the entire twisted cycle as commonplace. We needed life force, so we hunted. Cut and dried. It isn't that she was aware of having no regrets. She just didn't think about it at all. Enviable.

"What now?" I asked.

Before us lay the dark water, behind us a rusted train track stretching into the city. Beyond the tracks were faded nondescript buildings too old to be of much interest.

"We wait," she answered. "Someone always turns up."

"How often do you come here?"

"A few times a year. Something told me you'd like this place."

"I do."

Wind from the sound whipped up again, blowing my hair into slightly damp tangles. I heard voices. They came from the left. Masculine laughter. Maggie turned to look.

A party of three walked down the railed sidewalk, all about seventeen years old, all wearing torn jeans and T-shirts. One wore a leather coat. No earrings. No shaved heads. No makeup. They weren't skinheads or part of a gang, probably just some guys trying to get out of the house.

Maggie stepped out in front of them when they got close enough, but she didn't smile. "Lookin' for a date?"

The classy-lady-down-on-her-luck routine had vanished. She was just playing a hooker—except that her face and form were too perfect to be working the pier.

All three of the boys froze. I leaned back against the rail and let her take over.

"Yeah, but I'm broke," the one in front said. He was the tallest.

"How about some blow?"

That sounded stupid to me. She didn't look remotely like a cocaine addict. But then, some people hide it well, and it might explain why someone like Maggie would be willing to sell herself.

The blond in the leather jacket said, "I can take care of that. What about your friend?"

"She goes where I go."

"Good."

The blond had hard eyes, like empty glass. The tall guy in front seemed uncomfortable but was staring so intensely at Maggie I thought his tongue might break off. The third guy was smaller, built slight, with a white scar below his right eye and a nervous air about him— probably been kicked around since he was three years old.

The tall one had halfway decent manners and introduced himself as Travis. The blond was Jeff, and they called the little scar-face Dodger.

"Where to?" Maggie asked.

"A friend's place," Jeff answered.

I stepped up and slipped my hand into his, hoping Maggie caught the gesture and wouldn't peg Travis to feed on. Jeff glanced down at me without a flicker or hint of surprise. Cold and hollow, he would have made a good vampire.

When we started walking, Dodger fell in behind without a word. Maggie and Travis paired off, speaking in low voices, but that didn't mean anything. She'd probably follow my lead when the time came.

"You don't talk much," Jeff said.

"Do you want me to?"

"Not really."

I didn't know whether to respect his honesty or despise him for being such a bastard-in-training. Would my gift work? That was the trick. Men like Travis or Derek back in Portland had such soft hearts they were easy to manipulate. But I could never bring myself to hurt people like them—except in a few cases of emergency. It bothered me a little less to feed on hard cases like Jeff, but he was more difficult to reach, to seduce into cavalier mode.

We crossed the tracks, and I tripped on purpose, emanating uncertainty and helplessness. As though it
would never occur to him to do otherwise, he turned
and caught my arm. There was still a bit of human in
him somewhere. Good.

His highly uncharacteristic action brought stunned
expressions from both Travis and Dodger, but he didn't
seem to notice and kept walking. I turned off the power
for a while, knowing it worked if necessary.

"Listen," I said, "when we get to your friend's place,
can you go in by yourself?"

"Why?"

"Deals scare me. Maggie went in to get some stuff
with a couple of guys last month and almost got busted.
I don't like cops."

"Yeah, okay. But you ditch me, and I'll kick your
teeth in. Me and Travis gotta trade a few free runs to
pay for this shit, and I don't use it myself."

Charming.

"You're crack runners?"

He shrugged. "Sometimes. Depends on cash-flow
problems. I don't like cops either."

We stopped by a run-down apartment building.
"This is it," he said. "Be right back."

He disappeared inside.

Maggie kept up small talk with Travis but glanced at
her watch a few times. After three minutes she said, "I
need to find a ladies' room." She pointed up the street
toward a dimly lit gas station. "You meet us up there
when Jeff comes out."

Travis wavered for a second, not quite sure if he

should let her leave, and then nodded. "Yeah, sure." Why would she take off when he was getting her what she wanted?

I followed her at a normal pace until we were out of sight. Moving around the nearest shack, we doubled back down an alley, entering the apartment building from the other side. As far as Dodger and Travis knew, we'd gone down the street to a gas station, and Jeff was on his own making a deal. People disappear all the time over money, coke, or crack. He might never come back out of the apartment, but no one would suspect a couple of hookers who'd gone to pee at the local Exxon. His friends would be confused and angry and scared, and in an hour they wouldn't know what to think.

Inside, the staircase smelled like rotting vegetables. Since we didn't know what room number Jeff had gone to, we just leaned inside the stairwell of the second-floor landing and kept watch.

Footsteps sounded a few minutes later as Jeff came down from an upper floor. Surprise crossed his features briefly. "I thought you'd wait outside."

"Got cold," Maggie answered. "Your friends are in the lobby."

He didn't seem to find that unusual and nodded. "Got the stuff. We can go to my place."

Of course, when we reached the lobby it was empty. "Where are they?" Jeff looked around.

"I don't know," Maggie said. "We should wait, though."

Stepping into the darkness under the bottom stairwell, I motioned to him with my hand. "Come in here."

He smiled slightly for the first time and walked over, ducking his head to move inside the shadows. He pushed me up against the back wall. I couldn't see anything, but smelled spearmint gum on his breath. This was Maggie's usual trip, not mine, so I let him lead for a few seconds. His mouth moving up my neck felt alien. I didn't like it.

Too fast, I struck under his chin, catching the top layers of his throat but missing a solid hold. He actually screamed and rammed my backbone against the wall.

Careless on my part. Too fast.

Releasing my bite just long enough to get a better grip, I clung to him desperately, but he felt my teeth withdraw and pitched me off. He bolted back out into the lobby. I ducked after him in time to see Maggie grab his short blond hair.

She didn't try for a grip, but just jerked him back, bit down once at the full extension of her mouth, and ripped. Dark blood sprayed her dress. His face was horrible, not some sleepy, half-conscious sweet dreamer like Gunner had been last week. Twisting panic and disbelief contorted Jeff's mouth, and he lost consciousness while still kicking and gasping.

When he stopped moving, Maggie dragged him back under the stairs. We took turns feeding. I tried not to think or feel anything as I saw flickering images of his life pass through my mind while drinking his blood . . . comic books, beer bottles, an angry mother who hated herself.

I pulled away from his throat and closed my eyes.

Using a knife she always carried in her handbag, Maggie cut jagged slashes in the torn flesh of his throat, making it look like someone had done a poor job murdering him. I took his wallet, and we walked out the back, leaving him for the janitor to find—if this dive had a janitor.

"There's a pint of blood on my dress," she hissed.

"I'm sorry."

Staying in the shadows, we made our way back down to the pier. Once we reached it, she climbed over the rail down to the rocky beach and knelt to try and rinse herself with salt water.

My knees buckled slowly down beside her. "I'm really sorry."

"What exactly happened back there?" she snapped.

"He was touching me. I don't know. His neck felt close enough . . . I just missed. That's never happened before."

"Well, it's a good thing you weren't alone. This is a safe city for me. I'm careful. One screwup, even one close call like that, could end everything. Do you understand?"

"Don't give me a safety lecture. I hunted in Portland on my own for over ninety years, just different from you."

"Like how?"

"Different. You play a lot more games. Take more time. I used to just stand outside an alley somewhere looking scared and someone always stopped to either help or hurt me."

Turning away, she splashed more water on her dress. She wasn't angry at me, just shaken. "You're so strange, Leisha. Not like one of us at all."

"Then why do you keep me? Why do you let me stay?"

"I don't know."

We sat on the rocks like that for an hour, neither one of us saying a word.

chapter 7

F ive weeks later I sat by the fire in Maggie's living room watching her play chess with William. He often forgot the rules, and she patiently but firmly reminded him that his bishop could move only diagonally on the same color.

"No, William," she said. "That's your rook. It moves ahead or backward or to the side."

The stimulation of someone new had made William more interested in his surroundings. Maggie was good for him. She had changed a great deal since our arrival as well. Every time I brought up the subject of leaving, she'd say something like, "Don't worry about it yet."

I thought about the hate-filled look on her face the night after we arrived, when she had told me to keep William out of her sight. Maybe she feared being forced to remember. William was such a stark image of the link between our own dead era and the present. We were all tied to the same dark secret: Maggie, Philip, Julian, myself, and Edward. William was the keystone, a blinding, undeniable example of what could be.

But Maggie surprised herself by discovering what I had always known. There was joy in William. He wasn't an abomination. He was our history. It was okay to look him in the face and smile . . . and remember.

"Checkmate. I win." She laughed.

"Eleisha lets me win."

"Eleisha lets you cheat, and that's why you win."

He looked to me for support, his long, wispy hair hanging at odd angles around a narrow, once-handsome face. I did let him cheat. For some reason, Maggie found it very important that he play everything by the rules. I had little concern for most rules.

"Cheating helps him. It makes him think," I said in my own defense.

"Yes, but he'll never learn anything that way. You've spoiled him for anyone's company but yours."

Oh, that was rich, as if people were beating the door down to spend time with William. Maggie must have realized how stupid her last statement sounded because she dropped it.

"One more game?" she asked him.

"I'm tired. I'll stoke up the fire."

He didn't know how to stoke or build a fire, but it was something he liked to talk about. A few minutes later he was sleeping in his chair.

"We're going to have to call Julian pretty soon," I said. "We've been here six weeks. He'll need to know what's going on."

"He already does."

"What?"

"I called Philip last week and told him what happened. He said he'd take care of it. Julian won't care who you're staying with as long as he doesn't have to see William."

I sat stunned for a moment, and then said, "You should have told me."

"Why?"

"Because you don't know Julian like I do."

"Oh, spare me the martyr syndrome. He wants you out of sight and out of mind. That's all."

"No, I didn't mean that. You just shouldn't . . . You're putting yourself at risk for us. What if you get hurt?"

The hard lines of her face softened. "Don't worry. I can take care of myself."

Guilt was a new emotion for me. I hated it.

"Maggie, there's something else. Something I didn't tell you."

"What?"

"Do you remember me telling you about that cop who felt Edward die? The one who fell on the lawn?"

"I told you that's impossible."

"No, he felt it. I know because . . . I felt him."

Her expression sharpened again. "What do you mean, you felt him?"

"He was inside my head. I didn't want to tell you earlier because you might make us leave. He tracked me into a bar in Portland. That's why I sounded so scared the night we came here. I was just sitting at a table in a bar, and pictures from his thoughts flashed into my head."

"What did you see?" Her voice was tight.

"Half-decomposed bodies in Edward's cellar, the

photograph of me over his mantel, and the oil painting of me from his storage room. The police have all
those things. He thought in scattered waves about
his partner, Dominick, too. They both were chasing
me."

"How close was he before you felt him?"

"Inside the room."

She sat back in her chair, thinking, staring at William's sleeping form. She didn't seem angry or anxious.
Now that we were openly discussing this, I had a lot of
questions. Except for Edward, I'd never had a chance
to talk like this before—and he didn't know much more
than I did.

"Maggie, why do we see images when we're feeding . . . I mean of our victim's thoughts and life?"

Her head jerked at the word "thoughts."

"I don't know," she answered.

"And why are there so few of us? I used to read accounts of mortals dealing with our kind all over Europe. Now there are six—five, with Edward gone." I
paused, remembering a painful talk I'd had with Edward a hundred years ago. "What happened to the
rest? Edward told me . . . he thought Julian killed some
of us, but he didn't know why."

"Stop it, Leisha." She closed her eyes.

"Don't you ever wonder why we all came from the
same generation? That we were all made within thirty
years of each other?"

"It doesn't matter!"

"How can you say that?" I was angry. It seemed so
foolish to fear discussing our own state of existence.
"You think you're some woman of the world and I'm

this ignorant little girl who doesn't know anything beyond caring for an old man. But you follow Julian's and Philip's laws. You don't ask any questions, and you've been rotting in this house by yourself because they said you should!"

My outburst disturbed her, but I realized that even if she did know more, she wasn't going to tell me. Opening her eyes again, she stared at me—as if she was frightened.

I got up and moved to her. "You're glad we're here, aren't you? Otherwise you never would have called Philip."

"What do you want me to say?" Her low, breathy voice shook slightly. "That I didn't expect things to turn out like this? Okay, I didn't. That I'm scared you might take William and leave? Okay, I am. Is that what you want?"

I got down on my knees and laid my head in her lap. "We're not going anywhere if you want us to stay. But those cops are still looking for me."

"I don't care," she said. "Could that man who's tracking you be one of us?"

"No, I'd have picked that up. He's confused."

"I don't think he'll find you here, then. Not if he has to be in the same room."

She reached out and began stroking my hair. I stopped talking and enjoyed her attention. Her emotions toward me were difficult to read, but I seemed to fit in a niche somewhere between sister and daughter. William had become father or grandfather. We were forming a family. I thought it natural. She thought it strange.

"Let's get dressed and go hunting," I said suddenly. "We need to get out for a while."

"Should we wake William and feed him first?"

Her concern for the old man touched me. Last week, she and I had set up rabbit hutches in the backyard. Her willingness to help with something so menial surprised me. But she had simply said, "It's been a long time since I built anything."

"No," I said to her question about feeding William. "Let him sleep. I'll feed him when we get back."

Maggie called for a cab. Twenty minutes later, we were both made-up, miniskirted, and out the door. We decided to head back for Madison.

The streets downtown were busy. I didn't feel like sitting in a bar, so we just walked around talking to people we knew. Maggie was still a bit shaky about our earlier conversation. I didn't want to hurt or confuse her, but she could be such a sheep sometimes.

The streetlights felt good.

"Why did you leave Philip?" I asked suddenly. I'm sure she was sick of my questions, but now that the floodgates were open, I couldn't seem to stop.

She didn't brush me off. Instead, she kept walking, looking for words. "You had to know him before he was turned. We had one of those stupid, storybook romances where he was willing to give up his title and his family home just to marry me." She smiled cynically. "It was all quite romantic unless you knew the whole truth. His father was a bastard, beat him with a riding crop from the day he learned to walk . . . even burned him once with a lit cigar. His mother was no help, too spineless to do anything besides needlepoint. Philip needed an escape."

"And he picked you?"

"Yes, and then he disappeared for a few months. I couldn't stop crying. But he showed up in my bedroom in Gascony one night with white skin and wild eyes. He couldn't remember my name."

"After he was turned? Why?"

"I don't know. But for some reason he'd lost all memories of his mortal life. Perhaps because he'd been so unhappy, but my Philip, my schoolgirl's-wet-dream Philip had died, leaving a sorry stranger in his place."

"When was all this?"

"It was 1819. I was twenty-three. Philip had just turned twenty-nine. Some of my friends were planning a birthday party for him." She whispered now, lost in her own past. "He kept coming back late at night, like an animal that's forgotten its home but still remembers its master. For a long time he couldn't talk in complete sentences or hold my hand. Then, about a year later, just as things started getting better, one night he pinned me to the floor and—you know how the story goes."

"Yeah, I know."

"He thought it would bridge the gap between us. And it did for a while. But I never stopped missing the way he'd treated me before."

"Is that why you left?"

"No, he went to Harfleur in the winter of 1825. Said he needed to spend some time with Julian. I was glad to see him happy, to see him visiting. But he never came home again, not to live, only to visit now and then, and he was always nervous after that. Something happened to him that winter."

Her beautiful face seemed on the brink of sorrow, so I dropped my questions, feeling almost guilty. Why did my own past make me so insensitive to the needs of others? Just because blood and pain and violence colored the path of my own memory didn't make me an exclusive victim.

We neared the Seattle Center, where the white steel-boned Space Needle loomed up into the sky. Right outside the Coliseum I spotted a small crowd with a few vaguely familiar faces.

"Hey, Eleisha."

Two girls I'd met a few weeks ago at Neumo's were waving to me from the next block. Neither Maggie nor I had been in the mood to hunt that night, so we'd gone out dancing with a couple of Maggie's friends, Jennifer and Theresa.

"Wait, Jen, we'll be right there." I stepped off the curb.

Everything seemed fine, normal, one second, and then it hit me.

Wade's consciousness pushed its way into mine like a lost bull. He jerked out quickly in surprise, and then his thoughts scattered and began grasping at mine in panic. I couldn't see him.

"Maggie!"

My own screaming voice sounded far away. People stared. Wade's mind locked on to the images of bodies in Edward's cellar, the airbrushed photograph of me over his mantel, and the oil painting from 1872 in the storage room.

"Maggie!"

The sight of her running toward me cut through my terror. I felt her hands on my shoulders and realized I was kneeling on the ground.

"What? Are you hurt?"

"It's him. Run."

Her soft body stood up over me, and she looked around. The hatred in her eyes scared me more than the thought of Wade finding us.

"Don't!" I said. "You've got to get out of here."

I couldn't keep talking much longer. It was like living in the center of two distant worlds. Wade tried to run, but somebody had to help drag him. Glimpses of his sight line kept sliding in and out of mine. A wooden fence. A brick alley wall. The sweating face of his partner, Dominick. His fear of Dominick.

Maggie jerked my arm over her shoulder and bolted. I tried to keep up but kept going blind to what was actually in front of me.

"Hold on," she said in my ear. "I'll get us down to Blue Jack's. Ben will hide us."

Ben. I tried to concentrate on the thought of his broad face and palm-tree tattoo. Wade thought about his home. He'd been born in North Dakota, and his dad was a farmer. He wanted to know what I was. He wanted to know why Edward's death had caused him so much pain.

I became dimly aware that the farther Maggie ran, the more concrete Wade's thought patterns became.

"Wrong way," I tried to get out.

She didn't hear me. I tried focusing all my energy on pushing Wade out. For a few seconds it worked, but then the effort became unbearable, like swimming against a tidal current.

Maggie stopped.

I lifted my head and groaned. We were in some kind of alley, and Dominick stood panting and sweating in front of us. He was stocky and muscular, with dark hair and at least three days' growth on his face. Instead of a uniform, he wore faded jeans and a brown canvas coat—with Wade draped over his shoulder.

He dropped Wade and pulled a gun, a revolver.

"Freeze."

I couldn't talk. I couldn't separate my own past from Wade's. Could Maggie feel him, too?

Wade raised his head off the ground and looked at me. I remembered that he was tall, but the thin quality of his face suddenly struck me as beautiful and eerie at the same time. He was part of me.

"You," he whispered.

Why couldn't Maggie feel him?

"Put the girl down and step back," Dominick's voice echoed, flat and ugly.

No, he'll kill you.

Was that me or Wade? It didn't matter, and it was too late. Maggie whirled around, still holding me, and tried to run back down the alley. An explosion shook the graffiti-covered brick walls. The ground rushed up to my face, but it didn't hurt.

Crawling to all fours, I stared at a bloody, gaping hole in Maggie's back.

This can't be happening.

Was that me or Wade?

Dominick's footsteps sounded behind me. I half turned to see him, my mind screaming to try and grab hold of the gun, but I still couldn't clear my thoughts. When he reached down toward us, a flash of wavy, brown-black hair brushed over my cheek as Maggie suddenly pushed up off the ground and whirled around, swinging hard with her left hand and making a grab for his throat with her right. Her swing connected, and the gun landed on the ground with a thud.

"No," I tried to tell her. "Run."

But their bodies seemed locked together now, and they both fell backward. I could hear Dominick's desperate breathing. Undeads aren't supernaturally stronger than mortals. Pain stops people from running too fast or lifting too much or hitting too hard. But we don't have active nerve synapses, so that type of pain doesn't stop us.

I tried to crawl toward them, but the world started spinning, and my eyesight blurred again. When my vision cleared, he had her pinned down. Even without the pain to stop her, she wasn't a match for him. Creatures like us relied on our gifts. We rarely had to fight.

The light from a rooftop glowed off her dress and turned it dark orange. She looked so soft and violent. Blood covered one side of Dominick's face, but it must have been Maggie's.

She hissed and clawed at him—fighting for me—trying to freak him out. I couldn't move. Wade was still in my head, but out of my sight. Dominick had Maggie pinned with one hand, and a glint flashed as he managed to pull a long machete from a sheath under his coat. With his face locked in a mad grimace, he shoved the edge down against her throat.

"No!" I tried to scream, but the word came out in a rasp.

He didn't hear me. She made a gurgling sound. He kept wildly pushing the blade down, down through her throat to the bone at the nape of her neck. I heard a loud crack.

It's too bad undead can't cry.

The force of a thousand lives burst from Maggie's body, and Wade screamed. Maybe I did, too. Waves and waves jolted through and over and past me until I lay twitching on the alley floor. I don't know how much time passed. Seemed like hours.

Dominick knelt beside Wade. "What is it? What's wrong?" he kept saying.

Wade's consciousness was no longer inside me. His head lay at a twisted angle, and his eyes were closed. Maggie's headless body lay on the ground by a trash can.

She died for me. I struggled to my feet, choking in disbelief.

Dominick looked up in surprise and scrambled toward his absent gun. His china blue eyes and black facial stubble burned a permanent picture in my memory. Murderer. I couldn't fight him. I didn't know how. Instead, I turned and ran like a child down the alley.

He yelled something after me, but didn't follow. I stumbled on, lost in a nightmare. Maggie was dead, and I'd led her killers here. Now there were four of us. Only four.

My first thought was to race home and move William, but then my head cleared. Of all the places in the country, how had they known to look for me in Seattle? I could think of only one connection. Moving wasn't the answer. Running wasn't the answer.

I had to kill Wade.

chapter 8

Ten minutes later, I doubled back about two blocks behind them and crouched down. I waited for Wade to wake up, not knowing how close he needed to be for mental contact. I wanted to stay as near as safety allowed, but with enough distance to get away from him if he tried to track me down.

It was hard not to think about Maggie, hard not to wallow in hatred. I'd never seen a man so unaffected by Maggie's beauty. Dominick hadn't even flinched.

As my mind ran back over the horrible scene of him pinning her to the ground, I began to focus on a few things more clearly. He hadn't seemed surprised when his gunshot didn't kill her, even though he'd caught her square in the back. The memory of his face floated in front of me so solid and sharp it might have been there. The emotions flowing across it had run a rapid course—fear, hysteria, hatred—but not surprise, never once surprise. Why? Wade didn't know what I was, so he couldn't possibly know about Maggie. Yet Dominick severed her head. How had he known to do that?

The only way to permanently destroy one of us is to

somehow destroy the body: decapitation, fire, explosion . . . A stake through the heart is not enough. I've read that old European vampire hunters believed after staking an undead they also had to cut its head off—something about saving the soul. A stake through the heart would probably incapacitate any of us long enough for some zealot to perform a decapitation. The shock alone would cause temporary paralysis.

But how had Dominick known what to do?

It suddenly occurred to me that his gun had been lying on the ground somewhere close to me after the psychic pain of Maggie's death faded away. All I'd had to do was pick it up and shoot him. But no, I'd run off like a scared rabbit.

Something began stirring softly inside my head. Wade was awake. Without attempting to push him from my mind, I thought about nothing. I pictured a huge black hole covering the world. He would still be able to read my presence, but hopefully couldn't pinpoint my location or extract any information.

I didn't try to read his thoughts or do anything besides crouch there, picturing a black hole. He cast about for me in weak thought patterns and then stopped, probably exhausted. I moved toward the alley until Dominick's voice became audible.

"Just stop it then! She's long gone by now. If I had half a brain, I would've gone after her. Jesus, Wade, I thought you were dead."

When Wade answered, he startled me. Dominick's voice sounded exactly like he looked—mean and ugly. But Wade's voice was clear, kind of breathy. It didn't match his roughly scattered thought patterns.

"You killed her, Dom! You killed that woman. What are we going to do?"

"We're going to get the hell out of here. Can you walk?"

"We can't just leave her. There's a bullet from your gun in her back."

"No, come here and look. It went straight through her."

"Then it's still here somewhere. You know the routine. They'll find it."

"Come on, Wade. She looks like just another hooker. Nobody's gonna search this alley."

I'd never seen a dead vampire before. I mean . . . we're undead, but Maggie was *dead* now. Edward once told me that our bodies would begin cracking within moments, and then start turning to ash. This would eradicate any evidence of her existence. I had a sick feeling Dominick knew that or he wouldn't have been so flippant about the missing bullet.

Their argument grew muffled, and I could pick out only bits and pieces. Then they started moving. I kept the black hole in my mind in case Wade tried to search again, but I was beginning to realize that he didn't know much more about focusing his psyche than I did.

I followed them as closely as possible. It would have been a lot easier if I simply could have gone inside Wade's head and viewed his physical surroundings through his eyes, but that would have given my position away.

They eventually ended up on Fourth Avenue and got into a silver Mustang. I panicked for a second. Having to follow them in a car never occurred to me. The dark streets were nearly empty. Then I spotted an overweight teenager unlocking a dented Ford Escort.

The Mustang pulled out from the curb.

I ran to the pudgy kid. "Hey," I said, smiling. "Do me a big favor? Quick. For twenty bucks?"

His face melted in a simultaneous mask of suspicion and interest. "What kind of favor?"

"Follow them," I said, pointing to the disappearing Mustang.

He stared at me. "You're kidding."

"Just do it, okay?"

"Old boyfriend?"

"Something like that."

"Okay, get in."

"You're a prince."

He was actually pretty good behind the wheel and caught up to the silver moving target within a few seconds.

"Not bad," I said. "You practice this?"

He lit a cigarette and held it between thick lips. "My girlfriend dumped me for a hockey player. I used to follow 'em around sometimes."

"What happened then?"

"I got over it."

"Good for you. I heard hockey players make lousy lays, anyway. Too many bruises."

"Yeah." He smiled. "That's what my dad said."

Dominick drove all the way out to old Highway 99 and parked by a single-story motel called the Rosewood. But daylight was only a few hours away, so whatever I was going to do had to be fast.

"Here's my stop," I said. "Everyone please depart in a calm and orderly fashion."

The kid laughed softly, and I handed him thirty dollars.

"Thanks a lot," I said. "I gotta go."

"Hey, wait." He wrote something quickly on a book of matches and gave it to me. "That's my number. If you get over this guy, give me a call."

Sometimes I forget that I look seventeen. "Just might have to do that. Always did like a man who can drive."

As he pulled back onto the street, I fell out of charming mode and crouched down behind a Chevy pickup. Dominick slipped into room 6. Wade went into room 10. Instinct told me to ignore Wade and cut his partner's heart out, but common sense pushed that vision away. Dominick might know more than he should, but he was useless and blind without Wade.

For a moment, I considered knocking on Wade's door and taking him by surprise when he opened it. But the scene of Maggie's death flashed by me, and I decided he'd have to be caught while sleeping. For that I'd need a key.

The lobby of the Rosewood Motel was dead at three o'clock in the morning. A middle-aged clerk sat reading a tattered issue of *Playboy* behind the front desk. After peering through a set of glass front doors, I used my teeth to tear my own left wrist open and then smeared blood all over my arm and face before staggering into the lobby, bleeding on the cheap, indoor-outdoor carpet.

"Please, help me."

The clerk's stunned expression would have been comical at another time. Dropping the magazine, he hurried toward me, muttering, "Oh, dear. Oh, dear."

I hadn't heard that in years.

"Did someone cut you?" he asked, grabbing my arm.

For an answer, I started crying, and his face contorted in distress.

"This way, dear. Come back here and we'll tie up your arm and call someone to help."

His manner was so sweet and reassuring that I didn't like the idea of hurting him. With one hand on my shoulder and one holding my injured arm, he led me around to a TV room behind the front desk.

"Just a minute now and we'll have the bleeding stopped," he said. "Put your fingers here behind the wound, and I'll get you a bandage."

He trotted off and came back quickly with a first-aid kit. "Now, let me see."

When he leaned over to take a closer look, I brought my right elbow down on the back of his head hard enough to drop him. He fell like a sack of grain and lay unconscious.

He'd been nice. It bothered me to give any kind deed such a shoddy return, so I made sure he was breathing and then pushed two hundred dollars into his jacket.

The keys were hanging in shiny rows on nails behind the front desk. Wade must be asleep by now. I quickly found the key to room 10 and bolted out the door.

Room 10 was close. Putting my ear to the door, I listened for him. Nothing. Tentatively, I cast about with my mind, trying to pick up conscious thought patterns. Nothing. The key fit smoothly into the lock.

Click.

We have several advantages that I rarely, if ever, think about: like night vision. Many of my concepts of vampire lore were picked up from American culture. Film portraits of some handsome romantic undead hero bemoaning the fact that he'll never again see the sunrise have always made me gag. Edward and I used to go to the theater when we were bored and giggle during those silly scenes. We probably annoyed a lot of people. But after the first few adjustment years, I never missed the sun. My world is dark, and if I want light, I just stay home and run up the power bill. Why should anyone living an unnatural existence long for natural light? Ridiculous.

From the doorway I watched Wade breathing softly on his bed. The curtains by his head moved slightly in a night breeze. Moving in, I let the door close behind me. His clothes lay neatly across the back of a chair with his shoulder holster positioned on top. A streetlight outside the window reflected glittering points off the handle of his gun. This would be too easy.

I quietly unsnapped the little leather thong over the trigger guard and found myself pulling out a 9mm Beretta. It felt heavy and alien in my hand. For some reason, I had a feeling it had never been fired outside a target range.

Wade's breathing changed slightly, but he just rolled over in his sleep. How had Dominick known to cut Maggie's head off? I just couldn't get that out of my mind. How much did Wade know? Who else had they told about all this? Who else believed them?

Without really thinking, I walked over and pointed the gun at his head, but not close enough for him to grab.

"Wake up."

He stirred.

"Wake up, or I'll just kill you now."

Two very light brown eyes looked up at me from a narrow face.

"You stay out of my head," I whispered.

He gasped and sat up.

"Don't," I said. "Is this thing loaded?"

He nodded slowly, realization dawning. "What are you doing here?"

"Murdering you."

"No! I didn't know Dominick would kill your friend. We never talked about that. He's just gone off the deep end trying to figure this thing out."

"What thing?"

"You know."

"Don't cops have their own laws? If you're so sorry then why didn't you do something? Why haven't you at least turned him in? Shooting a woman in the back and then cutting her head off might be construed as slightly overzealous. Don't you think?"

He didn't answer for a moment, but watched my face and the gun. He seemed fascinated, like he wanted to spit out a thousand words but couldn't find them. "I can't turn him in."

"Why not? You jack-offs stick up for each other? Even for something like this?"

"No, it isn't that. It's . . . We don't work for the Portland Police anymore."

At first, that surprised me, but then again, I remembered Dominick was no longer wearing a uniform.

"Then why are you here?" I asked. "Why are you following me?"

He struggled for an answer. The corner of his left eye twitched as if with effort. His almost-white hair looked as if it had once been worn short and layered, but had long since outgrown its cut and simply rested in shaggy, messy tufts over his ears.

"Eleisha, I can't—"

The sound of him speaking my name made me jump. "Don't do that."

He pushed the blankets back and put his feet on the floor. All he had on was a pair of gray drawstring pajama pants.

"No, listen. I won't hurt you," he said. "I can't believe you're standing here, but I don't know how to tell you all this. It would take forever."

"I've got some time."

"There's a faster way." His face was guarded now.

"No."

"I want to help you!" he almost shouted. "Please . . . put the gun down and come here. Aren't you curious? If you just got inside my head for two seconds, you'd believe me. Please."

I didn't move.

"You need to see my thoughts when we aren't running," he rushed on. "I've been dreaming about this since that first morning when you reached inside my head."

Reached inside his head? He had pushed into mine.

"I can read everybody's thoughts." His voice was shaking. "No one but you can read mine."

How should I answer? Somehow, on some level, his words meant something to me. It's hard to explain. I still hated him for what he had helped do to Maggie, but I couldn't stop listening to him.

"You can read other people's thoughts?" I asked.

"Yes, everyone's." He nodded excitedly. "I can . . . Eleisha, just come here. We don't have to use words."

Slowly, I put the gun down. He looked tall and slender and white-blond—almost like an angel sitting there in his pajama pants. An angel. What a joke.

"What now?"

"Just sit down," he said.

"Don't touch me."

"I don't have to. But if you're standing you might fall . . . like earlier. It doesn't have to be like that."

When I didn't move any closer, he dropped down on the carpet. "Here, come sit on the floor."

It's strange how he judged me by normal mortal reactions, mortal fears. What did he think I was afraid of? That he'd rape me? Is that what he thought? I'd been playing the frightened little street urchin so long that maybe it just emanated from me. What would he think if he knew what I was really afraid of? That he'd find out I was undead. That I lived off the blood of others. What would he do when he found out about William?

"You don't have to show me anything," he said quickly, as though reading my face. "Just learn to focus. Just search inside me, and I can show you all of the past six weeks. I can show you pieces of my whole life."

It was urgent for me to learn about him and about

Dominick, why they were here, how much they knew, what they wanted.

Crossing over, I knelt down on the floor. Wade's features were animated, excited. We didn't say anything. For a moment we didn't do anything. Then, with my mind, I reached out cautiously and tried to see through his eyes. For nearly an hour, that's the last conscious thought I had.

chapter 9

Wade

Wade Sheffield was born in North Dakota in 1977, the fourth son of a wheat farmer. He was seven years old before realizing that no one else could hear other people's thoughts. His older brothers thought him weak because he cried while helping with daily chores like delivering baby calves or butchering chickens. His sisters sometimes cried when chickens were killed, but the men in his family couldn't figure tears over a new calf.

"She hurts so much," he would say, stroking the heifer in labor.

At the age of twelve, he began responding verbally to people's thoughts. This made several of his teachers nervous—especially the ones who quietly hated teaching, and Mr. Rhinehard, who was sleeping with a fifteen-year-old student named Phyllis Dunmire.

Wade knew all this. He knew what they thought of him. Most of the boys hated him because he was different, and most of the girls wouldn't be seen with anyone so unpopular. Lisa McKendrick had a secret crush on him for a few years, but she also worried much of the time about her private nose-picking habit.

By reading the thoughts of animals, he could always tell when a storm was coming. Animals knew a lot about weather.

One year, when he was fourteen, he stopped off for hamburgers with two of his brothers and mentioned to Mr. Masterson and Mr. Hinthorn that they should bring their cattle in early because of a thunderstorm. The weatherman on the radio had predicted no storm.

That night, every farm within a seventy-mile radius of the Sheffields' lost half their wheat. In anger and frustration, people blamed Wade because he'd warned them.

Within a week, three farmers caught him alone on the way to school and beat him with pitchfork handles until his left leg and four ribs were broken. His oldest brother, Joshua, put him in the back of a Ford pickup and drove him to the Whitman County Hospital, where he was also diagnosed as suffering from a concussion. The next few weeks were hazy. He didn't remember much besides a lot of bright lights, but when he woke up, a miracle happened.

Dr. Geoffrey Van Tassel leaned down over him and smiled.

"Welcome back," the round-faced man said. "Tell me what I'm thinking."

Wade had grown practiced at hiding the extent of his gift, but now he picked up bits and pieces of very focused thought patterns. "A garden," he whispered.

"Strawberries that your mother planted a long time ago."

The eyes above him grew warm. "I have an interesting proposition for you, young man, when you're feeling better."

Wade often viewed that moment as the real beginning of his life. Six weeks later, he arrived at the Psychic Research Institute of Northern Colorado, on a set of rented crutches, and began to realize his own self-worth. Suddenly, being able to do something no one else could do had turned into a plus instead of a severe minus.

Dr. Van Tassel was often with him then. Apparently, Wade talked a good deal while in his state of delirium. He'd been speaking aloud whatever the nurses happened to be thinking. Sheila Osborne, a young nursing student from the Psychic Institute, had been working on her internship at the Whitman County Hospital during Wade's stay.

The night before first seeing him, she'd experienced the worst blind date of her life. The guy her best friend had fixed her up with looked like he belonged on the cover of *Muscle Fitness*. He wouldn't eat the popcorn she bought at the movies because it had salt and butter. He called her babe and lectured her most of the night about the best kind of workout for slimming down her thighs. And then he actually expected her to sleep with him after his cellulite comment.

Slamming bedpans into the cupboard of a hospital room, she heard soft murmuring from the bed.

"I don't have cellulite. And I was wearing Levi's. What would he know?"

She stopped in shock. A semiconscious young man on the bed was rolling slowly in sweat-soaked sheets and whispering her recent thoughts. Forgetting her own hurt vanity, she leaned over him and wiped his face.

"Yeah, I had Levi's on," she said. "What kind of shirt was I wearing?"

"No shirt—that pink sweater your mom bought you last Christmas."

His voice was barely audible, but she heard him. Ten minutes later, she was on the phone to Dr. Van Tassel in Colorado. "I think you'd better come up here. There's someone you need to see."

That was the beginning. Sheila returned to the institute and remained his friend. Although he never did remember much about his stay at Whitman County, she related an embarrassing story about him exposing an affair between a prominent neurologist and his youngest male lab assistant. That hadn't gone over well in North Dakota.

Wade found some of the experiments he participated in to be pointless. But he continued high school with other young people like himself. Well, not quite like himself. No one in the history of the institute had demonstrated anything close to Wade's telepathic ability. He was the golden boy. Everyone wanted to be like him. But as the years passed, they kept asking him a lot of redundant questions.

"What do you see in my mind, Wade? Do you see words or pictures?"

"I see what you feel. Pictures, I guess. I don't know."

Scores of PhDs in fields he didn't understand wrote papers about him.

The frightened, barely literate farm boy from North Dakota slowly fell away, and a self-assured, young-adult version of Wade took his place. In time, he began to verbalize his responses on a higher level.

"What do you see in my mind, Wade? Do you see words or pictures?"

"What do you see when I speak?" he answered. "Do you see words coming from my mouth? How does your mind know what I'm saying?"

In his senior year of high school, he stopped studying for exams. Why should he study when the answers were right there in the teacher's head? He took Russian and began speaking the language fluently in three weeks just by concentrating on the instructor.

He lost his virginity to Sheila, but then left quickly afterward when she began thinking that he'd been okay but didn't compare to her last boyfriend, Steve.

His teachers started making him take his exams in a private room.

But most of them understood his sometimes difficult behavior. He *was* different, and they did not expect his schooling to be normal.

However, when new arrivals came to the institute, he was often put in charge of helping the young children adjust to their new environment. Early on, Wade exhibited strong—almost obsessive—tendencies toward protection over the institute's children, especially any who had been abused or neglected by their families . . . due to their abilities. He remembered all too well how it felt to be blamed and punished for his gift.

The children responded well to his assurances that everything would be different now, and he always let them talk to him, even though he could simply read their thoughts.

One thing Dr. Van Tassel did discover was that if he, or anyone else, put a conscious effort into blocking Wade, it wasn't difficult to lock the young man out. But the doctor never stopped thinking about the possibilities for Wade's gift.

"You could be anything you wanted, my boy. Anything."

The problem was that Wade didn't know what he wanted. At nineteen, his self-assured nature wavered when he was faced with choosing a university. The memories of fear and ostracism from his childhood had never quite passed away. The people in Colorado seemed to like him, and Dr. Van Tassel was the closest thing he had to a father. He hadn't seen his own since leaving for the institute.

His first thought was to go into social services—specializing in child protection. But he wasn't certain that his motivation was correct, and he had no idea *where* he wished to attend college.

The issue eradicated itself when he found out that he didn't have to make a choice. The institute arranged a full scholarship for him at Colorado State University in Fort Collins. All he had to do was go back and work with Dr. Van Tassel during summers and breaks on new tests or research projects. Relief flooded through him. That was safe and perfect.

"What are you majoring in, son?"

"I don't know. What should I major in?"

"That's up to you. As long as you continue working with the doctors at the institute several times a year, you can choose anything you want."

More choices. All his life he had hidden behind one wall or another. Now he was going back into mainstream society, where people had once beaten him with pitchfork handles.

College turned out to be quite different than he expected, though—full of pretty girls, liberal professors who questioned the government, and law students in black wool coats walking past Peace Corps soon-to-bes. It was amazing. But the pull to remain part of the institute, part of a safer world, still influenced him. He decided to major in psychology.

Dating, football games, and a part-time job in the university bookstore became part of his life and made him feel normal. Knowing how his girlfriends really felt about him wasn't an insurmountable problem. He simply took it for granted that even people deeply in love had evil thoughts about each other once in a while. He had long since grown used to reading the casual malice behind someone's smile. Those emotions were human.

His friends and lovers, however, didn't take his abilities so lightly. In his junior year, he fell hard for an anthropology student named Karen. She had long, brown hair and hazel eyes. He loved even the tiny freckles on her nose.

"This isn't working," she told him after six months. "I can't stand that you know what I'm thinking every minute, and you're a blank wall to me. I never know what you're feeling."

"Then ask me."

"I shouldn't have to."

That particular brand of pain and loss was new to him. He flunked statistics and had to retake it in his senior year.

After that, nothing of real note happened in his life until midway through graduate school. When he was twenty-three and working on his master's in developmental psychology, an inspector from the Los Angeles Police Department flew out and made an appointment to speak to him while he was on summer break at the institute. Dr. Van Tassel instructed Wade to make an effort to stay out of the inspector's mind.

"I'm Will Redington," said a tall man in a business suit, extending his hand. "Dr. Van Tassel's told me a little about you. We need you to do something for us."

"What?" Wade asked, immediately suspicious. This situation smelled as if he would have to make a decision.

"Just listen to one of our departmental psychologists talk to an officer," Redington said calmly. "That's all we want you to do. You'll be in a separate room with me, on the other side of a two-way mirror. You can see and hear everything that goes on. I just need you to tell me what the officer is thinking during the interview."

"Is he being accused of something?"

"I can't tell you that."

Wade looked to Dr. Van Tassel for help.

"It's your choice, son. You don't have to do anything you don't want to."

"What would you do?"

"I'd use my gift to help as many people as possible."

That wasn't much help. The inspector looked as if he flossed with a bicycle chain.

"Okay," Wade said uncertainly. "When?"

"Two days." Redington smiled. "We'll fly to California tomorrow."

Two days later, Wade found himself in an air-conditioned Los Angeles precinct. The interview room turned out much like Wade expected it to be—small and windowless, with an empty table and chairs. The officer in question's name was Mark Taylor. Wade was placed in an adjoining room on the other side of the two-way mirror Redington had promised. He was told to watch and listen to what went on.

Officer Taylor had a stoic, passive expression and answered the questions being asked him with all the emotion of a brass chess piece.

"Mark," the psychologist began, "how are you feeling about Christopher's death right now?"

"No one forgets something like that right away," Taylor answered. "I'm angry, but I'm dealing. It doesn't affect my job performance."

His answer sounded healthy and logical. Wade gently reached out into the man's mind, and then fell forward out of his chair in shock. Hatred and rage and visions of violent death flashed before him like an NC-17 film.

"Wade." Someone was shaking him. He looked up to

see Inspector Redington's face looming over him. "What do you see?"

"Christopher . . ." Wade choked. "He's dead. They cut his throat open and pulled his tongue through the hole."

Slight surprise registered on Redington's face. "Yes, we know that. But what is Officer Taylor thinking?"

"They killed Christopher," Wade shouted, "and you don't even care!"

"Sssssh, keep your voice down."

Wade started shaking. Christopher was Mark's partner. They'd been working undercover with some small-time cocaine dealers, trying to flush out big game.

"Who killed Christopher?" Redington asked suddenly.

Wade glared at him. "You know. You all know."

"Then tell me."

"Juan Merinchez and the rest of those spics."

Wade seemed to be lost inside Mark's mind.

"And Juan deserves to die, doesn't he?" Redington asked.

"He's already dead, you worthless piece of shit. Somebody had to handle it."

"If he's dead, then where's his body?"

"Eddy's Junkyard, in the trunk of a 'sixty-seven Fairlane."

Redington went to the door quickly and spoke to someone outside. Then Officer Taylor was taken away from the little room on the other side of the mirror.

"Wade," Redington said, "are you all right?"

Ugly pictures moving like worms crawled around

the inside of Wade's skull. He couldn't stop shaking or get up off the floor. Redington yelled out, "Somebody get me a glass of water!"

A uniformed policewoman came in with a paper cup. Redington held it to Wade's mouth.

"Drink this."

Cold water splashed between Wade's teeth. "Why did you do that to me?"

"We had to know. To be honest, I don't think I believed what Van Tassel said about you."

He leaned down to help Wade get up.

"Don't touch me!"

Redington pulled back slightly, withdrawing his hand. "I know you're thinking that none of this is fair. Not to you. Not to Mark. But our psychologist did an extensive evaluation and found him fit and ready for duty. Mark's been running around with a badge and a gun for two weeks now. Is that fair? Is that right?"

Wade's head was beginning to clear. "No," he whispered. "He shouldn't have a gun. He's dangerous . . . and racist. But he doesn't care about very many people, not even his wife. He cared about Christopher."

"That doesn't give him the right to kill someone."

"Did you know he'd killed Merinchez?"

"I had a pretty good idea. We just needed a body. And you may just have given us that."

Less than an hour later, two officers found Juan Merinchez's body in the trunk of a '67 Fairlane exactly where Wade had seen it in Mark Taylor's mind. Wade left the precinct as quickly as possible, flew home, and never checked back to find out what happened to Taylor. He didn't want to know.

Long ago, Wade had learned to slowly examine his feelings. Letting them all in at once caused poor or quick judgments. The experience in Mark Taylor's mind never left him. Those thoughts had been the ugliest string of images he'd ever seen. They would be with him always. But then anger set in . . . and guilt. That psychologist must have been blind. What if Inspector Redington had flown Wade out to California a few days earlier, before Mark Taylor had killed Merinchez? Could the situation have been averted? Perhaps Merinchez would still be alive, and Mark wouldn't be facing murder charges. Or back even further, what if Wade had actually been working undercover with Mark and Christopher? Could he have picked up that Merinchez had grown wise and then helped avoid Christopher's death at all? What if?

The questions never left him for long. After receiving a master's degree in developmental psychology, he went on to a PhD in criminal psychology at the University of Colorado in Boulder. Shortly before graduation, he applied to twenty-seven police departments around the country for a position as staff psychologist. He was offered three, and finally accepted a place in Portland, Oregon, because the department seemed friendly but overworked and in need of someone like Wade.

Wade wished to be needed.

"We'll miss you," Dr. Van Tassel said, smiling, "but I think you've made the right choice. You thought I wanted you to be a professor or a scientist, didn't you?"

"Sometimes, yes."

"It's your gift, Wade. We can study it and write about it. But you've been searching for something else your whole life. Perhaps you've found it. Come home for Christmas."

With the first phase of his life over, Wade moved smoothly into the next. He found a loft-style apartment that would have cost him twice as much in Denver. The weather wasn't to his taste. It rained a lot. But the trees were green, the city was old but not too old, vogue but not too vogue. He thought he could be happy here.

The job was difficult at first. He was responsible for the files on forty-four men and women. In spite of his own innate ability, there was a mountain of red tape to be danced around every time someone gave him cause for concern, especially when Captain McNickel wanted the officer in question back on the street.

A rookie named Joe Tashet got stabbed in the side while running down a fleeing mugger. After healing up and receiving a clean bill of health from a medical doctor, he was handed over to the police psychologist.

"No way," Wade stated flatly to Captain McNickel in private. "He's terrified. It's all too new. Give him a little more time."

"We don't have any more time. Unless you tell me he's going to piss on the street and then shoot a couple of old ladies, I need him back out tomorrow."

"What about his partner? Is it fair to send someone else out with a panicked rookie cop?"

"He needs to get back on the horse, Sheffield."

McNickel was the only person who refused to call him Dr. Sheffield.

But Wade found that understandable. After all, he

was barely twenty-seven and looked even younger. It would be hard for a crotchety old geezer like McNickel to refer to him by a title like "doctor."

What Wade didn't like or understand was McNickel's constant refusal to accept sound diagnoses. But the Joe Tashet case ended some of those problems.

Less than a month after Joe's psych evaluation, his partner was shot and killed by a drunken husband as the two officers were investigating a domestic battle. At the first sign of a gun, Joe bolted, leaving his partner with no backup.

McNickel listened to Wade more often after that.

Some of Wade's fantasies and expectations never came to pass. He didn't work undercover. He was occasionally asked to evaluate suspects and appear in court, but McNickel ordered him to "play down the psychic bit and just do your job."

Wade was often tempted to look inside McNickel's head and find out what made the old man so bad-tempered. Maybe his sex life was lousy . . . though Wade's own hadn't exactly been fireworks either. His job kept him hopping. Most of his duties consisted of helping exhausted, bored, and/or disillusioned cops whose work lives were drastically invading their home lives. Time passed quickly.

On November 7, 2005, at 5:32 P.M., Wade met Detective Dominick Vasundara, a transfer from New York. Wade was finishing up some paperwork in his office late that afternoon when a deep voice sounded from the open doorway.

"Captain told me to see you."

Looking up, Wade saw a man of medium height and stocky build, with stubble covering his wide jaw, and short black hair. He was dressed in faded jeans and a sweatshirt with the sleeves ripped off. The man wasn't large, but somehow he seemed to block the entire doorway.

"Can I help you?" Wade asked.

"Yeah, I'm Dominick. I don't know what you can do. The captain told me to see you on my way out. Something about starting a file."

Wade was tired. He'd had a long day, and the last thing he wanted to do was start a new file. He should already have this guy's records anyway.

"Are you a transfer?"

"Yeah, New York."

"Really? Did you request to come here?"

"All that stuff's on my application."

At that, Wade instantly entered Dominick's mind. He was too beat to play verbal volleyball.

Expecting the new arrival to simply sit there for a few seconds dripping in attitude, Wade read a few normal, sexually motivated images before he saw surprise flicker across Dominick's face.

"What the . . . ?" He blocked Wade. "Stay out of my head."

"Did you feel that?" Wade sat up, startled. "Could you feel me focusing in on your thoughts?"

"What do you think I am, stupid?"

"No, but you shouldn't have been able to—"

"Look, I'm not getting paid to be here yet. If you need anything, ask in a hurry and let me go."

This guy was some piece of work. First, he acted as if

setting up his psych file was an annoying chore, and then he acted as if someone pushing around inside his head was an everyday event.

"Do you want to get a beer?" Wade asked suddenly, surprising himself as much as Dominick.

"What?"

"I've been here since six this morning. There's a little sports bar down the street . . . good nachos. Why don't we finish up down there?"

The unshaven New Yorker stared at him for a few seconds and then shrugged. "Yeah, sure. Why not? I'm not trying to be a pain. People have just been jacking me around since noon. I thought I'd be out of here a couple hours ago."

Three beers later, they were sitting in Spankey T's Sports Bar watching the Seattle Seahawks get killed by the Chicago Bears on a large-screen TV. Wade sat there struggling for a way to broach the subject of how Dominick had known about blocking a psychic entry. The problem solved itself when his companion turned to him during a time-out and asked, "Hey, where'd you learn telepathy?"

For a moment the question threw him. "I didn't learn it anywhere . . ."

Wade had never considered himself bigoted or socially biased. But hearing a word like "telepathy" come out of Dominick's mouth surprised him. He usually imagined overmuscled guys with Bronx accents who wore torn-up sweatshirts would speak in one- or two-syllable words.

"I learned to focus it," he went on, "at the Psychic Research Institute in Colorado."

"Really? Did your folks sell you?"

"What? No . . . I wanted to go. My folks were ready to burn me at the stake. How'd you know to block me?"

Dominick put his beer down. "Spent a couple years with kids like you in high school. Some old guys, doctors, paid my folks a lot of money to borrow me for a while."

The tiny hairs on Wade's arms began to prickle. "Why?"

"I can touch things—almost anything—and tell you where they've been and who else has touched them."

"Psychometry?"

"Yeah."

"Were you involved with a research center?"

"A what? No, it wasn't like that. These guys worked for NYU, in this little building off campus. They had about six of us. They made us do a lot of stupid things. Pretty useless. One guy a little younger than me had what you have—telepathy. He and I used to practice on each other."

Wade sat there, fascinated. Even at the institute, psychometry was an unusual ability. Dominick spoke of it in the same tone he might use to say he was good at calculus.

"So what made you join the police force?" Wade asked.

His companion's forehead wrinkled slightly, as though he wasn't sure how to answer. "I couldn't always, you know, do it . . . when they gave me things to examine. Sometimes I could see dozens of pictures about an object, who it belonged to, where it'd been. But sometimes I didn't see anything."

Wade didn't follow him. "So that made you want to be a cop?"

"No. One day Dr. Morris—he worked with me the most—shows up with this guy in a suit. I was about fifteen then. Anyway, they take me into a back room and hand me a ripped-up white sweater with dried blood all over it."

Wade went cold. "What happened?"

"I threw up." Dominick's voice dropped, and he seemed to slide uncomfortably back into the past.

"I'm sorry," Wade whispered. The description was too close to home.

"It wouldn't have been so bad," Dominick went on, "but they didn't believe everything I told them."

"What did you see?"

"A dark-haired guy with green eyes, wearing a black tux. He tore this girl's throat open with his teeth and started drinking her blood. Since she was wearing the sweater, I saw it all through her eyes. I gave a full description of the guy. Three witnesses, including an informant bartender, claimed to see someone who exactly matched the description leave the Garden Lounge with her less than an hour before she died."

"Did they ever arrest anyone?"

"No, I don't think so. I was just a kid."

"So you joined up to help?"

"Yeah, something like that."

Wade looked into his glass at the foaming beer. This man sitting next to him certainly wasn't someone he'd actively seek out as a friend. But he felt a strange companionship, an understanding.

"I forgot you're the staff shrink," Dominick said. "You think I'm cracked, don't you?"

"No, I was just thinking about how you got involved with the force. We have a lot in common. Maybe I'll tell you sometime."

Dominick looked away. "I gotta go. It's getting late, and I just flew in this morning."

"Where're you staying?"

"I'm going to find a hotel. Someone told me apartments are pretty cheap. I'll start looking tomorrow."

"Compared to New York? Hell, yes. Hey, my couch folds out into a bed. You could crash there tonight. We can pick up a newspaper on the way home. You could go through the classifieds and call on apartments from my place tomorrow. I'll be at work all day."

"You married?"

"Me? No, if I was, she'd divorce me for criminal negligence. Job keeps me hopping." He jumped off the barstool. "Come on."

Dominick looked too tired to argue. They picked up a pizza and a newspaper on the way home. That was the beginning.

Dominick found a one-bedroom apartment only a mile from Wade's place. It often struck Wade as odd that the two of them had little in common and never discussed personal matters, but they spent four or five evenings a week together, just watching movies or going out for beer. Some nights, Wade would sit at his desk in the living room and work while Dominick just hung around entertaining himself. They seemed comfortable without having to talk.

Instead of sticking out like a sore thumb, Dominick fit in well at the Portland precinct. He was fair, hard, tough, never late for work, and wrote up reports with remarkable clarity and accuracy. He displayed a few eccentricities. For one, he carried a .357 revolver instead of a more standard-issue automatic pistol. He said he'd learned to shoot with this gun and refused to replace it. And two, he seemed to possess no sense of humor— none. But these things were minor in the grand scheme.

"I wish we could clone him," Captain McNickel said.

The one problem Wade had with his friend was an unfamiliar feeling of blindness. He hadn't realized how heavily he relied upon telepathy in his job. With Dominick, he had to actually judge facial expressions and reactions. Making a correct analysis seemed impossible.

"Why don't you let me in?" he asked one day while riding to lunch in Dominick's police car. "I'm trained at this, you know. I could make a decent evaluation if you'd just stop blocking me."

"No. How'd you like it if I picked up a pair of your underwear and told you who you screwed last week?"

Wade winced. "It wouldn't be like that. Most people think about sex forty times a day. I'm used to that."

"Just drop it."

Wade became so concerned that he suggested to Captain McNickel they assign Dominick's evaluations to another psychologist.

"I can't do it," Wade said. "I'm used to knowing exactly what they're thinking. A normal psychologist would be accustomed to relying on instinct, on judgment calls. I'm not."

"I hear you two have been hanging out together a lot."

"Yes, we have . . . we have some things in common."

"You two? Like what?"

"I don't know. We both like football."

"Yeah, right."

"Just think about what I said, Cap, okay?"

McNickel took the advice under consideration, but Dominick always played the role of the perfect cop, so nothing came of it.

Years passed and little changed. On the morning of March 2, 2008, Wade and Dominick were riding around at the end of a night shift with a rookie trainee. The shift had been boring and uneventful. They were almost ready to call it a night and get some breakfast when a female voice on the radio asked them to check out a noise disturbance. The rookie acknowledged the call, and Dominick rolled his eyes.

"Great, I'm starving, and we get to call a halt to a beer blast. Now, in New York, nobody would even notice. They got noise twenty-four hours a day."

Wade smiled.

They pulled up in front of an old Tudor-style home to the sound of classical music screaming out the windows.

"Jesus Christ, what is that?" Dominick growled.

"Tchaikovsky," Wade answered with mock snobbery. "*Francesca da Rimini.*"

"Oh, thank you so much. Now I can die happy. No wonder the neighbors are complaining."

All three got out of the car, but it was the rookie's job to handle the situation. As they walked up the lawn, a half-dressed man burst out the front door and onto the porch.

Before anyone could react or even blink, Dom had his gun out and aimed. That's another thing Dominick was always good for. As the man on the porch half turned before leaping off, Wade thought he saw dried blood in his hair and on his back. The whole world seemed frozen in a single moment. Wade's feet wouldn't move.

The man on the porch leapt off, crying out something none of them ever understood. On instinct, Wade reached out into his mind, looking for anything that might help. Then the impossible happened.

Fire from right in front of him lit up the morning sky. Flames burst from every pore of the man's skin, as if someone had dumped gasoline all over him and pitched a lit cigarette.

But Wade didn't smell any gas.

Then the pain hit him. His knees buckled.

"Dominick!"

Every muscle, every sinew of his body was being ripped open and left to bleed on the grass. All the separate little cords of his brain were exploding in an ugly mass. Pictures of a thousand deaths, a thousand lives lost, poured through him, and he was powerless to stop the visions.

He felt hands on his shoulders, holding him up off the grass.

"Call for help!" somebody yelled.

Then he felt her. The mind was feminine. He knew that from the first second of contact.

Pain.

Loss.

Terror.

Help me, he projected.

Then she was gone.

Incredibly strong hands lifted him and carried him through a doorway.

"Dom?"

Wade was four inches taller but twenty pounds lighter than his friend. Dominick laid him down on a couch as if he were a puppy.

"Wade, wake up."

Wade sobbed once and grabbed his own head.

"Stop it!" Dominick's voice cut through the echoing pain. "I don't know what to do."

"She's in here."

"Who's in here?"

"There's a woman in here, somewhere. Listen to me."

For an answer, Dominick grabbed his shirt collar. "It was him. That guy who ripped the white sweater. It's him. I saw his face. He's everywhere. I can't even think in here. You've gotta wake up!"

The agony in Wade's head began to clear at the panic in Dominick's voice. As he opened his eyes, the first things he noticed were coarse black hairs on the back of a hand grasping his shirt. Then he took in a pair of china blue eyes on the brink of hysteria.

"Get out, Dom," he whispered. "You should get out of here."

If Wade had been Dominick, he simply would have picked his friend up and carried him outside. But he wasn't. The ache in his head still lingered. He didn't know what to do.

"I need some water," he whispered. "And look for a woman. She's here. Where is that rookie?"

"I don't know. Are you awake?"

"Yeah, don't touch anything. Go outside and call for backup."

"It's him, Wade. The one they wouldn't believe me about. But he looked the same. Exactly the same as fifteen years ago."

"Do you see a woman?"

"No, why do you keep asking that?"

"She's here. She felt it."

"Felt what?"

"When that man died . . . it hurt."

It more than hurt, but he couldn't explain it. Dominick's eyes hadn't cleared yet. Something about the room had him nearly hyperventilating.

"Get me outside," Wade said. "I can't think in here."

Dominick dragged him outside. The porch seemed aged and faded, waiting to crumble like a yellow leaf in November. They moved past it and sat on the weed-filled grass, staring at the burning spot on the lawn.

"Do you smell gasoline?" Wade asked.

"No. Did you pick anything out of his head?"

"I didn't have time."

"It's him. It's the same guy."

Wade didn't know how to respond and thankfully didn't have to. Two squad cars with blaring, screaming sirens flashing red and blue lights pulled up. Uniformed men were running all around them.

"Where's the body?" someone asked.

"Right there," Dominick answered coldly, pointing to the burning spot on the grass.

"What happened?"

"You figure it out."

Dominick looked back at the house. "We have to go back. Can you walk?"

"Yeah," Wade answered, "but you aren't going back in that house. The cavalry's here now. Let them check into it."

"If you won't come with me, I'll go by myself."

"It can't be the same man. Think about what kind of a coincidence that would be. The same murderer from New York living in Portland—after you've transferred to the local police force—and you just happen to be on duty the morning he decides to cash his own ticket? I don't think so."

"Then come back inside with me."

Wade was exhausted, almost beyond caring. He needed to sleep this off. But something in Dominick's voice made him listen. Dom could be aggressive and high-strung and difficult to know, but he wasn't irrational.

"One condition," Wade said.

"What?"

"You let me in your head the whole time. If I feel you losing it, we leave."

Dominick's face darkened. For a moment, Wade thought he was going to hear the usual "No way."

"Okay," Dominick answered.

"You'll leave if I tell you?"

"Yeah, just come on."

For months Wade had wanted permission to read his friend's mind, explore his thoughts. Now that it was actually happening, he felt almost too drained, too numb to go through with it.

Upon reentering the house, the first thing they heard was one of the other cops choking in the kitchen.

"There." Dominick pointed to a large photograph over the hearth. He walked right over and put his hands on it.

The girl in the picture was different from anyone Wade had ever seen. She reminded him vaguely of a stalk of wheat. Her age was difficult, impossible, to peg. She might have been thirteen or twenty-eight. Her huge hazel-brown eyes complemented her pale face and blond hair. She sat on a forest-green velvet couch, with shelves of leather-bound books behind her head.

"Who is she?" Wade whispered.

Dominick's eyes remained closed. When he didn't answer, Wade gently reached into his mind and was blocked instantly.

"Stop it, Dom."

No answer.

"Hey, you guys," a middle-aged officer blurted out, running into the living room. "Hurry up. Jake found something downstairs."

"What?" Wade snapped.

"Loose boards and a stink you won't believe."

Dominick opened his eyes.

"Bodies," he said. "Jake found bodies."

Wade stared at him. "How do you know that?"

Dominick pulled his hands off the photo and moved quickly toward the stairwell. The first thing Wade noticed in the cellar was the smell—different, sweeter than the stench from the kitchen. Dominick dropped down to help Jake tear at the floor.

"They're here, under the boards," he said to Jake. "You smelled them, didn't you?"

Wade had completely lost control of the situation. He'd lost control of Dominick, lost control of reality. Then he looked up from the sight of the two men pulling at the floorboards to a painting resting against the wall, a misty, ethereal oil painting.

"Dom, come look at this."

His friend ignored him and kept on digging like a man possessed. Wade walked over to the painting. Her face was unmistakable: the girl in the photo upstairs. Her eyes stared out at him as though she were right here and alive.

Down at the bottom of the portrait was an unintelligible signature and a date: 1872. Was it authentic? How could this girl be the same one in the photo upstairs? Her great-great-grandmother perhaps? He looked closer. No, it was the same girl. No two people could share eyes like that.

Jake began choking. Without turning around, Wade let his mind drift into the young, retching policeman's.

He saw through Jake's eyes and found himself staring at a half-decomposed woman with red hair. He wasn't surprised.

"Dom, please stop digging and come look at this."

A moment later, he felt his friend standing next to him.

"Touch it," Wade whispered. "It's the same girl, isn't it?"

Dominick stared at the painting for a long time. Then he reached one hand out and placed it over her face.

"What the hell are you guys doing?" Jake managed to spit.

Wade ignored him. "Is it the same girl?"

Dominick's china blue eyes somehow seemed even lighter than usual. His fingers ran softly over the painting as though in a caress.

"Yeah, it's her. I can't tell anything else. She's like a wall. Maybe the painting's too old."

"Will you two get away from that picture and call the coroner? We've got a mess over here." Jake's voice had grown stronger.

The room seemed small. Wade had turned to answer when Dominick's hand closed over his wrist. It hurt.

"They aren't going to believe us, Wade. They'll say we're crazy or put us on vacation."

Everything in Wade wanted to argue, wanted to play this horror by the book. To do otherwise would mean making decisions. But he knew Dominick was right. Captain McNickel wouldn't want to hear this, much less believe it.

"We're on our own," Dom said.

Wade didn't look at the bodies. He stared at a mass

of painted wheat gold hair. "Don't say anything yet. We still need the precinct computers. I saw a red Mazda parked out front."

Dom was aggressive and high-strung and hard to know, but this time he was right. They were on their own.

chapter 10

Wade pulled away from my mind suddenly and shut me out. For a second I felt disoriented. Who was I?

"Eleisha," he said aloud.

The past few hours came rushing back. Maggie was dead. I glanced at Wade's watch. An hour had passed. An hour, and I knew his life story—or most of it. I braced both hands against the cheap carpet.

"Let me back in. What happened after you found the bodies in Edward's cellar? Did you tell anyone?"

His narrow face glowed softly in the darkness. He didn't say anything.

"What's wrong?" I asked. "Why did you push me out?"

"I always wondered what that must feel like," he breathed. "I've read so many minds, judging sanity by what I see, but no one has ever . . . What do you think of me now?"

The intensity of his question threw me. I was worried about getting William out of Dominick's reach, and Maggie's death kept flashing by like a real-life horror film. Somehow, Wade wanted me to turn my thoughts to him, to the questions and fears that had haunted him most of his life. No, it wasn't even that. He didn't seem conscious of such a self-centered desire. But in one hour, he had poured his life—his private life—all over the floor for me to see.

How else could he feel? Yet such concern was difficult, almost impossible for me to achieve. I was a survivor.

Was my human life so far behind me that I no longer understood it? Maggie had told me, "I once lived with a professional baseball player for eight months." The concept had stunned me. Could she have comforted Wade? Could she have conjured up pretty words and put his mind at ease?

"What do you want me to say?"

He blinked. "I don't know. Say anything. Now do you understand why I've been following you?"

"No, you shut me out too soon."

"It hurt to relive all that. It started hurting too much, and I couldn't tell what you were feeling." His voice began to grow excited. Pale streetlight from outside the window washed over his hair, making its fine strands turn white. "It was you in the house that day, wasn't it? You felt him die, too, didn't you?"

The words cut like a sharp edge into my eyes. "Yes."

"What was he? What are you?"

"I can't tell you. I came here to kill you so you wouldn't follow us anymore."

"Us?"

"Stay away from me, Wade. I mean it."

"This isn't happening like I'd planned." The pain in his words almost moved me.

"What do you mean, 'planned'?"

He suddenly turned away and sat half facing the bed. "I took the painting with me when we left the house that day. That's why I shut you out. I didn't want you to see that part of the memory. The painting was physical evidence, and I took it."

"Why?"

"Because I couldn't stop looking at it. I kept asking Dom to touch it and tell me things about you. The girl in the painting had to be the same presence I felt inside the house, even if the painting was a hundred and thirty-six years old."

I stood up suddenly and started backing toward the window. "What do you want?"

He looked at me helplessly, the tiny lines in his forehead crinkling. "Someone to see inside my head . . . for once."

"Why?"

Maybe he really didn't know, because the helplessness on his face turned to misery. Moving back over slowly, I crouched down next to him. "Dominick knows more than he's telling you. He knows what I am. He knew what Maggie was."

"What do you mean?"

"He knew how to kill her."

"He shot her in the back."

"Yeah, and then he cut her head off."

Wade's expression shifted to confusion, as if he struggled to remember. "She attacked him."

"You were so out of it you don't know what happened." I paused, determined to learn the rest of his story. "What did you do after finding those bodies in Edward's cellar?"

He blinked and then looked down at the floor. "Once all six victims were recovered, we turned in the license-plate numbers on the Mazda and a few other cars, but Dom didn't think we'd get much out of that. So that night, we just started driving around. By then he believed me . . . that I'd felt someone else at the house, and he wanted me to try and pick up your location psychically. But he was talking crazy . . . He was so worked up that I just went along." Wade stopped and took a few loud breaths. "We looked in restaurants, bars, alleys, stores . . ." he said. "We just happened to walk into Mickey's—pure chance. My knees almost buckled. Nobody'd ever pushed into my head before."

"Why do you keep saying that? I didn't push into your mind."

"That's what it feels like."

I thought about that for a minute. Maybe Wade and I couldn't help getting tangled up in each other's thought patterns. Maybe there was some mental magnet between us that we hadn't learned how to control.

"But how did you know to come here?" I asked. "Why would you come to Seattle? I didn't leave a trace."

"How did we . . . ? Oh, that. Yes, you did. The next morning we checked back on the Mazda's registration, along with a few other cars, and decided to check out some addresses. When we got to twenty-seventeen Freemont Drive, Dominick . . . he got agitated. We went up to the house, but no one answered the door, so he picked the lock—I told him not to—and we found a lot of British antiques inside. He touched a hairbrush in the bathroom and went into convulsions."

That was almost too much for me. The thought of Dominick breaking into our house and digging through our things made me tense up. "Nothing in that house would have clued you in to looking for us in Seattle."

When I said "us" again he glanced over curiously but didn't push it.

"No." He shook his head. "I dragged Dom back outside . . . By then he seemed to be having waking nightmares. We hadn't slept in two nights, and I was getting dizzy. We went back to the precinct, and I ran a check on all the airlines out of Portland. I caught two tickets to Seattle charged on a MasterCard registered to a Shelby Drake at twenty-seventeen Freemont Drive . . ." He faltered, looking up at me.

My stomach lurched. How could I have been that stupid? I led them right to Maggie. It was my fault.

He went on. "Dom was never the same after we left your house. He told Captain McNickel and our sergeant everything . . . They put him on suspension pending psychiatric investigation."

"McNickel did that? To Dominick?"

At the time, neither Wade nor I found it strange that I spoke of Captain McNickel as if I knew him. The visions from Wade's past were as real to me as they were to him.

"Dom just sounded crazy, even to me, and *I* believed him. The next day he quit and told me he was driving up to Seattle to look for you."

"And you quit, too?"

"What else could I do? He's my friend, and he was right. They're all too blind to look for the truth."

"That's Dom talking, not you."

He winced, and I sat there watching the streetlights from outside reflect off his cheekbone. I didn't hate him anymore. Maybe I couldn't feel like Maggie. Maybe I couldn't understand his nature or comfort him, but I felt that I *knew* him, and I wouldn't hurt someone I knew.

"You have to stop tracking me, Wade. If Dominick finds me, he'll kill me."

"But what are you? Tell me what you are."

"I can't."

His fingers dug into the carpet. I watched the blue swirl of veins under the flesh on his hands. "You're so perfect . . . The images I pick up from you don't match. I can't even follow some of your thoughts. So cold. They aren't human."

Did he even know how close he was to the truth?

I stood up. "Wade, please. If you care about Dom, you'll get him to stop tracking me, or I'll kill him. Don't let him know about this. Just pretend you can't find me. I'll find a way to disappear, and you'll never see me again."

"Is that what you think I want?" he asked harshly, sounding frustrated. When I didn't answer, his voice lowered. "So none of this, none of the trip down my memory lane, means anything to you?"

What did he want?

I walked to the door. "Just keep him away from me. I didn't ask you to quit your job and come here. I didn't ask to see your life. Remember that."

Before he could answer I slipped out the door. But his narrow, intelligent face lingered in my mind, his troubled expression.

What did he expect me to do?

In the back of my mind, a very small part of me wanted to know.

chapter 11

The next night, I sat in a chair by the fire at Maggie's, watching William dodder around the room. Reflections from orange flames flickered off dark mahogany end tables and danced down the wall beside me.

"I can't help it, William. We have to find someplace else."

"No, no, no. Just got here. Maggie will be home soon."

"Maggie isn't coming home."

"Call Julian. Time to call Julian."

"We can't."

His attitude concerned me. What if I couldn't get him to leave with me? Not that I blamed any of this on him. He'd lived ninety-six years in the same house. I'd dragged him out on a moment's notice and taken him to a strange place, only to tell him we had to move again. It was too much.

And I'd told Wade I would disappear . . . but now I wasn't sure where to go, even if I could get William out the door.

Would we have to fight it out here?

Maybe not. Could Wade be trusted? Thinking about Maggie, a part of me almost hoped Dominick would come hunting us again.

I got up and walked down the hall into Maggie's bedroom. Her cream lace bed draping smelled softly of floral perfume. Something white lay on her cherry-wood nightstand. I picked it up and read a list of things-to-do, written in her perfect script.

1. Have dry cleaning dropped off.
2. Get William a new bedspread.
3. French-braid Eleisha's hair.

"Maggie."

She was gone. I'd led them right to her. Lying down on her satin comforter, I closed my eyes to the sight of Edward jumping off his porch again. How many weeks ago? Edward, Maggie, Dominick, William, Philip, Julian . . . they all kept spinning around inside me until my stomach tightened in sharp rebellion. And what about Wade? He occupied my thoughts almost as much as William. It amazed me that someone so intelligent couldn't recognize insanity in his own partner. Mortals always use pretty euphemisms like "caught in an obsession" to sugarcoat realities like madness.

"What do I do?"

I didn't know and there was no one to tell me. In a rare moment, Edward had once whispered, "When we die, our maker will feel the pain halfway across the world. The pain of their children will always reach them."

If that was true, Philip already knew about Maggie's death. If I had taken the time to sit down calmly and write out a list of all the reasons for us to flee from this house and get as far away as possible, we might actually have made a decent run for Canada or New Zealand or maybe even China. But I wrote no such list, and I was tired of running. I'd told Wade we would disappear, and yet . . . if we ran now, we'd never stop. This house was perfect. It had been Maggie's, and now it was mine.

I got up off the bed and walked back out into the living room. William paced back and forth between the fireplace and the dining room, muttering bits and pieces of "Rapunzel," which Maggie had read him almost every night.

"No packing," he said to me suddenly. "No packing."

"No, we don't need to pack. We're staying here."

For the first time, I felt sick at the sight of his aged, senile face. He couldn't help me. Why was he so useless? "Get away from me, William. I'm going out."

Without bothering to wait for an answer, I ran out the front door and down the dark side of the street. Single people and couples moved past me, doing whatever it is mortals do at night in the Emerald City, but I ignored them and headed toward downtown.

Mad Dog 20/20 littered the chipped sidewalks like pebbles in a stream. I hopped easily around them without thinking, and for once didn't stop to give the homeless bums any money.

Moving by a tattoo shop, I stopped at the sound of two raised voices.

"Yeah, yeah, I'll be back by two. You lock that door on me again, and I'll kick your teeth in."

The shop was empty except for a young woman with greasy hair, smoking a cigarette, and a stocky, dark-haired man pulling on a jacket.

"Where're you going?" the woman asked.

"Out."

"What if a customer comes?"

"Tell 'em we're closed. I don't care! Go to bed or something. Just don't lock that goddamn door."

He hurried out, lighting a cigarette, and walked quickly toward a beat-up Ford Pinto parked near the curb.

"Why don't you get a key?" I asked softly.

"Huh?"

He half turned in annoyance, and then stopped sharply at the sight of me leaning up against the building.

"Why don't you get a key for the front door? Then you wouldn't have to worry about being locked out."

"Do you always hang out listening to other people's problems?" he asked.

"Not usually. Why don't you have a key?"

"She chains it from the inside." He had a stocky build, a hard face, dark hair, and china blue eyes, like Dominick. "What do you want? You need a ride or something?"

For once I didn't fall into my helpless act. He didn't seem to need it. But my recently adopted hooker's pose didn't fit right either. Besides, going out hadn't been on my agenda, and I was wearing a long broomstick skirt with a white tank top, in spite of cool April night air.

I walked out to him slowly. He was about five foot six, and I had to look up to see his face. My small size had always been a turn-on for short men. Julian did a good job choosing me as William's caretaker.

"Yeah," I said. "Some friends are waiting for me down on the pier."

He motioned with his head toward the car door. Loose ashes from his Marlboro scattered lightly on the pavement. "Get in."

Soiled McDonald's and Burger King bags covered the passenger seat. He gathered most of them up and threw them in the back without apologizing. It took him five tries to get the engine started.

"Where on the pier?" he asked.

"Just down by the aquarium. Where are you going?"

"No place. I just had to get out of there. Couldn't breathe."

"Do you actually put tattoos on people?"

He glanced over. "No, I bake doughnuts, and the tattoo sign just lures hungry people in. What do you think?"

"Do you have any?"

"Any what?"

"Tattoos."

"Yeah."

"Can I see them?"

This time he slowed the car down slightly. "How old are you?"

"Twenty-one."

"Bullshit."

"Want to see my license?"

He stayed quiet for a minute, and then said, "You want to blow off your friends and go have a drink someplace?"

"Why don't we just get a bottle and drive to Union Park?"

For the first time, he smiled at me. "Look in the glove box."

I popped it open and found a half-empty fifth of Black Velvet. "Nice. You shouldn't keep it there, though. That's the first place cops look."

"I never speed."

His teeth were yellow and the stench of three-day-old perspiration drifted over to my side of the car.

"What's your name?" he asked.

"Does it matter?"

Mortals never cease to surprise me. He looked about as bright as an antique fire hose, but he suddenly realized this situation was a bit out of the ordinary.

"Hey, what are you doing with me?"

"I was bored. You looked bored."

He still seemed uncertain, as if he thought maybe I was going to get him off and then ask for a hundred bucks.

He pulled into Union Park, grabbed the bottle out of my hand, and stepped outside. The lights on the water were beautiful at night. Black, cold water so polluted no one could swim in it, but tugboats drifted gently across the surface, in and out of the harbor, at all hours. I loved it.

My companion walked halfway up a grassy hill and sat down. The place was deserted. We could hear cars and distant voices, but couldn't see anyone. I sat down next to him and took a shallow drink from the bottle, even though warm, straight Black Velvet didn't appeal to me.

He reached out for another drink and grabbed my wrist instead. His hand surprised me. The bottle fell and shattered on a jagged rock. Instinctively, I tried to pull away, and he pinned me down beneath his chest. Bile rose in my throat as I tasted warm whiskey and stale French fries on his mouth. He was too strong to push off, and panic set in. He ripped the back of my tank top, and I managed to pull my face away.

"Don't."

"What's wrong?" he breathed without letting me up.

His eyes looked like Dominick's, cruel and flat. This must be the way Dominick made love, too. I pretended he was Dominick and felt my own control returning.

When he kissed me again, I didn't struggle. Memories of watching Maggie flooded past me, and I kissed him back the way she would have, openmouthed, with no pressure at all. His tongue pressed in violently.

The grass felt soft, and his body felt hard. Running my hands lightly up his chest, I listened to a sharp intake of breath. He rolled over with a groan and let my lips move down his unshaven cheek.

Touching him made me sick, but I just kept seeing him as Dominick. As my face buried itself in the crook of his neck, I reached up with one hand, grabbed his hair and bit down so hard that hot liquid spurted out in a tiny, pulsing fountain on the first strike.

His body bucked once, but I ripped upward with my teeth and bit down again so fast he went into shock. The blood tasted good, sweet. I tried to shut out all the ugly, shabby images of his life flowing through my mind. The faster I drained him, the fainter he got. With each swallow his arms grew weaker until they stopped pushing at me altogether.

Even when I couldn't take in any more, his heart thumped in his chest. I dragged him down the hill and rolled him into the bay, watching him sink, glad he was dying.

It was an unexpected experience, standing over the black water, blood all over my face and arms, rejoicing in someone else's death. So far I'd always hated killing. Tonight was a first.

Was the world changing or was it just me?

chapter 12

Twenty minutes later, home was just a few blocks away, and I was wishing for a coat. I'd tried to clean myself up, but had only made the mess worse. Between the torn tank top and the blood drying in my hair, I looked like a battered teenager. Only a few people passed me on the street, but my appearance stood out enough to be noticed, even in the dark.

Relief flooded through me when I saw the porch light at Maggie's.

Almost there.

The iron gate creaked slightly as I slipped through. Poor William. He would need comfort and to be tucked in bed with soft words. My earlier manner with him had been harsh and unfair. None of this was his fault.

The path to the door seemed endless, and then something soft and tentative touched my mind. My legs froze. I looked up wildly.

Wade sat on the front stairs, gazing out through a pair of tired eyes, his white-blond hair hanging in messy tufts.

Neither one of us moved or spoke for a full minute.

"What happened to you?" he finally asked. "Are you hurt?"

"No. I'm . . . No."

He was wearing a pair of torn jeans and a faded Colorado State sweatshirt.

"Is that your blood?"

"What are you doing here?" I asked, ignoring his question.

Maybe it had always been there, but that moment was the first time I noticed a sadness etched in Wade's face. He'd led a strange life so far, colored by bizarre abilities he'd never asked for. Rather like me. And maybe it was because my world felt so alone, but he looked familiar. His serious, narrow countenance was an almost welcome sight. I walked up toward the porch and sat down on the stair below him—instinctive deference—not caring what he thought of the blood and ripped tank.

"Dominick came to my room this morning, a few hours after you left," he said softly. "We had a talk . . . that turned into an argument."

"About me?"

"He said a lot of crazy things about you. I had to see you again."

What did he want? Was he here to prove Dominick wrong? If so, he would have a rude awakening. Maybe he should know the truth. So far I hadn't used my gift on him, but in his present state of mind, seducing him into a protective position wouldn't be too difficult.

"Wade, I'm a mess. Do you want to come inside?"

His brow creased in uncertainty. I had a pretty good idea what Dominick told him. But then a question struck me.

"How did you know where to find me?"

"I saw pictures in your head the night your friend died. I drove around until I found the right neighborhood."

"You didn't tell anyone else, did you?"

He winced. "What do you think I am? Didn't I show you last night that I could be . . ." He trailed off for a few seconds, and then his expression tightened and he nearly shouted, "I'm trapped! I quit my job and my best friend's a stranger. You're the only one with answers, but you're just sitting here without a scratch . . . covered in blood . . . worried about yourself!"

Okay, that did it. His anger unsettled me, and I immediately focused on his need to protect. Staring at a discolored stone on the stairs, I crossed my arms as though cold and whispered, "I'm sorry."

Worked like a charm.

"Eleisha." His expression instantly melted to regret. He dropped down on the step beside me and pulled my head into his chest. I let him touch me because William and I needed someone on our side, or that's what I kept telling myself. Wade's skin felt warm through his thick sweatshirt, and his fingers were soft on the back of my hair.

"I don't want to hurt you," he said. "But there's no one else left. I can't see into Dom's head. Everything's gone dark."

"Come inside with me. You need to meet someone."

"Who?"

"The other half of the 'us' I mentioned in your room last night. The someone I bought the second plane ticket for. But whatever you do, don't try to read his mind. At least not yet."

Whatever Dom had told him encompassed the ugly aspects of my kind. I didn't have a choice anymore about showing secrets to Wade. It was either tell him or kill him, and he didn't deserve to die.

He followed me cautiously into the front foyer of Maggie's house—I still thought of it as Maggie's house.

"William," I called. "Where are you?"

Wade's head turned at the sound of shuffling feet. Sweet William wandered out of the living room in his burgundy smoking jacket and wrinkled trousers. By the frightened look on his face, he remembered my earlier harsh manner.

"Chess game's set up," he mumbled. "Won't cheat for Maggie."

"Not tonight. We have company."

He peered out into the foyer. "Someone we know? Julian?"

"No, this is Wade. He's a new guest."

Glimpses of long-forgotten pleasantries came over William. He shuffled forward, right hand extended. "So pleased to meet you. Sorry Katherine's not here. She sets a fine table."

Wade's reaction didn't surprise me. Maybe that's why I let him in. Anyone else would have pulled back in revulsion at William's pale, corpselike visage.

"Glad to meet you," he answered politely, shaking William's shriveled hand. "Don't worry about the table. I had a late supper."

"Fine, fine. Come to the fire for brandy?"

"Later," I put in. "Wade and I need to discuss some business. You go on ahead, and we'll join you in a while."

William smiled, pleased that he had handled himself so well, earlier fears forgotten. "I'll stoke up the fire."

Leading Wade down the hall, I whispered, "That's one of the 'killers' Dominick is hunting. Quite dangerous, don't you think?"

For some reason, I wanted him to see Maggie's bedroom. The opinions of mortals mattered little to me, but he needed to see, to feel, what Dominick had wasted, had destroyed.

"Jesus," he murmured, looking around. "Did you do this?"

"Me? No, I could never do anything like this. I wouldn't even think about it. This is . . . was Maggie's room."

"Your friend?"

"Yes."

"She was beautiful."

That pleased me. "Yes, she was. But you should have seen her back in—"

"In?"

"Do you trust me?"

"Should I?"

"You don't know how hard this is for me or what you're dealing with. But if I show you what happened, if I show you how all this began, will you trust me?"

His face twisted in indecision, and I found him handsome. He wasn't a fool. "I don't know," he answered. "But if you even try to help me, I promise to help you."

"Sit down, on the carpet, like we did in your motel room."

He'd been so eager to show me his past, to share it with someone, anyone. I had been blind to his feelings because of my own fear at the time. Now his emotions seemed clear. I understood. For so long my past had been buried in dirty, black secrets.

When Wade sat down on the floor by Maggie's glorious bed, I reached out and grasped two of his fingers. Not to seduce him, not to trick him into protecting us, but just to help him connect.

Then I looked up into his eyes and dropped the shield covering my thoughts. This is what he saw.

chapter 13

Eleisha

Eleisha Clevon was born May 19, 1822, in Glamorgan, Wales, near the shores of Cardiff on the Bristol Channel. Icy wind blowing against cold flesh was the most vivid memory of her childhood, besides hunger. She considered the kitchen of Cliffbracken to be her home until the age of six—upon being informed by a cook that she and her mother only slept in the pantry through someone else's charity. After that, the concept of "home" simply didn't matter, even though she grew up within the confines of Lord William Ashton and Lady Katherine's walls.

Her mother's beauty faded early from hard work, malnutrition, and sorrow. Her father remained a mystery. Gossips of the manor hinted he'd been a French soldier who once served under Napoleon. Others said he was a traveling merchant, but Eleisha never knew what to believe and her mother refused to tell.

As a child, Eleisha discovered that the most worthwhile talent a little bastard kitchen wench can achieve is invisibility. The less the cooks saw her, the safer and healthier she remained. Lord William's enormous stone manor struck her as damp and cheerless, but filled with wonderful places to hide. Richly dressed people discussing private matters often walked right past her, never realizing she was there. By the age of eleven, flitting about the house became far preferable to scrubbing pots in the kitchen while watching her mother stare for hours into space, dreaming of something no one else could see.

Eleisha had been wearing the same brown dress for three years on the day she finally met Lady Katherine. Cliffbracken bustled with life. Apparently, young Master Julian, Lord William's son, was home after being away on business for several years. Eleisha found all the wild activity disconcerting. Why all this commotion?

She was making a poor pretense of dusting the banister when animated voices rose up the staircase, accompanied by sounds of light-clicking heels.

"What do you mean, 'she's disappeared'?"

"I can't understand it, my lady. We've searched everywhere." This voice was masculine: the house steward, Mr. Shevonshire.

Eleisha slipped quickly behind a large red vase on the first landing. Who had vanished?

"Well, you'll simply have to replace her. There are twenty people on the guest list, and Marion cannot serve dinner alone."

"What do you suggest, my lady?" the steward asked dryly. "That we set up interviews in the study? We have three hours."

"Serving girls are not my concern. Why you can't deal with these trivial matters yourself has never ceased to—" The female voice stopped. "Come out of there."

When Eleisha realized she'd been noticed, she stopped breathing. But survival instincts took over, and she stepped into view.

"What were you doing back there?" demanded a tall, auburn-haired lady with dark circles under her eyes.

"Dusting," Eleisha answered with downcast eyes.

"Who are you?"

"Eleisha Clevon. My mother helps in the kitchen."

The lady stared at her for a moment, taking in her hair and thin stature. "How old are you?"

"Twelve."

Tossing her head as though having made a decision, the woman turned to sweep back down the stairs. "Put her in a uniform," she said offhandedly to Mr. Shevonshire. "And have Marion give her the course list. She'll have to do."

Eleisha found herself standing alone with the angry house steward. They expected her to serve a formal dinner?

"Oh, no," she said. "I can't hold trays for proper ladies and gentlemen. I wouldn't know which one to bring out first."

"Be quiet." The expression on his face suggested he'd rather drop her down the stairwell, but he sighed and headed for the salaried servants' quarters. "Come with me."

Marion, the head serving maid, turned out to be so glad at the prospect of help she actually smiled and went over the menu several times, explaining carefully when each dish would be served. "Don't be worrying. You just follow what I do and keep your eyes down."

Eleisha's fear faded slightly at Marion's calm manner. She'd never been in one of the hired servants' rooms before. White walls and a little four-poster bed made the atmosphere pleasant.

"Did the girl I'm replacing really disappear?"

"Got shipped off more likely." Marion frowned. "Some of these girls what keep flirting with their betters deserves it, I say. Pretty face and a round bum, and they think some squire will lose his head and forget who he is."

Such stories sounded romantic to Eleisha. "Who was she flirting with?"

"Who? Master Julian, that's who." Marion's frown relaxed into a thoughtful, distant look. "You mind my words and stay away from him. Something ain't right with him." She trailed off, and then smiled again. "But you're a good girl. I can tell. Let's find a uniform, and I'll pin up your hair."

Serving dinner turned out far differently than Eleisha expected. The house and its inhabitants had never seemed so alive. Lord William, dressed in a handsome black suit, laughed amidst gold-rimmed champagne glasses, and toasted his son's return. All the guests, dressed in exquisite splendor, grew intoxicated by his mood, and cheerful voices emanated from the great dining hall.

In her short life, Eleisha had known several girls who dreamed of being noble and wealthy, of drinking champagne and wearing silk gowns. Although she herself had no such aspirations, the silver trays and crystal chandeliers gave the evening a magical, almost unreal glow. Only one thing dampened her impression of the glorious dinner: Master Julian himself.

Sitting near his father, Julian neither smiled nor raised his glass. Taking in the sight of them together, Eleisha thought it nearly impossible that two men with such similar features could still appear so strikingly different. She wouldn't have placed them as father and son. Despite its fine tailoring, Julian's suit brought him no elegance. His dark hair had outgrown its cut and hung at uneven angles around a solid chin. Nearly black eyes glittered coldly in his pale face. Over six feet in height, he actually seemed taller but expressed arrogance rather than pride. While he did not partake in his father's exuberance, he did not appear bored either, and talked at length with several of the guests.

"You're right about the young master," she whispered to Marion while they refilled soup tureens. "He's odd."

"Look at the few people he'll actually chat with," Marion whispered back. "Only blue bloods. He won't even look at Lady Eleanor Endor. She married into her title, and he don't consider her to be one of them."

Julian's obsession with noble bloodlines meant nothing to Eleisha on that first night. She only sensed that he was a creature of few or deeply hidden feelings—someone to be avoided.

His dim shadow passed when he left a week later, and Eleisha was offered a real position with a moderate wage as Marion's assistant. She and her mother were assigned a small, whitewashed room in the east wing. For the first time in Eleisha's memory, they had a space of their own.

Time passed. Eleisha began taking a strange satisfaction in her work, quite different from before. The prospect of setting out lovely breakfast trays for Lord William (especially when somebody else had to do the washing up) evoked a nurturing instinct. If he had been anyone else, her feelings might have been different. But on her second morning of service, she forgot her place briefly and smiled at him when he walked in for tea. Instead of having her chastised or dismissed, he smiled back.

Their surface relationship never developed beyond small things—her extra care in setting his place, the occasional newspaper next to his plate, preparing his tea with the right amount of milk—but he made it clear she was to stay in the dining room until he had finished, and two weeks later her wages doubled. She grew to like his hunting jackets, his quiet manner, and the thin structure of his aging face. Something sad drifted behind his gray eyes, distant and lonely.

Lady Katherine never came down to breakfast or luncheon.

As with that first animated dinner party, dark spots in Eleisha's life occurred only with Julian's infrequent visits. One night in 1836, he burst unannounced through the great front doors, two guests in tow.

"Father! Come look," he called as though drunk. "You'll never guess whom I've brought."

Both Lord William and his wife were in the study, sipping brandy after supper. Eleisha followed them out to see Julian and the guests.

Julian stood laughing in the entryway, his cape covered in mud, his mouth smeared with streaks of blood. On one side of him stood a handsome, similarly mud-covered man. But all eyes turned to his other side. Even the eerie laughter, even the red smears on his lips, could not hold attention in light of his second guest.

Rather than pale, her skin glowed a soft ivory. Perfect features, framed by a mass of chocolate-black hair, almost detracted from the low-cut, red velvet gown she wore.

Eleisha decided later that it was not mere beauty, but something more, something exotic that drew such stunned and wordless stares.

"You all remember Miss Margaritte Latour? Maggie?" Julian bowed low in mock chivalry. "Philip's whore fiancée? You must ask her to tea sometime, Mother."

Lady Katherine's eyes clouded in anger. Perhaps she was the source of her son's belief in dominant nobility. Perhaps she was simply jealous of Maggie's overwhelming attraction. Perhaps both.

"Philip, my boy," Lord William said, walking over to clasp Julian's other guest in a quick embrace. "Good to see you. How are the vineyards?"

"Julian, wash your face," Lady Katherine hissed while the others fell into speaking French. "Eleisha, go fetch a washbasin and pitcher."

Only too happy to leave this macabre scene, Eleisha hurried down the hallway. Were they all half blind? Julian had blood all over his mouth and openly insulted one of his companions. Why did no one react? Why did no one ask him where he'd been?

She quickly returned with the water basin, and then fled the study before anyone noticed her. There was something else, something terrible in the room. Fear. It had been slight in the entryway, but grew stronger each moment he was home. A sickening, uncontrollable fear flowed from Julian and filled her with a panic she'd never experienced.

Locking her bedroom door for the first time, she crawled under the covers with her sleeping mother and passed a restless night. The previous evening's events felt like a bad dream the next morning while she set out trays of breakfast choices for Lord William.

"Will Master Julian be joining you for lunch?" she asked timidly.

"No." His gaze drifted into space. "He's gone back to Yorkshire."

Relief like tart water flooded into her mouth. Good. Let him stay there.

The following year, Eleisha turned fifteen, her mother passed away quietly, and Lord William began to forget things. Small things at first, like where he'd left his hunting jacket—while he was wearing it—and the names of books he'd just read. As he was well into his early sixties, these spells seemed simply a part of growing older. But then his actions grew puzzling. One afternoon scarcely an hour past lunch, he walked in and sat down at the table.

"Are you hungry, sir?" Marion asked.

"Hasn't my lunch been prepared?"

"Yes, sir. You've already eaten. Poached sole and greens."

His eyebrows knitted, and he looked at the mantel clock. "Oh, yes, of course . . ." He seemed about to say more, but then stood up and left abruptly. No one talked about it afterward.

Slight changes began taking place. Fewer and fewer dinner guests were invited. Lord William forgot the names of people who had just been introduced and kept asking them the same questions over and over. Marion stopped going over the menus with him and began giving the cooks lists of dishes he'd always liked. Lady Katherine stopped having brandy with him in the study after supper.

One morning at breakfast he spilled his tea and cringed with embarrassment.

"Oh, this is nothing," Eleisha said, toweling up hot liquid. "Last week I tripped over a bucket of mop water in the upstairs hall. That was a true mess."

"Would you read me the paper?"

The question surprised her. But why should it? People's eyes often gave them trouble at Lord William's age.

"All right, but I'll have to spell out the long words, and you can tell me what they mean."

Lady Katherine might have fallen into a fit if she had walked in right then to see Eleisha sitting at the dining table reading her master his morning paper. Five minutes after she read one column, he asked her to read it again.

Marion peeked in once to see if the silver breakfast trays had been cleared away. After listening for a few moments, she cleared them away herself.

When he was done hearing the morning paper, Lord William said, "Come pheasant hunting. Good hunting by the pond."

Eleisha's duties did not include going hunting with

the manor lord. But Marion's head suddenly poked back in. "Go on, child. I can take care of setting up lunch."

It occurred to Eleisha that everyone else, including Marion, seemed to be avoiding Lord William. Did his condition distress them? Was it frightening or merely an annoyance?

She found some old boots and spent the entire morning tromping through the trees looking for pheasants. Lord William forgot to bring his gun, but that hardly mattered. They talked of senseless pleasantries like food and the manor gardens and then sat for a while by the pond pointing fish out to each other before she reminded him it was time for lunch.

While donning her nightdress for bed that night, she heard a knock on the door.

"Come in."

To her shock, Lady Katherine—quite striking as usual in a deep blue satin gown—walked in with a stiff, unreadable expression. "Good evening. Were you retiring?"

The question itself stunned Eleisha speechless. In the three years since their first encounter, those were the first words beyond instructions or commands she'd heard from her mistress.

"I am sorry to disturb you," Katherine went on without waiting for an answer, "but I couldn't help watching you today with Lord William. I have a good view of the fields from my window."

"Oh, forgive me, my lady. If you would prefer I remained at my normal duties . . ."

"No, it isn't that." She paused as though searching

for words. "I've been thinking for some time about hiring a companion, someone to watch over my husband during the day. But the right sort of person is difficult to . . ." Her face clouded. "No matter how it may seem, I love my husband very much, and I won't have someone patronizing him, even if I can't stand to be in the same room with him myself."

The raw, messy emotion Katherine displayed to a mere servant embarrassed Eleisha. "Of course, my lady."

"You care for him, don't you? Not just as your lord, but you seem to truly care for him."

"Yes, he is a kind man."

"He is." Katherine's eyes flashed with pride, perhaps of days long past. "Women of my state have little say in whom we marry. I was more fortunate than most." She paused, this time for several long moments. "I owe him something. Your position has changed. You will be his nurse, his companion. But only if it pleases you. Do you accept?"

"Yes, my lady."

"Your wage will be increased accordingly. I'll have you fitted for appropriate outdoor clothing. Lord William is happiest outdoors."

"Yes, I know, my lady."

"I think you do." She stared at Eleisha. "Doesn't it bother you to answer the same question fourteen times and watch the pain on his face as he spills his brandy?"

"No. I spill things all the time."

Eleisha added no title onto her last answer. Katherine's face fell into defeat, despair, as she walked out the door. "You will begin tomorrow. Marion doesn't need you anymore."

No, Marion didn't need her anymore because the house was declared officially dead. No more parties. No more dinner guests. People like Katherine couldn't be publicly embarrassed by a doddering old husband. Eleisha's feelings remained mixed for some time. She later found this to be the most tragic stage of William's illness. His manners and grace were famous about Wales. Cliffbracken was known and admired for its fine food, good company, and pheasant hunting. But now the festivities were ended, and Lord William was still mentally intact enough to be aware. He noticed Lady Katherine's discomfort. He knew the servants avoided him.

Over the next year, Eleisha's importance changed slowly, gradually, until she became indispensable. William often got lost in the house and believed himself to be a boy in Sussex again with his grandmother. Instead of correcting him, Eleisha often played the part of whatever past relation he believed her to be, and soon he'd slip back into reality without knowing he had ever slipped out. She fed him all three meals and was silently given license to go anywhere in the manor. She was allowed to take him out in the carriage—indeed, encouraged to do so. No one called her too bold. No one insinuated she was living above her station. No one envied her at all. They simply prayed she would continue to occupy Lord William's days and be the one to deal with his illness.

When he ceased sleeping through the night and began to wake, crying and lost, she moved a cot into his bedroom and slept there. No one said a word.

Lady Katherine kept to her rooms, but she and Eleisha avoided each other. Something behind the mistress's calm face began to grow: hatred. It waxed clear that she hated herself and hated Eleisha even more. The need—to need anyone as much as she needed Eleisha—drove the proud woman to malice. Her revulsion toward William induced guilt that became obvious.

"You look out for yourself after the poor master passes on," Marion whispered one night. "She'll send you off, she will. No one's to blame, but she's got hard feelings for you."

"Why? I'm doing what she wants and being paid more than Mr. Shevonshire."

"'Cause she needs you. Every waking minute she's afraid you'll have enough of him and leave her to be the one."

"That's ridiculous. I'm not leaving."

"'Course you ain't. But she don't understand." Marion paused. "None of us do. How you spend nearly every waking moment wiping his chin and telling him where he is again. It's uncanny. It's odd. You make her feel a sorry excuse for a wife and in the same thought she's frightened you'll leave. Do you hear my meaning?"

"No."

Eleisha found them all pathetic. William was simply ill, not repulsive, not a threat.

When Eleisha turned seventeen, Lady Katherine began to show signs of age herself. Guilt turned to agitation, and she appeared to be waiting wildly for something. But what? When the servants began to avoid her more than William, Cliffbracken became a lonely, frightening place. Only Eleisha seemed to thrive.

One late night in November, she sat reading parts of *The Iliad* to William while he gazed into the study's burning hearth. They both jumped when Lady Katherine fell through the door, smiling madly, her satin dress torn at the waist, wine stains on her skirt, and wisping strands of red-gray hair floating about her face.

"He's here, darling," she said to William. "He's come back to help you."

"Who's here?" Eleisha asked.

Katherine's eyes narrowed. "You may retire."

Servant-master relations long forgotten, Eleisha was about to question her mistress further when a cold, dimly familiar essence floated into the room. Fear. "Master Julian's home?" she asked.

"Get out, you insolent bitch."

Gasping in spite of herself, Eleisha turned toward the voice to see Julian's tall, dirty form standing in the doorway. To get out, she'd have to slip under his arm.

But William drew his attention, and he entered the room, giving her a space to bolt. She stopped short outside. What was he doing here?

"I knew you'd come." Katherine's voice drifted out.

"After twenty-seven messages, you grew difficult to ignore."

"Help him. Save him."

"You ask the impossible, Mother." Julian's tone softened. "Let him die quietly. Remember him as he was. It's a kindness."

"But he isn't dying! Just fading away like some mad circus clown. Every day a little worse until the sight of

him sickens me. Bring back his dignity. You can. I know
you can."

"I can't."

"Then you never loved him. You never loved me!
What good is your immortality if it gives nothing to
those who gave life to you?"

"And then what? Then what, Mother? Do you want
to see him feeding on the stableboys? Living forever
with a young mind and aged body? Without peace?
Without rest? He isn't like me. He was always better
than me. Killing to live would only hurt him. Don't ask
me to do this."

While their exact words made no sense, Eleisha did
grasp one surprising thing from this argument. Julian
loved his father, understood the psychology of William
far better than she ever imagined he could.

"Help him," Katherine whimpered. "For God's sake."

"No."

"Eleisha!" A ringing bell and screaming mistress
brought Eleisha flying back into the room.

"Yes, my lady?"

"Take your master up to bed. He is tired."

The expression of profound relief on William's face
at the sight of his young companion was not lost on
anyone, least of all Julian.

"Eleisha, child," William said. "It's time to sleep."

"Yes, quite late," she said, smiling. "We won't dream
tonight."

Toward the wee hours of early dawn, fear crawled into
Eleisha's slumber, and her eyes opened to see Julian's
nearly black ones directly above.

"Don't," he whispered before she could move or cry out. "No one will come."

Angry words gathered in her mouth. Terror overwhelmed them, driving them back down her throat.

"What's wrong with my father?" Julian asked.

His question threw her, and then she noticed the worried lines across his pale forehead. He must be desperate, or he wouldn't have lowered himself to speak to her in the first place.

"Age, illness. That's all."

"Don't patronize me," he spat. "It's more than age. I've seen old age."

"Why are you asking me?"

His hand jerked back to strike her, and then he stopped, breathing in harsh, shallow gasps. "I want no part of this . . . My mother's words say nothing. She's mad. A cold bitch at heart. Not like him."

Unlike Lady Katherine's emotional deluges, Julian's evoked pity. "He was a good father, wasn't he?" Eleisha asked. "Kind? Understanding?"

Julian lowered his hand. He walked over to the sleeping form of Lord William. "Yes, a good father. Wouldn't hear of a riding master. Taught me himself. Never pushed me or asked for more than I could give."

"You were fortunate."

"And look how splendidly things turned out," he rasped. "He deserves more. Mother and I deserve less."

Part of Eleisha wanted to stop him, to urge his secrets away. These words were born of exhaustion and sorrow. Right now he needed someone to talk to. Tomorrow he would despise her for knowing his weakness.

Suddenly, that didn't matter.

"Things don't always work out the way we plan," she said. "Your father is proud of you. He always has been. Don't you remember his laughter at your party? Not false or forced—a happy night."

"Does he remember me? Does he know who I am?"

"Of course."

"How long have you been sleeping in here?"

"Two years. He has trouble sleeping. Bad dreams."

Eleisha watched Julian's tall form as he stood for a long while beside William's bed. Then, without a word, he turned to the door.

"Sir?" she said quietly.

"What?"

"Tomorrow I won't remember any of this. I won't remember you were here."

He stared at her briefly and then walked out.

"Heartless thing!" Katherine wailed. "Cold and cruel, like a lake in December."

Why Julian didn't simply leave remained a mystery to the servants. Each night, his mother's railing grew worse. She hounded him in the halls, cried to him in the study. His face betrayed obvious horror, but he seemed unable to escape. Some invisible force held him at Cliffbracken, refusing to let go. He ate nothing, slept all day, and sat staring at Lord William most of the night. Eleisha grew accustomed to his presence and even slept well. A bizarre scene. Scandalous. A young lord, an old lord, and a serving girl spending each night in the same room. But no one said a word.

"It will be my fault if he dies," Julian whispered through the dark.

"Of course it won't," she whispered back. "Don't talk like that."

"No, it will be. Mother's right about that part at least."

This obsession grew worse, and Lady Katherine sensed it. "Why don't you help him? Why don't you save him?" she cried at dinner the next evening. Neither of them ate a bite.

The pressure built. The storm gathered for weeks before exploding into a nightmare. Eleisha heard Julian cry out from the study, and then the sound of books being thrown.

"All right! All right, Mother. But this is your doing. Your wish. If he hates me afterward, I'll kill you myself."

What was he going to do?

Fear closed Eleisha's throat. Julian swept into Lord William's room, eyes gone red. "Get out," he snarled at her.

"What are you going to do? I could hear you shouting from here."

Without answering, he grabbed her arm and threw her out the door. His hand felt cold. She hit the hallway wall and fell, scraping her elbow. Lady Katherine climbed up the last step on all fours, wispy hair hanging loose, an insane, triumphant look on her face.

"What is he doing?" Eleisha asked. "You've got to stop him."

"It'll be fine now, dear," Katherine whispered. "Just fine. Go to your room and stay there."

For reasons beyond logic, beyond fear, Eleisha got up quietly and did as she was told.

The next day, Lady Katherine did not emerge from her private quarters, and Lord William had vanished.

"Where could they have taken him?" Eleisha asked a sniffing Marion.

"I don't know. It's a loony house, it is. What with them shouting through supper 'bout God knows what."

"Lady Katherine's mad."

"'Course she's mad! They're all mad! You just noticing that now?"

The day passed silently. Several cooks and servants slipped away without collecting wages. No one blamed them. Julian's habit of emerging in the evenings made Eleisha wonder if she shouldn't follow suit and disappear before dusk.

But what about William? She couldn't leave him. And what if she interfered? Julian would kill her. That much seemed certain. If it had been anyone but Julian, her courage might have won.

Knowing she could not pack up and run, she simply went to her room before sundown and locked the door. Perhaps events would work themselves out. She would just wait. Despite Marion's outburst, Eleisha knew Julian hadn't lost his mind. To the contrary, if anyone had control of this terrible situation, he did.

The screaming began shortly after dark. Eerie, keening wails from Lady Katherine swirled up through the floorboards. She wailed on and on until nearly ten o'clock. Eleisha pulled a comforter off the bed and crouched down inside the closet. Around midnight, she had just drifted off when a loud, smashing sound jerked her awake.

"Where are you?" Julian shouted.

He was in her room. Sounds of the bed being jerked amidst gasping snarls terrified her into silence. Maybe he wouldn't think of the closet. Maybe he'd just go away.

The fragile whitewashed door flew back as its hinges were ripped out. Julian's hand closed over her wrist, his eyes bloodshot, his breath stinking of something stale and sweet.

"Please, please don't . . ." Fear drove every other thought away. In all her life, Eleisha had never begged for anything—not food, not money, not mercy, not pity. But she begged now, like a frightened, kicked dog. Her fingers clawed at his. "Please, let go."

"Quiet."

He yanked her up and toward the door. By the time they reached the hall, she was sobbing. A familiar face peered out from the opposite room.

"Marion, help me!"

No one answered. Marion couldn't stop Julian. Nothing could.

He dragged Eleisha straight to the end of the hallway and slapped the end wall with his free hand. To her amazement, it opened up to a black stairwell. Turning, he picked her up with one arm and descended the stairs rapidly. She stopped fighting and clung to his neck, too numb to think.

Soft light emanated ahead. Julian ducked his head

below a beam and entered a glowing open space with stone walls decorated by four torches. Lady Katherine sat in a heap on the floor.

Dead center of the far wall stood a door. Dead center of the door was a two-foot barred window. Julian carried her over to it.

"Look inside," he whispered.

Barely discernible muttering drew her attention before she made out the room's occupant. William paced back and forth in a ceaseless flow of motion, talking to himself.

"Lord William."

The sound of her voice caused him to whip his head around. She grasped the bars in helpless frustration, but then pulled back when he rushed up to her. His prominent wrinkles had deepened to dried creases, his flesh looked chalk-white, and dried blood covered his hair and cheeks.

"What have you done to him?"

"This place used to be a prison," Julian said. "Not a legal prison, but a place where my grandfather locked away troublesome servants and relatives. I used to play here as a child, pretending the cells were full of people. Father always hated it here."

"What did you do to him?"

"Made him immortal."

"No, you failed!" Lady Katherine cried from the floor.

Julian's body shook slightly, and for a moment Eleisha thought he might begin screaming himself. But his voice went on in low, controlled tones. "He is an abomination now, not what was intended. I worried about his reaction, his morality, trapping his once-sharp mind in an aged body, but never this. His illness is forever now. I've damned him to eternal senility."

Julian's white shirt was soiled and stale. He smelled of mold and something sickly sweet. Waves of fear washed through Eleisha.

"Please, put me down," she said.

"No. My father must leave this place. I can't bring myself to kill him, but he has no place here."

"You want me to take him away?" Her heart rose slightly. Julian might have slipped over the edge with his mother, but he might let her take William and run. That was almost too much to hope for. "I'll take him far away, as far as you like. Just unlock the door and let him out."

"It isn't that simple," he whispered. His jaw twitched. "You'll die in one lifetime, and then what happens to him?"

He walked over against the wall and slid down, holding Eleisha in his lap with one tightened arm. "Whether you believe me or not, I find this regrettable. You aren't the right type any more than he is."

She sobbed once and tried pushing him away as he grasped a handful of loose hair to pull her head back. "I'm weak and tired," he whispered. "This will hurt."

The world exploded into white. Awareness waxed dull, and memories grew dim. Eleisha didn't feel his teeth, but thought his lips were burning, crisping the flesh on her neck. Pushing at his chest, too lost to cry, she grew light and faint until the ceiling seemed inches away. Perhaps it was.

Her eyelids fluttered. His white face looked down from directly above, teeth ripping at his own wrist. He forced it into her mouth. "Take it back. All of it."

Warm.

Rich.

Liquid flowed freely into her mouth, and when it stopped flowing, she bit down to draw more. Heaviness filled her again, then darkness.

Eleisha woke up in the crook of Julian's arm, lying on the dirt floor, stunned to find she had both wet and soiled her nightdress. Lady Katherine was gone. William whimpered from his cell. How much time had passed?

When she sat up, Julian stirred. She stared at him. "Your wrist is still bleeding."

"Get cleaned up and pack a bag. Then do the same for my father."

"Where are we going?"

"Just do it."

An hour later, the three of them were traveling in a carriage at top speed down the coast road. Eleisha feared Julian was going to kill the horses.

"You're driving them too hard."

"Quiet."

"Where are you taking us?"

"I've booked two tickets on a ship to America. It's an old cargo ship, and you can't feed on the sailors. Don't try to eat any real food, or you'll be no good to anyone. Just manage by draining rats or whatever else is available. I've heard we can last up to three months like that if necessary. You'll have to hunt for my father as well.

Stay out of the sun completely, or you'll die. Are you listening to me?"

"Julian, I don't know what—"

"Just do as I say!"

She clutched tightly to William's shivering form and remained silent for the next two hours. When they pulled into a small wharf town, Julian hid the carriage in an alley and jumped out. "Stay here no matter what happens. I have to hunt."

Eleisha lost track of time. She sat, comforting William and waiting in terrified confusion. She almost sighed in relief when Julian's tall form slipped around the alley corner, and he climbed back up beside her. His face looked fuller, healthier.

"You have to feed before boarding. At least once." Using his own teeth, he tore at his wrist again. "Here, drink this."

"No."

He grabbed her head and forced his wrist in again. The warmth grew overwhelming. A hunger touched her mind, and she bit down again, this time consciously hating his closeness but unable to stop. He finally pushed her away.

"What am I?" she asked without emotion.

He didn't answer, but turned instead to William. "Open your mouth, Father."

William tried feeding, but spat and choked blood on the carriage seat.

Eleisha grasped his shoulder. "What's wrong?"

"I don't know," Julian answered, troubled, confused, but perhaps beyond caring. "That is your concern now.

Besides sending you money, I wash my hands of this. He is your charge, your responsibility." He pushed a velvet bag into her hands. "This should see you to America. My banker will open an account for you in New York."

"I don't know anything about banks . . . I don't know anything about America."

"Come with me."

Helping William, she followed Julian down to the dock. A stocky man dressed in a blue uniform awaited them. "Yes, sir," he said nervously. "I've prepared a space in the hold, as you asked."

"The old man has a skin condition," Julian said. "He's not to be out during the day. His maid will stay with him at all times."

"Very good, sir."

Julian handed the man a pouch of money and walked away. He never looked back.

Three nights later, hunger struck. It was faint, uncomfortable at first. They had no rooms to speak of, only blankets laid on the ship's floor in the windowless cargo hold. William crawled around, sniffing the blankets like an animal.

"Lunchtime, yes, it is. Must be lunchtime."

Remembering Julian's last words, Eleisha cornered and caught a squealing rat, amazed at how swiftly her body worked and how easily she had sniffed the creature out.

"Here," she murmured through cracked lips. "Bite down on this and suck."

William snapped down as though the rat were a juicy

bit of fruit. She watched in dull horror as he drained every last drop of blood and fell back in exhaustion without choking or spitting as he had with Julian.

Wanting to vomit, but finding herself unable, Eleisha lay on the floor and stared into darkness.

"What am I?"

chapter 14

Wade pulled out of my head and lay back on the carpet. Funny how he was always the one to jerk away first.

"What's wrong?"

"I can't look anymore," he choked out. "Need to stop."

"Are you okay?"

"It hurts."

My hands shook from intense emotion, and I realized why Wade asked so many questions after letting me read his memories.

"That old man downstairs is the same Lord William?"

"You know that," I answered. "You can recognize him."

"The memories are hard to take. What Julian did to him. What he did to you."

"It's more complex than that. The nobility labors under a pride you could never understand. Julian epitomizes that mental trap. He got lost in it."

"That doesn't make him any less of a bastard."

"No," I said slowly, regaining my composure. "It doesn't."

"I thought Dominick had lost his mind," he whispered. "You do live on blood, don't you?"

"Yes."

"Did Maggie?"

"And Edward Claymore."

Long-fingered hands drew up to cover his face. "Your thoughts were so different back then. You were so—"

"Ignorant? Naïve?"

"Compassionate."

"That was a long time ago." I laughed. "Julian left us to fate, hoping we'd drop off the earth and fall into whatever pit waits for incompetent vampires. But we didn't. Edward showed me what my gift was, and I taught myself to use it."

"You'd do anything to survive, wouldn't you?"

"Probably. So would you."

He sat up suddenly and fingered the bottom edge of Maggie's satin comforter. "What do you want, Eleisha? Showing me that past was painful. I could feel how much it hurt. You never would have let me in without a reason."

"Could you feel everything as I experienced it? Like you were there?"

"Yes." The psychic in him canceled out morality for a moment. "Everything—fear, horror, love, pride—like being inside a movie, watching your life flow past me."

"Did you have any emotions of your own?"

His eyes dropped. "Pity. Frustration."

"Frustration?"

"That I wasn't there. That I couldn't do anything."

His reaction caught me off guard, as I wasn't emanating my gift. "You couldn't have helped us, Wade. No one can stop Julian."

"You still haven't answered my question about what exactly you want."

"I've changed my mind about leaving. I want to keep William in this house—moving terrifies him—and I want Dominick to leave us alone."

"He won't quit."

"Then make him think we've run. I can charge a set of airline tickets to Boston or Sweden or China. Pretend to track the charge card down like last time. Just help me convince him we're gone."

He stood up and walked over to the cherrywood vanity table, lifting a small crystal bottle of perfume. "How many people a month do you have to kill?"

"What?"

"How many?"

"Don't judge me. I didn't do this to myself."

His shoulders were hunched forward. I realized how torn he must feel. How would I have reacted in the same situation one hundred sixty-nine years ago? How would anyone react? "If it makes you feel any better, William lives on rabbits."

"Rabbits?"

"Yeah." I almost smiled. "Want to walk out back and see my hutches?"

The corners of his mouth curved up slightly, but no words came.

Maybe he felt it a split second before me. The world slowed down, and I watched his knees buckle just before the waves hit. Psychic energy cut off my own physical control and passed through my thought patterns in rapid bursts. It was not agonizing, not like the death of Maggie or Edward. The release was milder, yet more vivid.

Visions of green fields, pheasants, a young Lady Katherine, rabbits, chess pieces, wolfhounds, and most of all, myself . . . image after image of myself. I could see his dreams, the focus of his undead energy leaking out, dissipating into space.

No!

It went on for what felt like hours. I couldn't move. I couldn't get up. I cried without tears, caught in the choppy sequences of his confused, beloved mind.

"Eleisha." Wade's sweating face looked down into mine. He was gasping for air. His eyes were wild. "Dominick's in the house," he breathed. "William's dead."

We both knew it was true, but I still cried out, "No!" and struggled up on all fours.

"You can't help him! He's gone."

This was too much. Too much. I couldn't think or cope or even feel anger.

"Hide here. Stay here," Wade rushed on. "I'm going downstairs. Whatever happens, don't open the door."

I should be protecting him. Hiding him. Fighting his battles. But I didn't. My William was gone, murdered, and I'd been upstairs, sharing memories with a mortal.

Frozen in sorrow and guilt, I just crouched there and watched Wade walk out.

William. My William. What did his body look like?

A sharp confusion struck me, and I could see an aged, headless corpse.

I was looking through Wade's sight line.

Without conscious awareness, we'd slipped into each other's minds. He experienced my sorrow. I saw through his eyes. It didn't occur to me until later to wonder at how easy, how utterly natural this feat had been.

"Dominick?" he called.

"Where's your girlfriend?"

I found it difficult to shut out Wade's surge of pity when his muscular partner stumbled through the kitchen door, a bloody shovel in his hands. My thoughts got tangled up in Wade's memories. What a good cop Dom had once been. Now dried food and old sweat stained his T-shirt. His black hair stuck to his skull in filthy patches, and quick, china blue eyes twitched back and forth, puffy from exhaustion, sunken by obsession.

"You killed this old man." Wade took in the sight of William's burgundy smoking jacket, wrinkled hands, head lying two feet from his body. "You murdered him. Does that get through to you at all?"

"He's been dead for years. Jesus Christ, Wade, you still don't get it, do you? How many people do you think this 'old man' murdered?"

"None. He fed on rabbits."

"Did she tell you that? She's lying. Remember her painting? The one you kept. I got sick touching it. That pretty face is a joke. It protects her, like a gun or armor. She'd rip your throat out in a second."

"That doesn't make you judge and executioner. Remember? You wouldn't even shoot at a fleeing criminal. You were good at what you did. Everybody wanted to be you."

Recognition, pain, flickered across Dominick's unshaven face. "This is different. Rules don't work." He walked over and looked down at William's body, as the flesh was just beginning to crack. "These things look at us as cattle. They butcher us to live."

This was war. And what if Dom was right? What if the last semblance of sanity still dwelled in him? Wade thought of Eleisha's tiny face, her frightened eyes, and his own growing fascination with her. What if he was wrong, the police were blind, and only Dominick fought on the right side anymore?

"She's not what you think," Wade said. "Her whole existence surrounded that old man. Now that he's dead, I don't know what she'll do. You have to report this, though. You've killed someone."

"No, I don't. In a few minutes there won't be a body."

"Where did you learn so much about these people?"

"Touching things. Her things and Claymore's. His house was a memory smorgasbord."

"Why didn't you tell me?" Wade asked.

"I didn't think you'd believe me."

"You could've let me in."

"My head? No." Dom's expression grew sad. "You're my friend. Trust me on this. My head isn't someplace you want to be."

"If you could just see her, talk to her—"

"Is she here?"

"No."

"Where is she, Wade?"

"I'm not going to let you hurt her."

"You can't stop me." Dom turned away from William's body and locked eyes with Wade. "What is going on here? You're on my side, remember?"

"You're out of control, killing people."

"They aren't people! Whether you understand this or not, I'm going to wait here until dawn and then search the house. She has to come home before it gets light. When she does, I'm going to cut her head off and this will be over."

"Get out."

"What?"

"You heard me. Get out. This isn't your job." Before his partner could speak again, Wade pulled the 9mm Beretta from the back of his jeans and pointed it.

Dom's eyes widened. "You won't kill me."

"No, but I'll blow a hole in your leg and then call an ambulance. By the time the paramedics get here, I'll be long gone."

"Why are you . . . ?"

Wade pointed the gun straight at Dominick's thigh. The burly man stepped back toward the door, his blue eyes narrowing.

"You don't want to take me on. You'll lose."

"Just get out," Wade repeated.

Dominick slipped out the front door, and Wade bolted it behind him.

I pushed myself up from Maggie's bedroom floor, removing my thoughts from Wade's, seeing through my own eyes again, and stumbled downstairs to the foyer. William's body was already turning to ash, the tiny cracks in his flesh spreading.

Wade dashed about, checking window bolts. "Did you see? Did you hear all that?"

"Yes," I whispered tiredly. "Through you."

"We've got to run. He's right. I can't take him on. I wouldn't even know how."

Sinking to my knees, I fingered William's smoking jacket. I couldn't bring myself to look at his severed head . . . across the floor. "It doesn't matter now," I whispered.

"Get up! Change your clothes."

"Dominick is nothing now."

"Twenty minutes ago you were begging me to get him off your back."

"Julian's coming."

Wade froze. "What?"

"You and I felt psychic waves only because we were so close. Julian made William. I think even halfway across the world . . . he felt it. He'll be coming."

"That doesn't change what's happening right now!" he spat. "We've got to get out of here."

"He'll find us."

"I just aimed a gun at my best friend for you!"

He had, hadn't he? I'd dragged him down into moral hell and now had probably killed him. No one could stop Julian.

"Where should we go?" I asked.

"Anywhere away from here," he said. "It'll be light soon, so catching a plane is out. You go upstairs and change clothes. We'll have to hole up in a motel for a day or two and figure something out." He knelt down next to me. "I don't mean to sound like this. I know what William was to you."

People say those words all the time—almost a cliché. But Wade really did know.

My torn, bloody tank hung at an odd angle over one shoulder. Knowing he was right about changing clothes, I stumbled back up to Maggie's room. Would it be the last time? Would her lovely room pass out of my life as she had?

Numbly, I got undressed and then pulled on a clean pair of jeans, and a long, oversized T-shirt. Then I found a knee-length wool coat, black but thin and lightweight.

A drawer slammed downstairs. I heard Wade's feet shuffling about rapidly, as if he was in a hurry. After saying good-bye to Maggie's room, her creation, for the last time, I went back down to find my companion stuffing a small box inside his sweatshirt.

"What's that?"

"Nothing. I'll show you later," he said.

Ashes floated up from William's body, like dandelions gone to seed.

chapter 15

I woke up the following night with lingering memories of Wade carrying me into a hotel room as the sun came up. What happened? Bits and pieces of memory floated back like a chill wind. William's death, Dominick's threats, Julian's inevitable arrival. Black world.

Wade had become more than a simple asset. My behavior the previous night embarrassed me beyond words. He'd taken over and protected me, dragged me out of Maggie's house, and checked us into a hotel.

Now I was lying in a large bed. I sat up and looked around. The room had decent decor—not that I normally cared about such things—in soft blues and grays, with a cedar wardrobe closet. Someone had covered the windows with thick blankets. Wade was sleeping in a chair a few feet away from me, his head lolling back, blond hair in a mess, the Beretta in his lap. He still wore his jeans and the faded Colorado State sweatshirt.

"Wade?"

His eyes clicked open. "Yeah?"

"Where are we?"

"Kirkland, northeast of Seattle."

"Did you hide the car?"

"Yeah."

We'd taken a taxi to a twenty-four-hour Hertz office, and then Wade rented a Toyota Prius. I didn't like the idea of using a credit card—in case Dom found a way to track us—but Wade assured me that his partner no longer had any form of police access. And we didn't have a choice. I can remember not too many years ago being able to pay for almost anything in cash . . . but not anymore.

By the time he got us to the hotel, I was falling dormant and no longer cared how he paid for the room.

Now he just sat staring into empty space.

"This is a nice room," I said.

"You like it? It's my first hideout."

"I should get out of here. When Julian finds us, he'll kill you."

"What?" His expression turned incredulous. "You're just going to leave? After last night, after everything that's happened, you're going to say 'thanks' and take off?"

"What do you want? If you stay with me, you'll die. If Dominick doesn't kill you, Julian will. No matter what you've seen of me so far, I'm faster than you, I'm probably stronger, and I know how to disappear. I also know how to make people help me."

"Like me?"

"You're different, and you know it."

"How?" He got up, grasping the gun, his voice bordering on hysteria. "How am I different? You aren't using me?"

What was I supposed to say?

His feelings actually mattered to me. "Last night when I saw you sitting on the steps at Maggie's, bringing you over to my side seemed like a good idea. I did use my gift a bit, but not much, and not anymore. If you help me now, it's because you want to."

He calmed slightly. "What are these gifts you keep talking about?"

"When we're turned, a strong personality trait grows into a hypnotic aura, impossible for mortals to resist. Maggie's was sexual attraction. Julian's is fear."

"What's yours?"

"Helplessness. People perceive me as small and frightened. Some feel a need to hurt or take advantage. Some feel an overwhelming urge to protect."

"And you kill them?"

"Usually the ones who fall into category A."

His gaze fell to the carpet. "Do you need to take a shower?"

The sudden change of topic relieved me. I was glad to talk about anything else. My T-shirt was still clean but wrinkled. "Yes, but I don't have any other clothes."

"Me either. All my stuff is with Dominick."

"Oh, that's right. Sorry."

"Doesn't matter."

I walked into a surprisingly large bathroom and stood under steaming water for ten full minutes. It felt good, comforting. Small bottles of hotel shampoo and conditioner sat on the tub. I washed my hair and face slowly, not thinking about reality or Maggie or William . . . or Wade. I got dressed in the same set of clothes I'd slept in.

Wade was lying quietly on the bed, watching television, when I came back out. His gun lay on the nightstand.

"You should probably order some food," I said.

He nodded. "What about you?"

"No, I'm okay. I fed last . . . Don't worry."

Something new passed behind his eyes. Something unreadable. "If we get stuck hiding, and you can't get out, could you feed on my blood without killing me?"

"What?"

"Could you?"

The thought frightened me. "Don't talk like that. You're my—"

"I'm your what?" he pressed, his brown eyes intense.

"Just don't say that. How can you think it?"

Slipping inside his head for half a second before he pushed me out, a startling desire flashed through—and I'm not easily startled. He wanted me to. The thought of my mouth on his neck excited him.

"It isn't like that," I said. "It's ugly and painful. Your throat wouldn't heal completely for weeks, maybe months."

Humiliation colored his face. He'd been casually reading everyone else's thoughts, needs, and drives since childhood. Fair turnabout shamed him. I felt bad for causing him embarrassment.

Everybody has weird thoughts sometimes. I didn't know what to say to make him feel better, so I crawled up onto the bed and laid my wet head on his stomach. A moment later, he reached out to stroke my hair.

"I love you," he said quietly.

No matter how abrupt or out of place this declaration might be, it didn't surprise me.

"No, you don't," I answered. "You feel close to me because we've shared private memories . . . because we're caught in the same trap. You don't even know me."

I'm sure my blunt dismissal must have hurt him, but it was for the best. He was quiet for a long time, and then he asked, "Have you ever loved anyone besides William?"

"Edward, but not like you think. I didn't live a mortal life long enough to learn much about human relationships."

"What was his gift?"

"Charm. And besides Julian's terror, it's the strongest pull I've ever felt. Everyone adored Edward, like Laurence Olivier and Peter Pan rolled into one."

"How many others are there . . . like you?"

"Only Philip and Julian as far as I know. They might have made others by now. But I don't think so. Julian hates most other vampires."

The word "vampires" caused him to wince. "It seems odd there are so few you know about. Did Julian turn Edward?"

"No, that's a long story." I paused. "Do you want to see it?"

Wade truly was unusual; the prospect of another trip down undead memory lane perked him up. "Yeah, can you start where you left off?"

Without answering, I sat up, grasped his hand, and let my focus flow back.

Back to Edward.

chapter 16

Edward

Eleisha felt only confusion when the heavy merchant ship stopped moving. The tiny hold space she and William shared reeked of rotting rat corpses. Sailors had long since ceased to check on the hold's two passengers.

"We've stopped, William," she whispered through cracked lips. "Perhaps we're in port."

"Time for lunch, then. Yes, yes, must be time for lunch."

Too weak to argue or answer, Eleisha left him and crawled up the cargo hold stairs. Their good fortune that the ship had reached dock at night suddenly occurred to her. What would have happened had they docked during the day, while she and William slept? Would the sailors have begun to unload wooden boxes around them?

"William," she called quietly, "we have to get off right now."

No answer.

She hurried back to find him crouched over. "What's wrong?"

"Can't leave. Haven't had tea. Haven't had lunch. Wait for Julian."

"Come on." She pulled his arm over her shoulder. "We have to get off now."

They also had to hide from the crew. Even without a mirror, she knew what a skeletal sight she must be. She only had to look at William to imagine her own condition. They both smelled of filth and dried blood. But she understood his fear. What sort of land was America? What sort of people lived in this place?

Peering up on deck, Eleisha saw a busy crew. No one paid attention to the hatch door. A wide plank extended to the dock. It was surprisingly easy for Eleisha and William to slip past the sailors, off the ship, and run toward some faded wooden shacks on the shore.

They hid in the mud by a decaying wall, William panting in wordless panic. Eleisha looked around. Now what? Not since Julian pulled her from the bedroom closet had she felt so out of control.

"Well, I must say." A smooth voice flowed through the night. "This is hardly what I expected. Two fugitives in rags?"

She leapt up, casting about for a stick or a rock. "Who's there?"

"Oh, calm yourself."

A man of medium height stepped into view. He wore the most outlandish costume she'd ever seen. His short, dark hair was topped by an absurdly wide-brimmed hat, and a black cape with purple silk lining billowed out over a too-large white shirt. "What do you think?" he said, smiling. "I thought to look the part. Julian has no imagination, you know." He stepped close enough to see Eleisha clearly. "Oh, dear."

Positioning her body in front of William's, she asked, "Who are you?"

"This is Lord William Ashton, is it not?" The man's foppish manner faded by the second.

Hope, or the barest hint of it, made her cautious. "How do you know that?" She stumbled from weakness and then caught herself.

"Julian sent me a letter by clipper ship. It arrived a week ago. He asked me to meet you here. I owe him a favor."

"Can you help us?" she whispered.

For an answer, he reached out and caught her as she collapsed.

"What have you been feeding on?" His tone sounded hard now, completely serious.

"Rats."

"My God." He grasped William's wrist. "Come, I have a carriage."

Eleisha didn't remember how he managed to get them both to the carriage. But her coherence returned as he led them into a building with red velvet wallpaper and a sign that read "Croissant House Hotel."

"I have guests," he snapped at the desk clerk. "Have fresh towels sent up at once."

"Yes, Mr. Claymore."

He led them into a room of braided rugs, velvet couches, curved wooden tables, and fringed, floor-length drapes.

"Are you a lord?" Eleisha asked.

"*Moi*? Hardly." Some of his earlier joviality returned.

"No one cares a whit for such things here. The only thing that counts here is money. If the Prince of Wales showed up tomorrow without a dime to his name, they'd ignore him completely. I am simply Edward Claymore."

"What's a dime?"

"Oh, dear."

He helped William over to a couch. "Would you like to rest, Lord William?"

"Time for tea. Yes, it's time."

Edward looked at Eleisha. "Is he delirious?"

"No, he's always like that. It's an illness."

"That's impossible. We can't become ill."

She sank to the floor. Nothing this man said made any sense. He seemed nearly as much at a loss himself. Her physical appearance stirred him into action again, and he hurried into a second room. She heard the sound of splashing water.

"I'm running you a bath," he said. "Go ahead and climb in. You'll feel better when you're clean. Then we must talk. I promised to meet you, not play nursemaid."

Eleisha walked in and beheld a porcelain tub with a metal spigot on one end. Steaming water poured from the spigot directly into the tub. She stared in amazement, then took off her clothes and stepped in. When the depth reached a dangerously high level, she called, "Mr. Claymore, how do you make the water stop?"

Her amazement grew when he walked in without even knocking. Startled for an instant, she leaned over to cover herself.

"Oh, please," he said. "I should think you'd be past that by now."

He turned some tiny levers, and the water ceased flowing. Then he looked up at her thin, pale body and dull hair. "How long has it been since you've really fed?"

She knew she should be burning with shame, sitting there naked . . . but somehow, she wasn't.

"What do you mean?"

"Since you've hunted?"

The warm bathwater felt soothing, but she stared at Edward in confusion, wanting to understand him, wanting to communicate.

"When did Julian turn you?" he asked.

"Turn me? The night we left, I think. He opened his wrist and put it in my mouth. Then he put us on the ship."

"Without telling you anything?"

"He told me to take care of William and stay in the darkness."

Edward fell silent. Small drops of water dripped from the spigot into the overfull tub. What was he thinking? Eleisha could tell that she and William were somehow a great deal more trouble than Julian had led this man to believe. Finally he picked up the soap.

"Lean back. Your hair is filthy."

"Shouldn't someone stay with William? He won't remember where he is."

"I put a blanket over him. He's lying by the fire."

"Thank you."

In a world turned upside down, Eleisha sat quietly in the water, letting Edward wash her hair and face and neck. Back in Wales, during her infrequent baths, she was so modest that she kept her shift on in front of Marion. But she somehow felt connected to this man standing beside the tub, as if his ministrations were commonplace. He was gentle and thorough, making her rinse twice. She tried to reach for a towel afterward, but he stopped her.

"No, don't get out yet." Indecision weighed heavily on his face. "I can't believe I'm doing this." Putting his own wrist to his teeth, he ripped pale skin down to open veins. "Open your mouth."

She didn't argue or question or even wonder at her own lack of character for obeying him like a child. The blood in his arm didn't taste like anything. Her consciousness barely registered the physical action of sucking or drawing at all. But heat and energy pushed through her with a tingling satisfaction unlike anything in her memory. Strength and speed and desire to live seemed tangible, attainable again. William must be cared for, protected . . .

"That's enough."

Edward's voice broke through as he disengaged her tightly clutching fingers from his wrist. Realization of what had just taken place sent her spinning into the void again.

"What am I?" she asked.

With an expression close to—but not quite—pity, her newfound caretaker dampened a cloth and wiped her mouth. "Julian should be disemboweled for this. An old man and a child. But I feel your gift . . . I think. We'll stay here a few nights, and you'll understand."

She watched him wrap a cloth around his wrist and

then let him dry her with a thick purple towel. Neither one spoke.

Sitting by the fire the next night, she felt safe and clean for the first time in weeks. Their hotel room delighted her senses with its reds and purples and velvet textures—nothing like Cliffbracken. Edward had somehow arranged for a black silk evening gown to be delivered, fit for Lady Katherine. Eleisha found it pretentious and a needless waste of fabric, but it brought coos of approval from Edward and words such as "marvelous." She wanted to please him. No matter what hidden emotions motivated him, his actions were kind.

While he might have been unwilling to answer many of her personal questions, he proved to be a wealth of information about their location.

"You landed in Southampton, one of the oldest cities this country boasts—still young by decent standards. Actually, I live on the lower west side of Manhattan. Wonderful place, teeming with life. The whole city keeps burning down, and they just build it right back again. Marvelous. We'll begin traveling back later this week."

He chatted on while boiling her a cup of mint tea. "Here, now," he said, "try a sip of this. It's one of the few mortal pleasures we can still enjoy—in weak doses. Something about the mint gives me a sense of comfort."

She sipped from a bone china teacup. "It's good."

"Wonderful stuff. But that's about the extent of what you can consume, except perhaps dark, very fruity red wine. Julian did tell you not to eat any food, didn't he? Our bodies can't pass waste anymore, so alien substances just sit and rot. I've heard terrible stories. But a few liquids in small doses seem to agree and dissipate."

"It's nice to drink tea again."

"Quite. Try to get Lord William to take a little. He's weak. I tried feeding him from my wrist last night. He wouldn't swallow, just spat and choked."

"That happened the night we left Wales, too. But on the ship, he seemed to draw more energy from the rats than I could."

Edward's dark eyebrows knitted. Tonight he wore well-tailored black trousers, a pressed white shirt, and a dinner jacket. She liked the way he combed his hair straight back so his pale forehead was bare.

"Can you tell me what happened before all that?" he asked.

Talking over tiny sips of tea, Eleisha started with Lord William's first signs of illness and worked her way to the nightmare journey to New York, watching Edward's face shift from wonder to disgust and back again. She left nothing out.

"Well, that explains my part in this," he said finally.

"What do you mean?"

"I'm a selfish bastard and Julian knows it. He's probably trying to absolve his own conscience without really helping you. He sent me a message to meet you, knowing I can't stand filth or imperfection. I should have cut and run, leaving—pardon my bluntness—an ignorant child to care for the old coot. You would have failed and probably been beheaded by some Irish immigrant from the old country. That great fear-emanating pig could comfortably blame everyone but himself."

Eleisha glared at him. "You're being unfair. Julian loves his father. He never wanted this. You didn't hear the things Lady Katherine said to him."

"It's quite rude to be loyal to someone I'm criticizing. Please don't do it again." He took her empty cup. "But we'll just disappoint him. I think you and Lord William might remain safe a bit longer."

She smiled up at him, thinking how vain and shallow the man behind this charming facade must be.

Not understanding him at all.

When she woke up on the third evening, Edward's bed lay empty. She searched the hotel room without finding him. A physical emptiness like hunger agitated her, and his absence brought her close to panic. William slept heavily on the couch, as though too weak to move.

Where had Edward gone?

This absolute dependence upon him bothered her, but nothing could be done about it now. To strike out with William on her own would be stupid, probably suicidal.

She was on the brink of walking down to the lobby and asking for messages when Edward swept in, carrying a struggling, yowling burlap sack, his handsome face etched in anger.

"For God's sake, help me."

"What is it?" Eleisha asked.

"An alley cat. Lord William has to feed on something. This is madness. If he can't hunt, he should be put out of his misery."

"No."

"Then you feed him! I've got claw marks up both arms."

"A cat? We have to kill a cat?"

"Have you a better idea?"

"Why do we feed on blood anyway? That's the madness, not William's age."

"It isn't blood; it's life force." Edward grew calmer. "And we ought to feed him so we can go hunting ourselves. I just hope this works. No one sells a handbook for the care and nursing of wrinkled-up undeads, you know."

He appeared so frustrated, Eleisha took the bag.

"William," she whispered. "Wake up."

His lids fluttered. Without thinking, she reached in, caught the cat with both hands, and snapped its back, not caring that it raked her hand. Weeks ago, the thought of breaking an animal in such a fashion would have sickened her. Now the act seemed merely an unfortunate reality. Biting into the cat's throat, she tore fur open to expose veins and white, daisy-chained vertebrae.

William's eyes snapped open.

"Here," she said, putting it to his mouth.

He bit down greedily, as though starved, red liquid spilling down both sides of his chin. Eleisha kept expecting to feel guilt or nausea but didn't. Edward left the room.

He came back a moment later with her black gown. "Get dressed. It's our turn."

"For what?"

"To hunt."

"Couldn't you have brought something back for us?"

"Oh, capital idea. Just waltz them past the desk clerk and dump their bodies out the window, I suppose?"

"Whose bodies?"

As those two words escaped her lips, Edward started in surprise. Some form of realization flickered in his eyes. "Get dressed, Eleisha," he ordered. "And do something with your hair."

Twenty minutes later, they were walking down a Southampton street, her hand inside his arm, striking the sharp image of a wealthy couple. But something felt wrong. She sensed it in his silence, in an intimate tension so thick she had to hold on to him to keep from running.

"Where are we going?" she whispered.

He didn't answer.

An enormous number of strangers passed them. How could so many people live in one place? How could there possibly be enough food and water? And they were all dressed in such various forms. Edward sported a tailored brown suit tonight. Similarly dressed gentlemen tipped their hats to him, and factory workers in rags moved out of his way.

"It's so crowded," she said.

"Wait till you see Manhattan." Her companion finally spoke. "There are sixty-four thousand Irish immigrants alone."

"Sixty-four thousand?"

"That's why I live there. No one is ever missed."

She pulled her hand away. "Why are you acting like this?"

"Because I don't know what else to do." He ran a hand across his face and suddenly motioned to an alley. "In here."

Pushing her up against a brick wall with his chest, his face moved closer until she could see tiny swollen blood vessels behind green irises.

"Can you read, Eleisha?"

"Let go of me."

"Can you read?"

"A little."

His grip reminded her vaguely of Julian's strength—only Edward moved more like a tree, flexible and solid at the same time. Unable to disengage him physically, she fingered the fabric of his jacket and dropped her gaze.

"You're hurting me," she murmured.

His hands jerked back as though she were on fire; a mask of fear flickered across his face. "Don't you ever try using that on me again!" he spat. "I'll drop you in the East River."

Her actions had been instinctive, without thought. "What did I do?"

Stomping his feet on the ground while walking in a small circle to regain control of himself, he muttered, "Should've thrown myself in the river when that clipper ship hit dock."

"Why did you bring me out here?" she asked.

"To hunt! You really don't understand, do you? I've never seen any vampire who could seep power like you before she'd even made a kill. God knows what you'll be like in a few months."

"What are you talking about?"

"How can you be so dense? Don't you have the

slightest clue? We are dead, Eleisha. And we aren't dead. We'll never get any older, but have to draw life from those we kill. I fed you from my own arm. Where do you think that blood came from? A cat?"

She stared at him. "You killed someone?"

"I've been killing for the past twenty-six years," he hissed softly. "That's what we are. It's what we do. And I can't believe that I'm actually standing here, explaining this to you."

"I won't murder other people."

"Then you'll starve. Life force from animals won't give you enough energy. After a while, you'll grow too weak to move at all and live forever in a state of frozen, emaciated agony. No one will take care of Lord William, and the same thing will happen to him. Isn't that a pretty scene?"

For the first time in her life, Eleisha experienced hatred, not for Julian who had done this to her, but for Edward who told the truth. Rational or not, she hated him for forcing the reality of existence on her and for leaving her no control and no way out.

"Follow me," he whispered. "Don't ask questions, and just follow me."

With no other choice, she walked behind him out of the alley and into a small pub. The smoke and human smells and crush of bodies caught her senses. Wooden tables, pints of beer, men playing cards, brightly dressed women in tight corsets . . .

What a different place. So busy and unaware of itself. Everyone so intent on individual activities.

Then she noticed Edward's face. All traces of stress and pain had vanished, leaving only foppish, cynical humor. "Gregory, old man," he called to the bartender, "marvelous apron tonight. Did you wash it?"

Several heads turned in pleasure at the sound of Edward's voice. Eleisha observed the cheerful effect he had.

"Black heart," one of the barmaids said, smiling. "Matilda's nearly wasted away just waitin' for you to come back in."

"How many times have you been here?" Eleisha asked softly.

"Once. Last week."

The extent of Edward's popularity kept everyone's attention on him as he flirted with barmaids, teased the bartender, and joked with customers. But his eyes never strayed far from the door. No one besides Eleisha noticed a lone sailor who paid his tab and left.

"I've kept you all from serious drinking long enough," Edward said a moment later. "Off to a late supper now."

Laughing over loud protests, he handed Eleisha her cape, and they stepped outside. What happened in the next few moments took place so fast she almost couldn't follow the order of events. They caught up with the sailor outside another alley, and Edward suddenly jingled a change purse.

"Excuse me," he said. "I think you dropped your pouch."

When the sailor turned to see who had hailed him, a relaxed smile curved his lips. "Oh, hello. Don't think that's mine. Someone else might have dropped it."

"Are you sure? It struck the ground right behind you."

Holding it out like an offering, Edward waited until the sailor leaned over to inspect the purse. Before the actual movement registered, both men disappeared inside the alley, and Eleisha heard bones cracking.

Just like the cat.

Her companion had chosen a good time and place. No one else passed by to hear the struggle. Not that it was much of a struggle. She moved into the dark alley mouth only seconds later to see Edward leaning over a slumped form.

"It's time," he said.

"I can't."

But as she looked at the open throat, exposed veins, red fluid running down onto the ground, a hunger—and not a hunger—sent her memory into a wavering haze. Had this source ever talked and moved and danced? Or was it just a source? A wellspring?

"This pulls at you," Edward whispered. "Don't let yourself think."

He reached out and gently took her wrist. No pulling back. No fighting. She let him draw her forward, and then knelt down on her own.

The experience was similar to feeding on Edward's arm but more intense. The warm liquid was sweet. Heat raced through her while pictures of ocean waves and fistfights and a brown-haired woman etched themselves into her brain. After the initial physical connection, she was no longer conscious of her mouth on the sailor's throat, only the strength and pleasure and energy his life force brought.

Just as she could take no more, she felt his heartbeat stop. When she lifted her head, she saw torn-edged flesh and two dead eyes staring up into empty space.

Euphoria faded.

Edward's hand touched her hair. Turning, she hid her face in his chest, forgetting she might get blood on his jacket, not hating him anymore.

On the fourth night, they began traveling to Manhattan in Edward's carriage.

"The trip should take three days or so if we don't dally," he said, falling into his charming fop routine. Perhaps he played it so often the personality had become part of him. "I know a delicious little dress shop on Market Field Street. It's divine. We'll buy you something low-cut in red taffeta."

A handsome pair of bay horses trotted ahead of the carriage, pulling it away from the Croissant House Hotel. Eleisha felt sorry to be leaving. The hotel room had grown comfortably safe.

"Once more into the breach, dear friends," Edward called, snapping his whip in the air.

Despite the fact that he seemed genuinely glad to be heading for home, he was also avoiding any serious conversation. Not that she blamed him. What could they say? Last night had been brutal and emotionally exhausting. She didn't want to think about it, much less discuss it. And getting William into the carriage had been a nightmare. Although stronger from feeding on the cat, he was also more aware of his surroundings and terrified that Edward might be taking him back to the ship. Eleisha's coaxing and comforting did little to help. In the end, Edward lost his patience, slapped William hard enough to daze him, and then carried him outside like a sack of potatoes past the openmouthed desk clerk.

All in all, it hadn't been an easy night. Edward's empty chatter soothed Eleisha while she rocked William back and forth, assuring him there was no ship in sight.

She felt surprisingly safe beginning a new journey so soon after finishing the last one. But her trust in Edward was profound. He may not have been an overwhelming force like Julian, but he was strong and careful, no matter how frivolous he might pretend to be.

"Do you live in a house?" she asked.

"No, a hotel suite. You'll like it." He glanced over at William. "Can you put him to sleep?"

"Maybe. Why?"

"Because we'll have to cross W-A-T-E-R in a short while, and he's going to throw a fit."

"Can't you go another way?"

"No. Haven't I shown you a map of New York yet? We're on Long Island. Southampton's cut off by a small bit of the Peconic Bay. Just a sliver, but we need to take a ferry."

"How much farther?"

"About ten miles."

She hated to talk in front of William as if he weren't there, but Edward made sense. She continued rocking the old lord until he drifted off. Ten miles later, the carriage moved right up onto the ferry without stopping. William slept through the entire process.

"Capital," Edward sighed when they had safely crossed. "I was afraid I'd have to hit him again."

"You need to be more patient."

"If I'd resorted to patience, we'd still be sitting in the hotel."

His tone waxed humorous, though, good-natured. She smiled up at him, pretending they were a brother and sister escorting their grandfather on holiday, playing Edward's foppish game and forgetting reality if only for a little while.

Here, Wade became aware of himself briefly as the clear images of Eleisha's story switched to flashes and impressions rapidly shifting past him like the pages of a book.

Yet he still felt what she had once experienced.

Upon arriving at Edward's "home," she was delighted with his lavish hotel suite, and the new world that he showed her. But no longer a servant, she'd had trouble at first adjusting to the hotel staff waiting upon her, laundering her clothes, lighting the fire, cleaning the rooms . . . changing her bedding.

Images raced by as time flowed on.

The next seventy years passed in a flash of scenes. Edward moved his little family to a new hotel suite about once a year, and Eleisha was glad to let him handle their living arrangements, their money, ordering their clothes . . . their entire existence. She always hunted with Edward. Otherwise, her only concern was to care for William, and she was content to let Edward take care of everything else.

Still half lost in her mind, Wade could not truly pin-point when the change began.

But one night, she wanted to order a gown to her own taste—something simple. Then sometime later, she wondered why she did not have her own bank accounts for the money Julian sent.

She said nothing of this to Edward.

But their world was changing.

She started hunting alone.

The scene crystallized again, and Wade forgot himself.

Eleisha ripped the bastard's throat out and watched him fall back with a soundless scream. Pig. A nearly black Manhattan alley hid his flailing arms from the outside world, not that anyone cared. With one hand, she pulled up the torn shoulder of her red taffeta dress, and with the other, grasped the back of his head.

This time the blood tasted good through her teeth, over her tongue, dripping in warm rivulets down her bare shoulder. She saw pictures of rape and whiskey, a red-haired girl being beaten, the hanging of an Irish steelworker, no beauty, no music.

She finished feeding and dropped him, feeling less remorse than usual.

Wiping her face carefully, she slipped back out onto the street. A white-bearded gentleman in his early fifties stopped at the sight of her torn but expensive gown.

"Are you hurt, my dear?"

Human nature still escaped her. This man possessed

kind eyes, his concern genuine. But had her face been painted and her dress cheap dyed cotton, he wouldn't have stopped to nudge her dead body. She didn't really want his gallant services, but walking around with ripped clothing would attract attention.

"No, sir. Thank you. I walked past an exposed nail." She glanced about in pretended distress. "Could you please hail me a cab?"

Pleased to be of assistance, he stepped toward the street, found her appropriate transportation, and lifted her inside the cab as though she were a kitten.

"You are most kind, sir."

"Not at all," he said, bowing slightly like a knight standing over a slain dragon.

The cabbie pulled out and followed her directions to Bridge Street, to Edward's hotel suite. She'd never stopped viewing any of their various residences as Edward's.

Apparently the aging Sir Galahad must have paid for her trip, because once she stepped down, the cabbie pulled away without a word.

Eleisha turned and headed up the stairs of the Green Gem Hotel to find Edward sitting on a velvet couch reading the newspaper.

"Hello, angel," he said over a cup of tea.

She smiled absently, noticing how comfortable he always appeared inside a lavish hotel suite they would simply abandon in another few months. Didn't he ever wish to stay in one place and make it a home?

William tottered out of his bedroom, messy silver hair hanging in his face. "Eleisha," he said, smiling in a moment of coherence. "Time for supper?"

He and Edward had begun avoiding each other of late. Instead of becoming accustomed to William's condition, Edward was growing more repulsed with each passing year. This bothered Eleisha.

"Yes, time for supper," she said. "Just let me change, and I'll get you a rabbit."

She'd arranged for a local butcher shop to bring in live rabbits—for a substantial fee. Money meant nothing. From what she understood, Julian sent them enough money to support ten people in style. Edward believed he was doing her a service by managing their finances. He supplied her with spending money, and he always told her, "You only have to ask."

But for some reason, lately, she didn't like having to ask.

"Why are you changing clothes?" Edward lowered his paper and looked up over the top of his teacup. He was especially dashing tonight in a brown silk waistcoat.

"A thief on the pier tried to rob me," she answered.

"Is he still with us?"

"No."

"Good girl."

He could still make her smile.

Two years later, Eleisha stood staring out yet another hotel window.

She didn't hear him approach, but wasn't surprised when Edward peered over her shoulder.

"See anything you like?" he asked.

She didn't answer.

"Shall we go to Delmonico's?" he asked in a bright

but forced tone. "Have something upscale for supper?"

She tilted her head back to look up at him. His green eyes were sad.

Neither he nor she seemed able to speak of anything beyond the moment. They rarely hunted together anymore—or rather she rarely wished to hunt with him.

"Of course," she said, feeling guilty. "I'll get my cloak."

He nodded in relief, but his eyes were still sad.

Summer was approaching.

William was sitting on the velvet couch one night, carving a new set of checkers and talking quietly to himself. It troubled Eleisha that he only ventured out into the main sitting room now when Edward wasn't home . . . No, it more than troubled her.

Tonight, she wore a comfortable muslin dress—that she'd purchased herself—and was walking around the hotel room in bare feet.

"Are you tired of carving, William?" she asked. "Would you like to play chess?"

"No, no. I'll stoke up the fire," he said.

"All right."

She knew this was his answer for when he was content with his current activity. So she looked about the suite, wondering what to do with herself, trying not to let herself think. Lately, all she could do was think—to mull doubts and questions over and over again.

She had longed to ask Edward for the answers for years now, but at the same time, she resisted having to accept anything from him, to need him, to depend on him.

And so a few weeks ago, she'd gone to a library to do research on the undead. The wealth of material astounded her. She was bursting to know . . .

Turning her head, she heard Edward's light footsteps on the stairwell, and a moment later, he swept in through the front door with a "Tallyho" and a bottle of red wine.

"Hello, darlings," he called. "Daddy's home. Look what I've found. A bottle of 1865 cabernet sauvignon. We should celebrate."

"Celebrate what?" she asked.

"Oh, I don't know. Think of something. You're the clever one." He frowned, staring at her. "Good God, what are you wearing?"

William stood up and quickly shuffled toward his room.

Suddenly, the whole facade of their existence came crashing down around Eleisha. She wanted to scream but did not know how. She whirled to face Edward, and his cheerful expression shifted to caution.

Her feeling of hysteria faded, replaced by a cold sense of calm.

"Edward, how many of us are there?"

He put the wine down on a polished table. "Well, there were three of us the last time I counted. Has someone come to visit?"

"That isn't what I meant."

"I know what you meant. Why on earth would you ask me that now?"

"Because there should be more. Because we had to come from somewhere. Who made Julian?"

This conversation was difficult for both of them. But she had to know.

He looked older somehow, almost defeated, just standing there, locked in her eyes. Finally he moved over to the fire and sat down in a mahogany chair. "I thought you might ask me where I came from . . . a long time ago. But you didn't. Did you never wonder who made me?"

"Julian did."

"No."

Eleisha froze, still staring at him.

"Don't look at me like that," he snapped.

She didn't speak, and he glanced away.

"Where do you want me to start?" he asked.

"The beginning." Her voice sounded cold to her own ears.

"I don't know anything about that." He ran a hand through his slicked-back hair. "I only know of a Norman duke from the twelfth century who was turned. Nobody knows who made him, but in the early nineteenth century, he made three sons: Julian, Philip Branté, and a young Scottish lord named John McCrugger."

Now that he was actually speaking of these things . . . of things that mattered, she didn't want him to stop. She walked over and sat on the floor beside his chair.

"Which one made you?"

"McCrugger." The tight tension faded from his face, as if he, too, suddenly wanted to talk of the past. "I was just an ignorant young man looking for work—and failing. He came to London on business, and I tried to pick his pocket. He took me back to Scotland and gave me a job as his manservant. Later I took over the house accounts, and finally, he turned me out of convenience."

"What?" she gasped.

"Sounds coldhearted now, doesn't it? I don't know. Maybe he just wanted to experiment with his power, but he said that he'd trained me well and never wished to go through such training again."

"What happened to him?"

"Julian hunted him down and killed him . . . and I think he killed the old Norman lord as well. I don't know why. To the best of my knowledge, neither one had wronged him. He seemed to be going on some sort of murder spree, but he never went after Philip or Maggie."

"Maggie?"

"Margaritte Latour? Philip's whore? Did you never meet her?"

The memory of Maggie remained vivid. "Yes, once. She's not someone you'd forget."

"She's the final player. There are only six of us left as far as I know."

"As far as you . . ." She trailed off as something he'd said struck her. "Why did you say 'murder spree' if he only killed two other vampires?"

Edward paused for a long moment, as if deciding how much to share. "Because later, Maggie and I corresponded out of . . . concern for ourselves, trying to figure a few things out. She hinted there were others."

"What others?" Eleisha asked in fascination, moving closer.

"I don't know!" He closed his eyes briefly and opened them again, trying to calm himself. "Remember I was only a servant. Except for Maggie, the others were noble. I was certainly not in the loop."

"You said Julian left them alone, but he left you alone, too?"

His face grew pained. "Yes. My master had gone to Harfleur that winter, and I was managing his French villa in Amiens . . . He owned homes in several countries. He showed up one night with no warning and told me to pack, that we were going back to Scotland. We went down together to give instructions to our grooms . . . and Julian came out of the shadows by the stable. I watched him cut McCrugger's head off and then he just turned around and said, 'Go,' like some homicidal, self-important god. I ran like a coward for America and never looked back."

Eleisha's mind raced.

"But I've read . . . Edward, don't be angry with me, but I've been reading at the library. Some of the accounts suggest larger numbers of us across Europe."

His green eyes widened. "You've been . . . ?" He leaned back and looked up at the ceiling. "I know those old stories, too. All myth and folklore. We each feed at least once a week. What if there were even twenty vampires living in Manhattan? Twenty deaths a week? We'd depopulate the area too quickly for secrecy."

He was right, of course, but the picture still didn't make sense. Those written accounts couldn't all be fictitious, could they? Mass hysteria?

"What if—"

"Enough!" he snapped, and then his expression softened. "Enough for one night." He looked down at her simple dress and bare feet in disapproval. "What are you wearing?"

"It's comfortable." She paused. "And I would like to buy a few more—just for evenings at home." Her jaw clenched. "I'll need some money."

"You only have to ask."

She looked over to note that William had not come out of his room.

Less than a year later, Edward came home to find her standing by the window again.

She was holding an envelope in her hand, the address written in a familiar black script of blocky letters and numbers.

"A love letter from Julian?" Edward asked flippantly. "What does the old boy have to say?"

Then he saw her face, and he stopped walking. "What's wrong?"

"Nothing." She held up the envelope. "He's agreed to begin sending our stipend to me directly . . . in Oregon."

Edward blinked, as if she were speaking a foreign language.

"I'm taking William, and we're leaving," she said.

His mouth fell open in shock. He dropped into a chair, his dark eyes shifting back and forth.

"William's grown afraid of you," she rushed on. "Admit it, Edward, the sight of him makes you ill. I've arranged to buy a house in Portland, Oregon. We need to start over . . . someplace new."

"You can't be serious," he choked. "You're just doing

this to frighten me, to make me treat the old nutter more kindly. If that's what you want, you could have just said so."

"I am serious. We leave next week. I've booked a private car on a westbound train."

Edward stood up stiffly, slowly, and walked past her, even closer to the window. He was composed now, unable to express himself, trapped by his own facade. They were both quiet for a moment, and then he said, "I'm keeping the painting."

In the early 1870s, he'd befriended a visiting French Impressionist named Gustave Caillebotte. They shared several weeks of intense conversation—typical of Edward—and in the process, Caillebotte made a portrait of Eleisha sitting on a green velvet couch. She found it vain. Edward adored it.

Moving up beside him, she wanted to comfort him, but didn't. Neither one spoke. They had nothing more to say.

chapter 17

This time I broke off first.

"Don't stop," Wade said, grabbing my hand.

"No more. When you're inside my head, I see his face like he's in the room."

Visions of Edward hurt far more than I'd imagined they would. He'd been so alive, so original.

But Wade's questions kept coming. "So, you went to Portland?"

"Yeah," I managed to answer. "Edward followed two years later. He stayed in different hotels until 1937, then bought a house. He'd just grown too used to company."

"You lived with him in New York for seventy-three years?"

"I'd almost forgotten. Seems like another lifetime."

I needed to stop talking about this, and I noticed Wade's eyelids flutter. How long had it been since he'd really slept? The previous night he'd been up playing Superman, and then he probably stood guard over me all day.

"Maybe you should rest."

I thought he might argue—still burning with curiosity—but he pointed to the door. "Not yet. There's another whole room out there."

"What . . . You rented a suite?"

"Seemed appropriate."

Walking out into the living room of a modern hotel suite surprised me, as if Wade had been kidding and I'd find myself in a hallway. The decor was sterile, predictable: a gray sleeper couch, dried blue flowers in a vase from Tiffany's, two assembly-line paintings of seascapes. But this probably cost six hundred dollars a night. Why would Wade spend that kind of money? To impress me? Maybe he just thought I was used to places like this? What a guy.

My mind needed a break. How long had it been since Edward jumped off his porch? Only six weeks. Couldn't be. The memories shook me more than I wanted to admit. That's why I pushed Wade out of my head. What if the three of us had simply stayed in New York? Would Edward still have lost it? He'd never liked Portland, but his attachment to me kept him from being happy alone in Manhattan. Was it love? Maybe. He could have cut and run that first night in Southampton, left us to die in ignorance, but he didn't. How much did we owe him? I didn't even have a photo, not even a photo.

And my William . . .

Stop it.

I wasn't ready to deal with his death. I wasn't prepared to mourn. Trying to mull over that loss and figure out my next move would only bring hysteria. What was my purpose now? Even if I did escape Julian and manage to live—which was doubtful—what was I supposed to do?

"We need to go out for a little while," Wade said from behind me.

"Aren't we supposed to be hiding out?"

"We're in Kirkland—miles from Seattle, and we'll go on foot. It'll be okay."

"I think you need some sleep. What's so important?"

"You'll see. First I want to go someplace and get a hamburger."

"Really? You always sort of struck me as the health-food type."

He smiled slightly. "Used to be. Back at the institute they served whole grain and greens three meals a day. Dominick got me hooked on beer, pizza, and burgers."

The mention of Dominick sent my mood into the shadows again. Wade turned away. "Sorry, I just don't have any other friends. Kind of sad, huh?"

"No, I don't have many friends either."

Getting out of the hotel turned out to be a good idea. The night was clear and cool. We walked in comfortable silence to a small diner called Ernie's and slid into a cushy booth where a matronly waitress who bore an astonishing resemblance to Alice on *The Brady Bunch* took our order.

"I feel like a kid on my first date," Wade said, holding his cheeseburger in one hand.

"Really? Maybe I should giggle a lot?"

He threw a French fry across the table. "Hey, is the room okay?"

"Room? The suite? Of course, it's fine." Why would he worry about something like that? "Listen, you should let me pay you back for all this. The hotel. The rental car. Everything."

"You don't need to. Anyway, where would you get that kind of money?"

"Me? Jesus, Wade, I thought you'd have figured that out by now. I'm . . . pretty well off: three rotating CD accounts in Portland, an account in Zurich, stock in Coca-Cola, Starbucks, Hewlett-Packard . . . Boeing."

He stopped eating. "How did you manage all that?"

"Accountants and stockbrokers. Money is the only thing that matters here. Julian has joint control of my Portland accounts, though. He doesn't care how much I spend, but if I'd pulled out four hundred thousand to buy a new house, he'd want to know why."

"Your accountants work with you at night?"

"Sure. If you're poor and strange, people call you mad. If you're rich and strange, they call you eccentric."

He finished his dinner without another word and paid the check. Somehow, our exchange seemed to have upset him. We walked down the street awhile in silence. "You think you've got us all figured out, don't you?" he said finally.

"No."

"Yes, you do. You take mortals at face value and then put them into neat little categories so you won't have to deal with anyone."

"Where are we going?" I ignored his statement, which struck me as pointless anyway since our relationship went far beyond face value, and I was certainly dealing with him. We turned into a park with green grass, slides, and a large swing set.

"Why are we here?" I asked.

"You'll see." His momentary annoyance faded, and he led me through the park until we found a patch of forest near the back. "Here, this is a good place."

"For what?"

Kneeling down, he lifted his shirt and pulled a thin box from the back of his jeans. "We're going to bury William."

My skin went cold. "What?"

"Don't look so surprised. When I was a kid, I had only one pet, an orange cat named Meesha. She got hit by a car, and I couldn't deal with it. My dad got disgusted, but my mom put her body in a box and took me for a long walk. She said, 'You can't put this behind you or go on with tomorrow until Meesha's safe in the ground, and you know where to visit should you need to.' That's the only thing my mother ever did for me that mattered."

"What's in that box?"

"Some of William's ashes. I got them while you were changing upstairs last night."

He began digging in the dirt with his hands. My knees sank down of their own accord, and I reached out to help him. Night wind blew through the leaves above us, and it seemed right to forget who we were, what we were caught in the middle of, and instead pretend to be just two people laying a ghost to rest.

"Do you believe in heaven, Wade?"

"I don't know."

The box fit neatly in its hole, and we gently patted the loose dirt back in place.

"We can't leave a marker," he said.

"It's all right."

For a long time we sat together, gathering our thoughts, thinking of the past, blanking out the future. Though still unable to mourn, I felt different now that perhaps William had found rest or even lived in a better place than this world.

"Thank you," I said, the words sounding inadequate.

Instead of answering, Wade stood up to leave. Our work here was done, and he wanted understanding, not thanks. The dirt beneath our feet changed swiftly into grass as we emerged from the forest patch into the park, walking in solemn silence like people leaving a funeral.

It was over halfway through April, and sweet scents of summer blossoms drifted on the air. Western Washington is a rainy place, often cloudy and wet, but the few clear spring nights Mother Nature doles out are a paradise of green leaves and bursting flowers.

My mind was almost at peace, drifting in several different directions, when I heard the first whimper. Wade stopped, listening. His expression went blank for a moment, and then twisted slightly.

"What is it?" I asked.

"Here, over here." He ducked away and pushed aside a shrub to our right. To my surprise, a small boy practically boiled out from underneath and darted in a beeline for the trees.

"Leisha, help me get him."

Gliding into instant motion, I flew past Wade, whose long strides were actually quite fast, and I focused on the spot the boy had disappeared into. Once inside the forested area, I was running blind and stopped to listen. Wade's voice blew past me.

"It's all right, Raymond. If you come out we'll get you something warm to eat."

Raymond?

How had he managed to pick so much out of a fleeing target's mind? Perhaps children are more open than adults.

"We should leave this place," I called. "When he gets tired, he'll go home."

"No, he can't go home. Go to your left. He's right ahead of you."

Children are an alien species. Hunting them for life force wasn't my style, and I couldn't remember ever having spoken to one. But Wade seemed dead set on catching this boy. Small shuffling sounds in the bushes ahead caught my attention, and I sprang forward, the tips of my fingers grasping a small arm. I struggled for a better grip.

He bit me. The little shit sank his teeth into my hand, hard enough to break skin. It didn't really hurt. Lifting his kicking feet off the ground, I whispered, "You wouldn't like it if I bit you back."

Wade bounded up beside me, his nearly white hair glowing like a beacon. "Here," I said. "You take him."

My companion's arms were more adept at holding children than mine. "It's all right, Raymond. No one's going to hurt you."

The boy stilled as Wade kept whispering soft words in his ear. The poor kid was a mess. About five or six years old, with dirty clothes and long, filthy hair. His eyes were wild, and low grunting sounds escaped his mouth. He seemed incapable of speech.

His short legs wrapped around Wade's waist. Wade put one arm around the child's back and the other beneath his bottom for support. Somehow the sight of Wade holding him moved me. Edward used to say it takes all kinds of people to make a world.

"What now?" I asked.

"He's been neglected. We need to get our car from the hotel and drive him to the authorities."

"Are you crazy? You're talking about cops, right? Cops?"

"It's eleven o'clock at night. Social Health and Welfare closed down hours ago. We don't have a choice."

"Sure we do. I'm not going near a police station."

"You have to! Dominick may be able to block his thoughts from me, but I can still feel him coming. This won't take long. We're just going to feed him and then find someone else to take over."

What was he thinking? We could now be linked to three bizarre deaths, and he wanted to walk right into a Seattle precinct to turn in a lost child? No way.

"You aren't listening to me!" Wade spat at Sergeant Ben Cordova of Precinct Seventeen in west Seattle. "He hasn't been beaten. He lives with his father and his father's girlfriend. They leave him alone for days at a time, with no food in the house. No one's ever changed his bedsheets as far back as he can remember. He hasn't attended any school. They don't wash his clothes."

Sergeant Cordova looked back with the eyes of a dead fish. "Are there any physical marks of abuse?"

"How about malnutrition, you stupid fuck?"

Oh, great, there it went. I'd been standing in the back of a crowded police office, watching Wade argue with this dispassionate sergeant for nearly twenty minutes. The more intensely bored Cordova appeared, the higher Wade's voice rose. And now he was swearing.

"There's no need for that, sir. This falls between social services and the boy's father."

"No, you can't send him back home for a few days. Not for five minutes."

I moved up behind them. "Leave the boy here. They'll know what to do."

"They don't. That's the point. The minute we walk out that door, this joker's going to call his father." He whirled back to Cordova. "Get your captain out here."

"He's not available, sir."

"Get him out here, now!"

"Is there a problem?" a deep voice asked from behind me. I turned to see an enormous man wearing a suit and tie.

"Yes, there's a problem," Wade snapped. "Your sergeant has his head up his ass."

"I'm Captain Baker. Can I help you?"

"No, you can help this boy. He needs a clean place to sleep."

"And you are?"

Until that point, my angry friend had avoided discussing himself, even though Cordova had asked for ID three times. "My name is Dr. Wade Sheffield. I've been the staff psychologist at Captain Joseph McNickel's Eighth Precinct in Portland, Oregon, for the past four years. If you like, we can call him at home and wake him up for verification."

That sounded dangerous to me since Wade had resigned under such odd circumstances, but maybe McNickel would back him up.

Captain Baker crouched down and smiled at Raymond, who pulled deeper into Wade's chest. "And how much do you know about this little guy?"

"Not much. His name is Raymond Olson. His father's name is Robert Olson. They live somewhere in Kirkland at an apartment complex called Greenwich Village—at least that's what the sign out front says. He's been starved and neglected . . . He can't even talk."

"How did you become involved?"

"I found him in the park a few hours ago."

The captain's brow wrinkled. "So how did you learn this much information if he can't speak?"

Wonderful. This kept getting better by the moment. Not only was Wade irrational, but he'd just backed himself into a corner. "Please, just check my story without sending him home. If you have any pity at all."

The room fell quiet for a moment. Then Baker said, "A friend of mine—well, my wife—works for social services. Let me go call her and have her come down."

Wade looked into the man's eyes for a few seconds, and then he relaxed. Turning to me, he nodded and said, "It's okay. He's not lying."

I'd never seen him like this, not quite this worked up. In all other aspects of his own self-image, he was sometimes unsure, often timid. But when it came to trusting his psychic ability, he exuded a confidence that made other people listen. Was he even aware how angry, how aggressive, he sounded?

We waited quietly together on a bench for nearly an hour—Wade still holding Raymond in his lap—until a middle-aged woman who looked overworked, underpaid, and slightly frazzled walked in. I didn't have to be psychic to figure out she was Baker's wife.

She spotted us in a hurry and flashed a tired smile. Wade's tight muscles unclenched. Even with her hair flying all over, this woman had kind eyes and a tough expression. Good combination.

I pulled back to let her speak alone with Wade. He took her phone number, said a few words to Raymond, and then handed him to Mrs. Baker. There was a moment of panic on the boy's part, but it passed. He was probably so lost by then that up from down didn't matter.

As we walked back outside to our car, Wade still didn't look happy. "I feel bad leaving him there."

"There's nothing else you can do. He's got even less chance with us right now than with his own family."

"That doesn't make me feel any better."

"You can't save the world. It's already lost."

What an unexpected chain of events. How selfish I'd been. The boy, of course, meant nothing. Children have been starving since the inception of time. Raymond was as common as dirt.

But Wade had offered his help, his services, to me so easily it seemed he almost wanted to be caught up in this horror. Not true. Had he wanted to spend half the night fighting with tired cops in a police station? No, but some part of his mental makeup drove him on. He could do something no one else could, and that responsibility pushed him past his own physical limits. That's why he had worked night and day for the Portland police. That's why he continued helping me. Was it pride, or some unfulfilled need?

In silence, we drove back to the hotel, parked the car, and went up to our suite. Blue and gray decor greeted us with its sterile cheerfulness, and Wade switched on the lamp.

"Do you miss your job?" I blurted out.

The question didn't surprise him. Perhaps he'd been thinking about it himself. "Sometimes. I need to be . . . useful. Pathetic really."

"No, it isn't. At least you contribute."

With William gone, what would my contribution be now?

"Maybe." He sighed. "I'm tired, but I don't want to sleep."

"What should we do?"

He picked up the *TV Guide*. "*Captain Blood* is just starting on HBO. Do you like Errol Flynn?"

"Sure, he's my hero."

"I thought I was your hero?"

"Fat chance."

He cracked a grin and looked around for the television remote. Two minutes later we were sacked out on the couch, watching pirates swashbuckle in shades of black and white.

chapter 18

I woke up in the bed alone.

We'd watched television until nearly dawn when my eyelids grew heavy. But we'd been out on the couch. I didn't remember coming in here.

Long, heavy blankets covered the draped windows to block out any light from the sun. Of course darkness had settled by now. Where was Wade?

Hopping up, I walked out into the suite's living room and found it empty. Didn't this guy ever sleep? He was definitely an original. I suddenly considered slipping out the door and disappearing before he came back. Somehow, his life seemed to be worth more than my undead existence. Leaving him here would cut him deeply, but staying could mean his death. And even more than that, what if he actually lived through this? Could he go back to being Dr. Wade Sheffield? Mortals often identify their self-worth with their occupation, as if what they do is an integral part of what they are.

But sooner or later, for better or worse—probably worse—a final-act curtain would drop down on this macabre play. Whoever was left in one piece would have to go on to the future. Did Wade remember that?

I heard movement outside the door, and then he walked in with an armload of shopping bags.

"Where were you?" I asked.

He dropped the bags. "Take a wild guess."

"Oooh, you're too funny." I walked over to see what he'd been up to. "Shopping?"

"Yeah, come look. We both needed some new clothes." He pulled out a pair of Levi's and a brown T-shirt with long sleeves. "Size four, right?"

"You bought me clothes?" He never ceased to astound me. "How did you know my size?"

"Lucky guess. Sorry this stuff's so basic. But we're going to be running a lot."

This was getting out of hand, and he'd seen way too many movies. I was about to give him our survival chances when he yawned. "Did you sleep at all today?" I asked.

"A little this morning," he said.

"You won't be good to anyone like that. Come on. Lie down for a while, and I'll stand guard over your prone, helpless body, okay?"

Hiding my concern behind humor had always worked well for me. He didn't even argue. While he got ready for bed, I went into the bathroom and changed clothes. He even bought me new underwear and socks.

"Do they fit?" he called.

I walked out to find him under the blankets, eyes about half closed. "Yeah, you did a good job. Thanks, Wade."

My approval pleased him. "Wake me in a few hours."

"Sure, I'll be in the living room."

He was already breathing softly. I closed the door and went to make a cup of tea. We were going to have a long talk when he woke up. What did he think tomorrow would bring? Endless running and living in fancy hotels with me? He had absorbed my memories in detail. Didn't he realize what we were up against?

The room suddenly felt cold. Where was the thermostat? Glancing around, I saw movement by the curtains. A shadow.

"Didn't think you'd ever notice me," a soft voice whispered. "Lost in thought?"

Three facts registered instantly. Masculine. French. No available weapons.

I drew back against the wall. "Philip?"

Only once. I'd seen him only once before. How shortsighted. Julian felt William die. The possible threat of Philip had hit me the night Maggie died, but a great deal had happened since then. Concentrating so completely on Julian, I had forgotten about Philip. How did he get in here? Had Wade left the door unlocked?

"You have some stories to tell, little one," he whispered in a heavy accent. "What happened to my Maggie?"

He stepped out of the shadows, and I looked at him, wordless. He didn't look like Maggie . . . but he *was* so much like her. His beauty must have blinded hundreds, thousands. He was tall—slender and muscular at the same time. Thick, red-brown hair hung halfway down his back, and amber eyes stared out of a narrow, ivory face. He and Maggie shared the same gift. But this time, the pull affected me.

It felt as if I were staring into the sun at noon.

Gifts.

He was a killer without thought. Snuffing out my existence and Wade's meant less than nothing. I was not immune to his gift, indeed probably more susceptible since it was new to me. But then again, he wasn't immune to mine either. I crossed my arms in fear and looked at the floor.

"Philip, don't hurt me."

Concentrate. Emanate. Get him on his knees.

"You're finally here," I said. "I kept hoping. I didn't know what to do."

His expression flickered. Could he feel it? Did he know what I was doing, or was he lost in some overinflated sense of forgotten manhood? He was so perfect. I'd never seen anything like him in my life—except Maggie.

A humorless smile curved the corners of his mouth. "We seem to be at a standoff, little one. Unexpected. Maggie tried to warn me, but her words were often exaggerated. Yet right now I feel an overwhelming urge to throw my body in front of a moving train to rescue your handkerchief."

A lie, and a stupid play. Showing that he already knew the score gave me an advantage. He liked to show off.

"How did you find me?"

"Followed you from Maggie's." He motioned with his head toward the bedroom. "Who's your pet?"

"No one. He's been helping me. If you sit down, I'll tell you everything."

I didn't tell him to sit down; that's the key to handling men like Philip. You can't tell them to do anything. You either ask them or make it seem like their own idea.

He crossed to a chair, expression guarded. I felt torn for a moment. Sitting by his feet would give me the best psychological advantage, but getting that close to him was dangerous.

"If I had come to kill you, you would be dead," he said in a voice that sounded more sad than angry. Sorrow was no mystery to me, at least not anymore.

Moving to the floor by his knee, I focused on his black Hugo Boss pant legs and not his face.

Don't look at his face.

"Odd little thing," he said. "More than I expected."

"Do you remember the first night I saw you?"

"No, have you seen me?"

My words pleased him. He might have had some depth hidden away, but he thrived on attention.

"Yes, at Cliffbracken. You came in with Julian and Maggie late one night, but that was a long time ago."

"A long time ago," he echoed. "What happened to my Maggie?"

"How much do you know? She said she called you once."

"Only that Edward Claymore destroyed himself and mortal men chased you to Seattle."

Part of me wanted to say anything that would make him leave. I wanted him to go away. Wade slept helpless in the next room, and I knew no way to protect him. But another part of me understood Philip's confusion, his pain. Maggie had been a deadly work of art, and she'd barely outlasted two lifetimes. She should have gone far into the future. And now it was as though she'd never been.

"A policeman killed her," I said quietly, "named Dominick Vasundara."

Starting with the first night at Edward's, I gave him my version of the past six weeks, letting him know the kind of hunter Maggie truly had been, so competent and skilled—and still graceful. No matter how sick it sounds, that was my comfort for his loss. Perhaps that's another gift I'd developed, instinctive recognition of what others needed to hear. I left out Wade's psychic ability, though, and played up Dominick's psychometry.

"You cared for her?" he asked.

"She was good to me . . . and to William."

"I was close to the house when he died."

His words startled me, leaving no response. For the first time since watching him step away from the curtain, I looked into his eyes. Reckless or not, it felt like the right thing to do. He was searching for words, like a computer accessing memory banks for a correct response and finding none. No residual trace of humanity remained in Philip.

"It's all right," I told him. "You don't need to say anything."

"Julian would think us mad, no? Like two old ladies sad for things past."

I didn't know how to answer that, so I just sat there, looking at him.

"Maggie's voice changed the last time she telephoned," he said abruptly. "You gave her something I could not."

"What?"

"You tell me."

"Maybe she was just tired of being alone."

"Our kind lives alone, hunts alone. It's the way."

If he really believed that, he was as cracked as Julian. But Philip's expression reminded me of faces I hadn't seen since going to church as a child. Religion? Did we have a religion? If so, Edward certainly hadn't mentioned it.

"Why are we supposed to be alone?" I asked.

"Your maker once said we are the despised of God's children. We live in darkness and deserve no comfort."

"That's ridiculous. We used to be mortal ourselves. If that's true, where did the first vampires come from?"

"Spirits. Before the world was made, a mass of black clouds existed in its place. When God made the world, spirits rebelled and entered the bodies of dead mortals."

What? Did Julian believe any of this? Maybe Edward had been some sort of heathen or atheist, because he had never talked like this—not that I was buying into it either. But does it make any less sense than other religions? Does it sound any less plausible than four billion years of evolution being condensed into six days?

"So why did you make Maggie? Didn't you want her to stay with you?" I pitched my tone to suggest deference, childlike innocence. Challenging him would have been a mistake.

The question threw him anyway. "A crime . . . but letting her beauty fade seemed a sin. Not before, not since, has anyone matched my Maggie." He smiled weakly. "Julian would think us mad."

That was it. Possibly not even in life had Philip experienced true loss, mourning. Emotion confused him, and this kind of pain was new.

"Why did you come here, Philip?"

"For you. I came for you."

The ambiguity of his answer brought fear rushing back. I rolled over and up, gauging the distance to Wade's door.

"Worried about your pet?"

"He's not a pet."

"You should silence him, little one. He knows what you are, doesn't he?"

I wanted to smash his face with a brass lamp, but I'd lose, and Wade would die. "No, please. He doesn't know much—just some guy I seduced for help. Don't hurt him."

That was a bad play, and Philip knew it. Vampires don't worry about each other, much less about one insignificant mortal.

"You are a curious thing," he said. "But when Julian comes, your pet will die anyway. Come with me, and he might live."

"Why would you want that?"

"Maggie helped you. Edward helped you. At the beginning, they were on the brink of despair. Oh, don't look so shocked. I know more of Edward than you think. He'd have jumped off a porch a hundred years sooner were it not for you." His handsome face grew intense. "What did you give them?" he demanded.

"Nothing."

"Come, tell me. I am more than Edward was."

Bastard. He was taking me whether I wanted to go or not. Defeat ebbed my power, faded my gift, brought anger to the surface. "You're nothing compared to Edward. Would you take in an orphan and a half-mad undead? Bathe them? Feed them from your arm? Don't compare yourself to him."

I might as well have slapped him. Perhaps no one ever spoke to him like that. He took a step toward me and stopped. "Odd thing. Cold without your gift."

"As you."

Gazing down, his eyes reminded me of Maggie's again. Did he have any of her fire for living? For hunting? Compassion for old cripples like William? Or was he empty?

And then it occurred to me that everyone else was really gone—except Julian, who didn't count. If I wanted companionship from my own kind, Philip was the last boy in town. Sorry thought.

"Come with me," he said. "Your little friend will live."

Wade deserved to live, more than the rest of us. But what would he think upon waking? That I'd deserted him? It didn't matter. Maybe he'd go back home and be safe.

Stopping only to pick up Maggie's wool coat, I got up and followed Philip.

chapter 19

"**D**o you have a car?" I asked as we stepped outside the hotel.

Instead of answering, he looked up and down the street, then walked to an early-eighties, dirty-blue Camaro and climbed in the driver's side.

He couldn't possibly have rented this. What a piece of junk. Hardly his style.

"You should lock your doors down here anyway," I said. "Somebody too drunk to see might steal it."

His answering laugh made me nervous. The interior looked even worse. Marlboro boxes, Hershey bar wrappers, and Big Gulp cups covered the backseat and floor. As I slammed my door, Philip reached up with both hands and jerked the steering column five inches out of the dash, exposing red, black, and green wires.

"What are you doing?"

"Rewiring the ignition," he answered casually, as if we were talking about fall fashions.

Later I felt ashamed of my own reaction. "You can't do that. It's illegal."

Laughing again as the engine roared, he squealed the

tires while pulling into traffic. "You are too tame. Or is this your gift again, eh?"

"Philip, stop the car. If the police catch you, they'll lock you in a cell."

Doing seventy-five as we hit the southbound on-ramp for Seattle, he glanced at me warily. "What are police to us? They are too slow to catch us. Bullets don't hurt us."

"So what do you do when you get pulled over?"

"I don't pull over unless I'm hungry."

He started weaving through traffic, the needle peaking at ninety. Steering with one hand, he fished around on the dashboard, found a crusty Black Sabbath tape, and slammed it in. Ozzy's voice screamed out two rear-window speakers. Whoever owned this car really needed to be told what year it was. I hadn't seen a cassette player in years.

"Where are we going?" I asked.

"Seattle Center. This city is new to me, but Maggie said hunting in the center was good."

"You want to hunt now?"

"Don't you? We just woke up." His accent seemed to be getting worse instead of better, making me wish I spoke French.

"No, I fed last night."

"So don't feed." He shrugged. "Just hunt."

Maybe Maggie had been right about me. Maybe I hadn't seen enough in my one hundred and eighty-six years. "You just want to kill someone?"

He took his eyes completely off the road and stared at me. "Is this for real or are you playing? What do you do all night if not hunt?"

"Take care of William, read books, settle the bank accounts, talk to my investment broker. I don't know, just things."

"No?" Amused, almost pleased, he pushed the needle up higher. "William is gone. You are immortal, with no need for books and investment brokers."

That's the first time the word "immortal" sounded absurd to me. Webster's unabridged defines it as "not mortal; deathless; living forever." I know. I looked it up once. What a crock. We may not get any older, but the body count hit three last night. Sounded pretty mortal to me. Maybe Philip wasn't keeping score.

Watching him drive—his long hair flying out the window, his head bobbing to the music, his face sporting an adolescent grin—made me try to see beyond his gift. What was he besides beautiful and careless? His black Hugo Boss pants and Calvin Klein shirt suggested his taste was not only good, but up-to-date. Edward always bought Savile Row and Christian Dior, which worked on him but was sort of "older crowd"—sort of.

Philip also cared what Julian thought. Why? Why would Julian's opinion matter?

"Turn down the Mercer/Fairview exit," I said.

Downtown Seattle is a mass of one-way streets, confusing signs, and heavy traffic, but my too-happy companion drove as if he were on a backwoods dirt road.

"Where'd you learn to drive?"

"Paris," he answered. That figured. He found a pay-by-the-hour parking lot near the Space Needle and jumped out. "We ditch this car now."

"Whatever you say." Instinct screamed that it was

time to ditch golden boy. But I didn't. Maybe he was the only true vampire among us—cold and fast and wild. Maybe Edward and I struggled too hard to hoard little bits of humanity and somehow never quite fit into either world. Philip didn't feed just on blood. He seemed to feed off the world, draining life and power and material wealth from anything unlucky enough to cross his path. And he did it without thought or remorse or pity—a purist in the true sense. Fascinating. Frightening.

"Look, a roller coaster," he said, smiling. Canned carnival music and bright lights flooded the scene. He bolted toward the bumper cars, and then stopped, looking back for me. "You like rides?"

"No . . . I don't know."

He jumped the few steps back to me, looking confused, as if he wanted to grab my arm but didn't know how. Again, his expression reminded me of a computer accessing data it couldn't find. Perhaps he'd forgotten how to touch someone he wasn't murdering.

"Come, Eleisha. Come on."

"How long has it been since you've hunted with someone else?"

His eyebrows knitted. "What year is it?"

What year? How could he be so up on fashion and not even know the year? "Don't you read the newspaper?"

That annoyed him. "Newspaper? For sheep and puppets. You start to believe your own gift."

"And you don't?"

The night lights and black corners pulled at him. I

could see it in his eyes, and in spite of myself, it called to me as well.

"Too much talk," he said. "Come."

Changing his mind abruptly, he steered away from the carnival and headed down toward the fountain. I followed about a half step behind him, watching a wide variety of people pass us. Philip ignored all of them like an overfed cat turned loose in a science lab. We reached the huge round fountain in Seattle Center's heart. Four teenage kids sat on the lawn, smoking and talking. Philip headed straight for them.

A tall boy, about sixteen with a shaved head and two pewter skulls hanging in the same ear, took a long drag and noticed us. Apparently he didn't want extra company, because his lips tightened angrily at our approach, and then Philip smiled. All four of them smiled back. Too weird.

"Bum a smoke?" my partner asked, pointing to the cigarette.

"Here." Pewter Skulls held out the pack. "Where're you from?"

"France, but I like your city."

Philip's communication skills with the kid actually surprised me. I don't know what I expected. But the sight of him sitting on the grass smoking and making small talk didn't fit my mental image. Pewter Skulls introduced himself as Culker. The rest of the group included a boy named Scott with a green mohawk, a blond girl named Becky with small eyes and a blue leather miniskirt, and an African-American girl named Jet in a pink, tie-dyed dress under a loose jean jacket.

They were all about the same age. I thought the mo-hawk was passé. Becky seemed to have about four working brain cells, but Jet's face caught my attention, clean and straightforward. Part of me actually wanted to talk to her, but that wasn't my place here, not my gift. Philip had them eating from his hand.

He leaned back on his elbows. A mass of silky red-brown hair hung to the ground.

"Who's that with you?" Culker finally asked him.

I'd been sitting quietly behind Philip, hiding in his overwhelming shadow. A safe place, almost pleasant.

"Eleisha, say hello to our new friends."

I fell into my routine and focused on the ground. "Hi."

Scott turned to Philip. "Hey, if we give you the money, will you buy us some beer?"

"Where did you plan to drink it?"

"At Becky's. Her folks are gone. You want to come?"

This was too easy. Although if we trotted down to the nearest 7-Eleven, picked up a case of cheap beer, and then headed to Becky's, how would Philip manage to get someone off alone?

As we fell into step toward a store, I noticed Jet walking beside me and gave her an honest smile.

"How old are you?" she asked.

"Seventeen."

"How old is he?"

"Twenty-nine."

She wasn't dumb. Due to our unnatural skin tone, our ages are often difficult to place. But Jet's questions struck a little deeper. Why would an incredibly beautiful, well-dressed, adult Frenchman want to hang with them when he had a pretty, seventeen-year-old girl-friend for company? It didn't make sense.

"You going out with Culker?" I asked to change the subject.

"Culker? No way. These guys are just my friends. I like your coat."

"Oh, thanks . . . Did you dye that dress yourself?"

"Yeah." She seemed pleased. "I do all kinds of stuff. Sell clothes at the Folklife Festival."

"What's that?"

"You don't know 'bout the festival? Where're you from?"

I smiled. "Portland."

She smiled back, and we talked all the way to a run-down mini-mart. Philip glanced back at me once. He went inside and came out with a case of Henry Wein-hard's Ale that must have cost twice what Culker gave him. Didn't this situation seem unusual to any of them?

"Awesome," Scott said. "My car's two blocks south."

Becky kept moving closer to Philip. I'm sure he noticed.

We all piled into a rusted Buick Skylark with ciga-rette butts falling out of its ashtray. We ended up driv-ing to Capitol Hill, but Scott spent twenty minutes trying to find a place to park.

Piles of dirt and garbage had been plowed to the sides of the road. One decrepit apartment building melted right into the next one. Every available parking space seemed filled with a dented Volkswagen Golf.

Babies cried through open windows, and some guy down the block kept yelling, "You bitch!" over and over again.

I wanted to go home, but we didn't have one.

Scott finally managed to squeeze the Skylark between two cars, and everybody climbed out. I'd figured out by then that Becky's parents didn't live in a house.

"We can't be too loud," she said. "The guys below us are crack dealers. One of them gets mad easy."

Charming.

Something about her apartment's interior touched more sorrow than its outside. Small arrangements of dried flowers sat on paint-splattered tables. An old mattress was covered by a hand-stitched quilt. Cheap lace curtains blew out from chipped windowpanes. Someone cared about this place enough to try to make it a home.

Culker broke open a Henry's. "We should've bought some chips or M&M's."

"Order a pizza," Philip said. "Isn't that what you Americans do?"

"Can't, I'm almost broke."

"I'll pay."

Could they possibly be this blind? Jet sat alone. What was she thinking? It's funny how Wade had given me a different perspective of mortals. On impulse, I reached out and touched her mind—as I would have with Wade—not expecting to get through. Psychic pictures come to us only when feeding or when another vampire dies. But to my surprise, her immediate thoughts flowed into me as though she were speaking.

Philip was the most perfect thing she'd ever seen, and she usually didn't go for white guys. But what was he into? Why was he here? If he was looking for some kind of threesome, he'd pick Becky. That was obvious. Not that Jet cared. Her baby boy was with a sitter, and she ought to get back soon, anyway. His ears were bothering him, and she'd need to take him to the doctor tomorrow.

I pulled out, reeling internally. How long had that taken? Had she felt me? Only seconds seemed to have passed, and she continued watching Philip with the same cautious curiosity. She had a little boy? I wanted to know more but didn't know how to deal with the moment's revelation.

Was I more like Wade than I realized?

Philip caught my attention suddenly by sitting down next to Becky and touching her bare thigh. I hadn't seen him touch anyone yet, and the movement of his hand was slow, light, gentle. That's why he hadn't grabbed my hand in the carnival. Touching was only for victims.

The room fell silent as he leaned down and kissed her. Everyone—including me—watched the gradual movement of his open mouth as he licked her lips and face. His pale hand moved up her side, feather touch, like a concerned lover. Nobody else moved.

What was he doing? This didn't make sense. If he wanted to lure her away from her friends, he should have just asked. She'd have followed him off a cliff.

The red polyester couch they sat on showed huge gaping holes of foam rubber. Becky's breathing quickened when he moved to her neck. Completely lost in his gift, she tried to put her fingertips on his face. The scene changed.

Click.

He ripped out a chunk of her throat before I could blink—right in front of her friends. Instead of falling into a hazy state of slow motion, the world rushed to a hundred miles an hour. Scott started screaming as blood shot out of her jugular and covered his T-shirt. Philip jumped over the back of the couch and landed on top of him.

"No way, man," Culker kept repeating from the center of the room. "No way."

Philip stopped Scott's screaming by flipping him onto his stomach and breaking his neck with a loud crack. Then he smiled up at Culker.

Until that point, I'd been too off guard to move. What was he doing? He wasn't even feeding, just ripping and breaking bones. But they'd seen us. Both Jet and Culker could describe us right down to "any distinguishing features."

"You son of a bitch," I said in despair.

He turned his head toward me, laughing savagely. Jet bolted for the door. I caught her by whipping my left arm around her stomach and pulling her back into my chest. She was nearly a head taller than me. Her mouth formed a scream. Hating myself, hating Philip more, I grasped her entire chin with my right hand and jerked. Her body hit the floor before the scream ever escaped.

Culker began crying.

"Do it fast," I hissed to Philip.

It sounds cliché to compare Philip to an animal, but that's what he reminded me of. I mean it. He couldn't even talk. Culker seemed to know running was a waste of time and backed up against the wall.

Please don't let him start begging.

Philip was on him in a flash, tearing at his neck, but this time I heard sucking sounds. Often frightened by my own kind, sometimes confused, that was the first time I ever felt ashamed.

"We gotta go," I whispered. There was no way we could clean this mess up. Better just to leave it.

Philip dropped Culker's body and stared at me as if he didn't know who I was. His eyes made me step back.

"No," he said, finding his voice, red liquid dripping down onto his black shirt and vanishing against the darker color. "Not yet."

I'd thought the worst was over, but it wasn't. Putting his own wrist to his teeth, he tore it down to open veins and held it out. "Here, like with Edward."

For a minute I didn't get it. Then what he wanted came crashing down, followed by revulsion. "Stay away from me."

"Like Edward."

"Philip, don't."

Jet's dead body lay between me and the door. But in the time it took me to glance down at her, Philip had his hand around the back of my head, gripping my hair.

"You know nothing," he breathed in my ear. "You need me."

Survival instincts told me to do whatever he wanted and get away as soon as possible—please him and run.

But I didn't. Something snapped. Grabbing his shoulder for support, I rammed my knee into his stomach hard enough to make him spit out a mouthful of Culker's blood.

"I don't need your arm." My own voice sounded unfamiliar. "I don't want you touching me. You're sick. You weren't even hungry, were you?"

He gasped once, eyes glazing over. He didn't hit me. "But I thought . . ." He looked confused. "You hunt with me now, like with Maggie or Edward."

"This isn't how we hunted! Any of us. Maggie left bodies sometimes, but at least she made sure they were drifters or dealers. She always took their ID, and she never killed anybody for any reason but to drain life force. Is this what you do in France?"

"We do as we want," he whispered. "We are not sheep, Julian and I. And how many have you killed in just this past hundred years? How many?"

"I'm not like you."

"You are. This moral piety will not comfort the dead."

His words hurt and left me wanting cool air. I ran into the hall and down to the street, not caring who saw me. The dirt and garbage still sat in large, ugly piles. The baby upstairs still cried.

"I don't want to hurt you," Philip said into my ear. He must have followed me down, swift and quiet.

"What do you want?"

"For you to be happy, like with Maggie or Edward."

Was that really his game? He'd been taught by someone that we have to live out our existence alone. Now was he questioning that? He and Julian had once thought me insane or weak for living close to other members of our kind. Did Philip want an instant family? He knew nothing of humans, and even less of vampires.

"You can't have everything you want," I said.

"Yes, I can." He smiled and threw his arms in the air. "We live forever. This is our heaven."

Before I could respond, he glanced around and spotted an old Firebird among the Volkswagens. "This way."

Not wanting to follow him, I looked down at my watch. Four o'clock. We'd been inside that apartment for over two hours? Felt like minutes. "All right, but we need to find a hotel. It'll be dawn soon."

He didn't answer but scowled at finding the car locked. Using his right elbow, he smashed the driver's window and opened the door, then unlocked my side. "Get in."

"Promise to take me to a hotel?"

"Wherever you want."

While he worked on starting the engine, I climbed in and watched him. "Why do you always take old muscle cars?"

"These are fast, solid, and they almost never have alarms."

"I thought you didn't care about police or getting caught."

He flashed me a dirty look and whipped out onto the street. My manner with him in the past half hour had been leaning toward foolish. If I wanted any control at all, I'd need to turn the manipulation beacon back on. He just made my skin crawl.

I was normally asleep by five or so. My eyelids felt heavy. "Have you ever been inside Maggie's place?" I asked.

"No."

"It's wonderful. I wish we could go there."

The passing minutes didn't bother me too much. Philip was doing ninety by the time we hit northbound I-5. I was actually beginning to relax when the first siren roared from behind us.

"Jesus, Philip, don't pull over."

"I hadn't planned to."

"Can you outrun him?"

For an answer, he laughed out the shattered window. "Now we are having fun, no?"

"No."

This was all we needed. A cop chasing us down in a stolen car with Philip's wrist torn open and his shirt soaked in blood.

"You'd better lose him. He'll be calling for backup."

"Too many movies," Philip answered, and then he glanced over at me. "Put on your seat belt. I'm not used to passengers."

Obeying him instantly, wondering how he could talk and drive so fast at the same time, I looked back to see the police car falling behind. A second siren wailed from our left.

Philip might have gotten me into this, but somehow I believed he would get me out. He wasn't scared or worried or putting on some macho show for my benefit—as a mortal would. His expression was focused but calm, every fiber, every muscle and reflex moving in rapid sequence.

Whipping to the right with no warning, he threw me off balance, and I grabbed the dashboard.

"Hold on," he said.

We flew off I-5 onto the Bothell exit. Philip never took his eyes off the rearview mirror. Sirens still screamed, but no lights were visible. He turned behind the office building of an old wrecking yard and braked the Firebird so hard I jerked forward against my belt.

"Get out," he said, shoving his own door open.

We ran among rusty cars, trucks, motorcycles, and army jeeps as the sky slowly turned from black to dark gray. Our speed felt good, too quick for most mortals to keep up.

Philip slowed down next to an abandoned barn. The changing sky bothered him a lot more than the cops had. Me, too.

"We better get another car and find a hotel room," I said.

"There's no time."

Tearing the barn door open, he slipped inside. The building must once have been part of the wrecking yard. Hubcaps, blackened socket wrenches, and even an aged engine lay scattered in the grass. I followed Philip to find him on his knees, ripping up floorboards.

"What are you doing?"

He didn't answer, but my question had been pointless. I knew what he was doing—making a hole under the barn for us to sleep in.

"Here," he said, "get under here."

"We can't stay in this place. What if somebody comes? What if somebody finds us?"

"You would rather take chances outside? No one has been here in years. We'll be all right."

My eyelids felt even heavier than my arms, and what choice did I have? He was right. We had no chance outside. The sun would be up in a few moments. Walking over, I slid down into the crawl space between the ground and the barn floor. Philip's body dropped down next to mine. Lying on his back, he put all the boards back in place over us.

Part of me wanted to thank him, but if not for his reckless behavior, we wouldn't be here in the first place.

"Sleep now," he whispered. "We talk tonight."

"I've never slept on the ground before."

"Never?"

"No."

His next words were a jumble, and his hard body relaxed slightly in dormancy. I don't remember anything else.

chapter 20

Upon waking that night, three different lines of thought pushed to the front of my brain. The first was Jet—not only my regret over her unnecessary death, but the experience of reading her mind. How was it possible? Could she have been special like Wade? If so, why didn't she sense my intrusion?

The second thought, of course, was Wade himself. By now he figured I'd ditched him and run off to save myself. The hurt feelings of one mortal meant nothing—especially in trade for his life—but I wanted to talk to him, explain Philip's unannounced presence. Ridiculous really. And irrational. Wade's good health depended on my absence, not my words.

The third struggling thought was a memory from long ago of a dog named Thorne. One of Lord William's female wolfhounds disappeared during a hunt, and then turned up three weeks later, running with a wild mastiff. Months later, she gave birth to a single puppy. I must have been about ten when he was born. I can still see his broad, swaggering little chest and hear him growling at everything that moved. He grew up use-less for anything men consider important. Indepen-dent, vicious, refusing to be touched or petted, he received no one's favor but mine. I couldn't scratch be-hind his ears any more than William could, but that didn't matter. I saved him kitchen meat scraps and cheese and gravy that the cooks threw out. He eventu-ally stopped snarling at me and even met me by the back door in winters when live game grew scarce. I didn't love him but respected his independence.

Two days after my sixteenth birthday, he attacked a small boy—one of the groom's sons—and inflicted permanent scars. The boy admitted to having thrown a stick at the dog, but no one listened. The groom shot Thorne an hour later. I heard his gun from my room. It wasn't as though I'd lost a pet who was dear to me. He just somehow seemed more important than the boy. Why should anything so strong and fierce have to die like that? I'd put my cloak on, left William in Marion's care, found a shovel, and had Mr. Shevon-shire lift the dog's dead body into an old wooden cart for me. Pushing the cart into the woods, I buried Thorne by the pond so he could hear flocks of geese coming home in the spring. I shed tears for him. His loss affected me in a way I can't explain. He was not a loss to me personally, simply a needless loss. He'd been magnificent in life, more worthwhile than most people could claim to be.

And why would Thorne push to the front of my brain after so many years? Perhaps I was lying next to his kindred spirit. This Philip. This purist who saw no contrasting shades in the world.

He stirred beside me and pushed up at the boards. "Eleisha, are you awake?"

"Yes."

"Come."

After climbing back up into the barn, we walked outside, night air breezing across cool skin, making me feel alive. Half expecting Philip to start looking for a car, I was surprised when he sat down on the grass.

"Sit," he said. "Answer questions."

I stayed on my feet. "You need a new shirt."

"That doesn't matter. Tell me things."

"What things?"

"You were afraid of being caught by mortals last night, no? Not a game. Not your gift."

His face and hair glowed like a candle in the dark, emanating his gift, but I didn't care.

"Why did Maggie leave you?" I asked.

That caught him off guard, and he stood back up. "She . . . We were different before. I can't remember how, but we were different. She cried for lost walks through vineyards in the morning, the sun on my face at dusk, the warmth of our hands. None of that mattered to me. Useless, human trappings of a world long past. There is nothing but hunting."

"Did you miss her?"

His jaw twitched. "I thought she had gone to Wales at first, so I searched for Julian. But she wasn't with him. He said that my chasing after an undead whore was insane. He said I must have been mad for turning her in the first place."

"You had a better reason for making her than he had for making me."

Walking over, I stood beside him, my head barely reaching his chest. He gazed down at me uncertainly. "Your voice is soft tonight. You don't hate me anymore."

His amber eyes searched my face when I didn't answer.

"You spat angry words at me," he said. "You called me 'sick.'"

We all have hang-ups. Philip seemed overly concerned about what others thought of him. An unexpected weakness. But that could work to my advantage, give me a little control, keep him from killing unless we found safe conditions to hide bodies.

"You just surprised me," I said. "You're so careless."

"And you've been keeping William safe forever."

"Forever."

That may have been the heart of my fear, of my shock at Philip's inhumanity. The prospect of a future without William meant either death at the hands of Julian or existence in isolation. Which would be worse? Philip presented a third option. But did I want his company? Did the seeds of friendship—or more likely respect—keep me here, or merely reluctance to be alone?

"We could leave the country," I whispered. "Go to Sweden or maybe Finland."

My words struck a chord, and his eyes widened. "Would you do that? Leave with me?" Then he smiled. "Julian will think us insane."

"Probably. We could get on a plane tonight. Be far away before morning."

"Tonight?" He frowned. "No, tonight we go to Maggie's."

"Maggie's?" I stepped back. "We can't go there. Dominick's been watching the house, waiting for me."

"You should have killed him nights ago, ripped his throat and watched him bleed. Maggie cared for you, little coward."

William never spoke to me except in garbled sentences about chess games and rabbits. Philip's use of "coward" sliced like a thin blade. Thinking myself above it all, above him, above pain, the shame made me choke.

Only because he was right.

"He knows what we are," I said. "How to really end us, not like a peasant with stakes. He used a shovel to cut off William's head."

"You and Maggie shared a weakness, having grown too dependent on your gifts. Not lions anymore, but snakes, waiting only for the right time to strike. William was no challenge, old and weak. I am still a lion, and I am not weak."

His words weren't a hollow boast to impress me. Philip wielded the truth like a weapon. But he barely mentioned Maggie's name after leaving the hotel last night. I thought his mourning must either be internal or past. Now he wanted revenge. What good would it do? We couldn't get Maggie back.

"Can't we just go, Philip? Just run? There's nothing left here. Killing Dominick won't change anything."

"Are you coming, or do I go alone?"

The thought of staying here by myself, wondering,

waiting, frightened me more than Dominick did. "I'm coming. But promise you won't play with him. He's dangerous. Promise we'll just do it and go."

"Whatever you want." He seemed pleased, like a little boy with a new puppy. He glanced around the old junkyard. "These cars don't work. We have to find others."

"Couldn't we just call a cab?"

A little over an hour later, we pulled up to Maggie's in a '79 Chevy pickup with Styx's "Pieces of Eight" flooding from the speakers—Philip had actually wanted to put in Boston. I was going to have a serious talk with him about music when we had time.

"Didn't you ever watch MTV?"

"What's that?"

"Forget it."

Somebody else must be buying his clothes.

The house looked dark.

Stepping from the car, I cast around with my mind for Wade. He wasn't here. That would be just like him, though, to come back here instead of running for Portland.

Philip walked out the front gate and came back a moment later. "There's a dark-haired man two blocks down the street in a silver Mustang."

"That's him." Fear crawled up the back of my neck.

"Good, then he saw us drive up. Do you have a key?"

"A key?" I tried to smile, but my teeth kept clicking. "Mr. Break-and-Enter wants a key?"

"If I know Maggie, this place will be locked like a fortress."

"Dominick broke in the night he killed William."

"Then somebody got careless—left a window open maybe."

Did we? I didn't think so. But that would be too much to bear. Guilt from William's death weighed heavily enough.

I had a set of keys, but getting past the multiple locks on the front door still took a few minutes. Philip had been right about that. There was also a dead bolt that someone would normally have to slide back from the inside, but Wade and I left in a hurry the night before last, out the back.

"Okay, we're in," I said.

"Leave the door cracked. I want him to waltz right inside."

"He isn't that careless."

"We'll see."

"Do you want another shirt? That one's all stiff."

We went upstairs to Maggie's room. I took my coat off and laid it on the bed, but then I watched Philip's face as he walked in. He disappointed me a little. Instead of gasping in awe at her wondrous creation, he stepped to the window and lifted up yards of satin drapes to expose a blacked-out window laced with steel bars. He stomped his foot once against the floor.

"Good," he said. "Hardwood floors beneath the carpet, Sheetrock walls. We can sleep in here if we have to. What's the door reinforced with?"

I'd never even noticed the bars before. Philip must

have known Maggie far better than I had. This room made me happy because of its beauty. But we definitely weren't sleeping here—too high off the ground. So, instead of answering his question, I went to the walk-in closet and found an oversized plaid flannel shirt . . . maybe from Maggie's baseball player?

"Here, this will fit."

He wrinkled his nose. "I am not wearing that."

Was he serious?

"Philip, no one cares how you're dressed right now. This is soft, and it will fit loose if you don't tuck it in. You'll be able to move." How could anyone with his fashion sense listen to Boston?

With an annoyed look, he began unbuttoning the stiff fabric of his shirt. Curious, I stood watching him undress. I wasn't disappointed, only surprised. The proportions of his arms, chest, and flat stomach were perfect, like his face. However, four ugly burn marks stood out on his left shoulder, marring the image.

"What happened to you?"

"Eh?"

"Your shoulder."

"Oh, that. Old scars from when I lived as a mortal. Since we keep whatever form we were turned with, they didn't heal."

"You were burned? How?"

"My father, I think. With cigars. That is what Julian told me."

My stomach clenched. "Your father did that?"

"I think. Almost everything from before being turned is lost, hard to remember."

"Not for me."

He nodded. "Or for Julian. He remembers everything."

I looked at his burns. It was possible he'd blocked his past out if his father abused him. We all think we're so cool, so above it all. But Edward cashed his own ticket, and Philip existed in a state of self-induced memory loss.

Casting around for Wade again, almost sure he'd come back here, my knees buckled when overwhelming emotions of hate and triumph hit me.

Dominick.

"He's in the house."

Philip whirled without putting the flannel shirt on. "How do you know? I don't hear anything."

"He's here."

"Where?"

Trying to locate him, I met with a mental wall and remembered how completely he could block Wade. "I can't tell. Downstairs somewhere."

Philip's expression stopped me. His eyes were anxious, almost repulsed. "How do you know this?"

"He's psychic," I answered in half-truth. "His presence can be felt, like images when you're feeding."

"Telepathic?"

"Psychometric. I told you that last night."

Partial relief crossed his face. What was he afraid of? Before I could push the matter, he slipped out and called down the stairs.

"Dominick, I know you are there. Come and play with me."

His voice sounded eerie, almost musical. Murdering those teenagers last night had been his idea of a good time. He'd felt no malice, no sense of anger toward them. What would he do to someone he hated? I moved up behind him.

"Are you afraid?" he called. "Used to fighting little girls and old men. Come try your shovel on me."

No one answered.

Philip's strength and speed made him arrogant; at least I thought so. Dominick fought with more than guns and shovels. He knew about us. He had touched and absorbed all the antiques and personal possessions at Edward's, their secrets spilled on the floor like aged wine. What we feared. How we died. He knew these things.

"Philip, come away from the banister," I begged.

Before he could answer me, Dom's first shot rang out. Long and loud, like dynamite. The entire left side of Philip's throat exploded, spraying near-black blood across the hallway. The next shot sounded almost instantaneously. It missed.

"You like games?" a deep voice echoed up. "How was that?"

Philip collapsed on the carpet, awake but stunned, his perfect mouth twisting in surprise. Running footsteps pounded up the stairs. Dominick's shadow grew large on the wall.

I panicked.

More through instinct than intent, I tried pushing my thoughts inside his mind, and I emanated pictures of Culker's death, Maggie drinking from the drifter near Blue Jack's, the tattoo artist sinking into Union Bay. I tried to force every ugly, violent image I could summon straight into Dominick's head, past his wall, past his mental block, into his consciousness. And I got through.

He screamed.

I fired out with memories of ripped throats and dead bodies with staring eyes . . . and I could feel that my forced invasion hurt him. I tried to hurt him more.

I still couldn't see him, but listened to him scream while I imagined my fingernails clawing, scratching, tearing at his brain . . . all my attention focused on his sound until it softened to a whimper.

Then I let him go and came back to myself—but only because I was certain he was down, and because I had to help Philip.

Turning quickly, I stumbled at the sight of an empty carpet. Philip had disappeared.

"Philip?"

"Don't move."

Dominick's sweating, gasping form stood at the top of the stairs. I was stunned to see him on his feet after what I'd just done to him. He looked dirty and smelled of stale perspiration. Greasy, outgrown black hair hung around his glazed eyes. He pointed a .357 revolver at me. Without waiting for him to fire, I bolted for the bedroom and paused just inside. He blurred across the threshold, his arm stick-straight, pointing the gun rapidly to the right, then the left. I slammed the door behind us and bolted it.

Focusing hard, I sent my impressions of this room— all the treasures in this small piece of the world— flooding into him. These mental attacks were exhausting me, but this was all I had. Images of lace fans, silver combs, perfume bottles, and cream satin soaked into his brain like water through sand. I was hoping to lose him in the images of Maggie's soft possessions, blinding him to everything else, so even if he gained coherence he might not know what was true or created.

He only had four bullets left in the gun.

"Aren't you tired?" I whispered. "Why don't you sleep?"

He fired twice more, the gun wavering in his hands. Maybe I could overwhelm him enough to make him drop it. His legs trembled.

"Close your eyes, Dom. Look at yourself in the darkness. You're alone. You have no one, not even Wade anymore." I dropped my voice even lower and whispered, "And you're so tired. Just close your eyes."

It was difficult to invade his mind, speak to him, and try to gauge the distance between us at the same time.

With a strength of will greater than my own, he gathered his thoughts and tried to force me out. Rage replaced his confusion, and he pointed the gun right at me. I saw my shoulder explode before hearing the shot or even realizing what had happened. It didn't hurt much, not like real pain, but the floor rushed up anyway.

His hand buried itself in the back of my hair, lifting me. Through the haze I tried to focus psychically again, but he smashed the gun handle into my jaw.

"You do that again and I'll end this right here," he whispered.

Rancid breath drifted into my nostrils. Why didn't he, then? Holding me by the neck with one hand, he opened the door and dragged me back into the hallway, to the banister.

"Call out to your friend," he said.

"No."

"Do it now!"

"I don't care what you do."

Jerking me back, he shoved the gun in his jeans and pulled a machete from a sheath under his jacket.

"Get out here now," he yelled to Philip. "Or her head flies down the stairs by itself."

My gift was useless, as Maggie's had been. Dominick's vision of reality had shifted so far from sanity that he viewed us as all the world's evil. If he could just erase us, everything else would fall neatly into place. Poor thing.

Looking up at his unshaven face, I said, "No matter what you do to me, he's never going to let you out of here."

"Shut up. You're the center of all this."

"I'm nothing."

"That's bullshit. Who's the guy with you?"

"His shirt's lying on Maggie's bed. Why don't you go in and touch it?"

That twisted his mouth into anger, and he let go of my hair long enough to slap me. Fool. I hit the floor, and my foot shot out to crack his kneecap. The pop reminded me of the sound from an overshaken champagne bottle.

He grunted and buckled. My left shoulder didn't work at all, but I kicked out again at his cheekbone and then tried to scramble away.

An iron grip clasped my ankle, and then somehow he was up over the top of me, snarling and using his weight. Steel glinted off ceiling lights. The blade was coming down.

Just like Maggie.

But it never connected. As though he could fly, his body floated upward. For a moment I thought I was already dead or hallucinating. Then Philip's bare arms shifted into view as he finished raising Dominick and threw him against the hallway wall.

Relief flooded my brain until I got a good look at Philip. The recently opened veins of his throat had closed off, but his chest and shoulders were covered in blood. Our regenerative powers work quickly, but how much life force had he lost first?

Dominick bounced off the wall and landed with a gasp. Dropping the machete, he grabbed the gun again.

"Shoot me," Philip hissed.

The dark ex-cop aimed for his neck and fired again, but Philip jumped up to catch the bullet square in the chest. "You're empty. I've been counting."

Anybody—anybody but Dom—would have slobbered and groveled and begged. Maybe he knew we possessed no mercy. Maybe he was just more like us than I cared to admit. But he grasped the machete again and said, "Then come and get me."

His right leg wouldn't hold him. I must have shattered his kneecap. The whole scene reminded me of this T-shirt Edward once gave me, depicting a hawk swooping down on a cartoon mouse with its tiny middle finger up. The caption read, "Last Great Act of Defiance."

Dominick wasn't a mouse—far from it. But he was already dead, and I'm sure he knew it.

Philip moved so fast nobody even got cut. He slapped

the machete out of Dominick's hand and then grabbed him, lifting him into the air. Stepping forward, Philip threw his heavy burden over the banister.

"Just kill him," I whispered. "You promised you wouldn't do this."

A dull thud sounded from below as Dominick hit the floor. Philip hopped over the banister himself, and I moved up to see him land in a comfortable crouch. Dominick tried crawling on one elbow toward the front door.

Something in my voice must have gotten through to Philip. He could have kept this horror show going another hour, but he didn't. After breaking a leg off one of the living room chairs, he walked over and rammed it through Dominick's broad back, into his heart, as a peasant would stake a wounded vampire. The broken, crawling form on the floor didn't even cry out. It just stopped moving.

I turned away from the railing and went downstairs, feeling no relief now, no sense of triumph, only a dim ache that hadn't quite registered yet. My handsome, blood-covered friend stumbled about the room, staring at his mangled victim. Maybe no mortal had ever fought back like that before.

"I did try to warn you, Philip, to tell you."

He looked up at me with liquid eyes—no pleasure, no triumph either. For some reason that pleased me. Perhaps Philip might have wept over Thorne's grave, too. Perhaps he was beginning to understand the sorrow of needless waste.

Instead of answering me, he just kept weaving back and forth like a jack-in-the-box.

"What's wrong?"

Then I noticed patches of flesh peeking through the blood on his chest. It wasn't just pale anymore, but nearly white. Reaching out, I caught him before he fell.

"Try to get your arm around my neck," I said.

The basement bedroom wasn't far, but I couldn't carry him. He shouldn't have jumped off the banister. It was a waste of energy. It seemed to take hours to drag him downstairs through the cellar, his head bobbing up and down with weakness. Would this ever be over? Would we ever get on a plane and just leave this nightmare behind? Was he dying?

No, I pushed that thought away while finally laying him on the mattress in Maggie's basement. He couldn't die. We weren't destroyed by mere wounds.

"Can you talk? Tell me what to do?"

"Blood," he mumbled.

Long ago Edward told me that vampires who refused or were unable to hunt fell into agonized paralysis, forever immortal, forever starving. Half of Philip's throat had been blown away. That he could speak at all amazed me. Maybe he'd simply lost too much life force.

"What do I do?"

"Like Edward."

My own shoulder wound had sealed itself and was regenerating slowly. But I'd been bleeding, too. "Don't go to sleep. Keep your eyes open."

I ran up the stairs and down the hall. Dominick's body was in the same broken position as before—like a filthy G.I. Joe. After pulling the stake from his back, I turned him over. Dead eyes stared up into nothing.

Would this even work? I'd never fed on a corpse, but he'd only been dead a few moments. Maybe I could still draw residual life force.

I drove my teeth into his neck. No pictures or visions or scenes from his life touched me. Nothing. But I felt something, some strength flowing from his blood . . . though it was fading fast.

After a few minutes I couldn't take any more and left him lying there.

His empty gun was still upstairs, and his ID was in his pocket. I didn't bother taking either one. Maggie was missing, and he'd recently gone rogue. It could be a while before anyone even found him, and then the police would be lost attempting to unravel what happened. Philip and I would be long gone by then.

Even in death, Dominick had lost. And who would mourn him? Would Wade?

Hurrying back to the cellar took only seconds this time. Philip's eyelids fluttered. He looked so pale lying there. I moved to the mattress and crawled over beside him. Opening my wrist savagely, I put it in his mouth.

"Bite down."

Having long since put aside the feeling of Julian's lips burning and crisping my neck, pain stunned me blind when Philip drew down. It hurt far worse than being shot. After about thirty seconds, he suddenly lashed out with his right hand and grabbed the back of my head, pulling me down beside him, still sucking hard on my wrist. His amber eyes were wide . . . wild.

I didn't struggle. I knew he was just hungry and desperate. Then slowly, the fire evened out and grew bearable. Had my body still been human, I might have stroked his cheek and comforted him. Those memories lingered, but not the ability to enact them.

Instead, I whispered in his ear, "Like Edward."

chapter 21

The next night, my eyes opened to the sight of Philip's red-flaked chest. Where were we? Peeling my hair off his body, I felt brittle and light, like Chinese paper. Maggie's cellar surrounded us.

I must have passed out on Philip's shoulder. He was a mess.

Dominick lay dead upstairs.

"Philip?"

Amber eyes flickered faintly. "Where . . . ?"

"The basement. Your throat looks better." I smiled weakly. "It's really over."

He pushed himself up off the mattress, lost and disoriented. "Are you hurt? Your skin is too white."

"No, I'm okay. The bullet went through my shoulder. I just couldn't get you to stop feeding once you'd started."

"Once I . . . ?"

Recent events must have flooded back because he suddenly grew embarrassed and turned away. "We should get cleaned up."

Nodding, I tried to follow. My bones made hollow cracking sounds.

"I'm going to need to hunt pretty soon," I said.

"Can you walk?" he asked, turning back.

"Maybe. Give me a sec."

Struggling up, I limped after him for the stairs. We both ignored Dominick's cold body and headed for the nearest bathroom.

"We don't have to look perfect," Philip said. "Just good enough to get around in public."

"You're the vain one, baby, not me."

"Get in the shower."

Pulling my shirt over my head seemed an effort. "Could you go to Maggie's room and find me something to wear? I'm not up to climbing more stairs."

"Yeah, be right back."

I finished undressing and stood beneath a steaming spray of water. Once all the dried blood had been washed away, my shoulder sported only an inch-wide hole. Our bodies hold together well. A bullet from a .357 Magnum should have taken my shoulder off. The wound had been much larger last night, though. I was regenerating quickly, my undead condition striving to resume the form it had been turned in—a blessing and a curse. We never change.

Philip came back in and started messing around with Maggie's bottles and hand mirrors. I could hear him outside the shower curtain. Maybe he was making a place to lay my clothes, but he was still being far less talkative than usual. He'd never been shot before—that was pretty clear—never seriously injured by a mortal. He thought himself a lion, indestructible, and I had fed him from my wrist. Not that it really mattered any-more. We were free from Dominick. Perhaps Philip would listen to me a little better in the future. I stepped out of the shower.

"Your turn."

He handed me a towel. "I brought you a dress. Will that do?"

I would have preferred a clean pair of jeans, but the dress was simple enough, black and sleeveless.

"Designer?" I joked.

"Yves Saint Laurent."

"You're serious? You actually looked at the label?"

"Don't you?"

Teasing him made the soreness in my arms less no-ticeable. I hadn't felt this weak since getting off that ship at Southampton. Philip stepped past me into the shower, his expression troubled.

"Eleisha?"

"Mmmmm?"

I got dressed, noticing he'd laid out his own pants and the flannel shirt I'd given him the night before. Maybe he couldn't find anything else that fit.

Behind the curtain, he stayed silent, not finishing his question, probably searching for words long forgotten.

"It's all right," I said. "You don't have to say any-thing. Let's just finish up and book a flight."

"Not yet. Not tonight."

I went cold. "What?"

"Julian's in the country by now, probably in this city. We can't leave, or he'll think we're running."

"We are running! Is that a news flash to you? No way.

There's no way I'm facing down Julian. And look at you. You couldn't take out a cat like that."

"There won't be a fight if we face him. We don't have to go anywhere, except maybe find a hotel room. I know his cell phone number. He'll come to us. Honor demands he look into this. But if not for Katherine, William would have died years ago. Julian may be pleased his abomination is gone."

"William wasn't an abomination."

"We just tell Julian I need to help you for a while," Philip said. "He'll believe that. He already thinks of you as crippled, that you can't function alone. But he sees you as no threat."

Could it be that simple? Could Philip convince Julian to leave me in peace?

"What if he wants me dead anyway?"

Sensing victory, Philip smiled slightly and shrugged. "I don't know. We could use Dominick's big gun. Another inch to the right, and I might have flown off to hell."

"That isn't funny."

Two hours later, we checked into the Bellevue Red Lion and settled into an attractive suite of soft tans and yellows—but too many windows with thin drapes. I ordered extra blankets and hung them carefully over the curtain rods.

Philip might have been shaken by his near-death experience, but he considered the event a fluke. I had been hoping he'd let me rent a car and drive fifty-five to the hotel. No dice. He ripped off an old Charger right in front of Maggie's house and ran two stop signs in the first mile. When a policeman flashed his siren, Philip stopped, knocked the officer unconscious, pulled his body inside the car, and told me to feed as if we were at a McDonald's drive-through window. This all took place on a busy downtown street. The really weird part was that nobody else stopped or even noticed.

My companion's disturbing nature seemed a small thing tonight, though.

Now that we'd checked into the hotel, there was only one thing left to do.

Philip made a quiet—very short—phone call to Julian. He spoke in French, but I picked up a few words . . . like the name of our hotel.

Torn between true freedom and fear of how it might be achieved, I tried not to listen while I paced about the hotel suite, fussing over the drapes.

"Is he coming?" I asked once Philip hung up.

"Soon."

I glanced away, not sure whether to be frightened or relieved.

"You know," Philip said suddenly, "once we settle this matter with Julian, we don't have to go up north. We could go to France."

"Even Paris?"

"Anywhere."

I'd never been to Paris. The thought calmed me, made me smile. "What's it like?"

"Good hunting. Few rules." He seemed about to go on when something unreadable shifted his expression.

"What's wrong?"

He turned pale, his features twisted, and he stumbled on an ottoman. Before I could move to help, Wade pushed inside my head.

Where are you, Leisha?

Stay away! I'm not alone.

Philip regained composure and snarled, then bolted for the door. I darted in front of it, blocking his exit. "Wait. Just listen to me."

"That's your little pet, isn't it? You've been lying! He's completely psychic, isn't he?"

"Not like it seems."

"That black-haired cop was psychometric, eh? And I believed you. You've been telling this little friend of yours all about us, haven't you?"

"No, and I didn't lie. But if you had known Wade could read minds, you would have killed him that first night."

"Of course! As you should have!"

"He helped me. Just meet him. Just talk to him."

"You aren't serious."

"Please don't hurt him. He aimed a gun at his partner for me."

"Well, isn't that what you do? Get weak-minded men to slay dragons for you?"

Cold, cruel, and inhuman, Philip's eyes flashed rage at me. He possessed so many different sides. Could I ever keep up? This was a worst-case scenario, defending one person who mattered from another person who mattered.

Someone knocked.

My legs froze. "Wade, is that you?"

"Open the door."

Philip brushed past me, jerked the door open, and grasped Wade's throat. This was too much.

"Philip, I fed you last night!"

He stopped, hand now up in Wade's white-blond hair.

"Don't do it," I said. "Just let him in. For me."

He stepped back slowly, as though with great effort. I knew the only thing holding him back was his strange desire that I remain in his company. The room felt small with all three of us standing in it.

A wave of anger swept through me. What did Wade think he was doing?

"You ditched me without a word," he spat.

Incredible. With a blood-crazed six-foot vampire standing right next to him, he wanted to argue about forgotten good-byes?

"Is that what you're here for?" I asked. "An explanation?"

"To start, yes."

"After everything I've done to try and save you? Who was stupid enough to give you a PhD?"

Our familiarity disconcerted Philip. Unlike Maggie, he'd probably never spent more than a few hours with any one mortal. "Your partner's dead," he snapped. "Staked through the heart. Quite poetic."

Wade didn't even flinch. "I know. I just buried him."

"Where?" Philip asked.

"In Maggie's backyard, behind the trees. I buried his gun, too, and I washed the living room floor. Then I moved his car four miles away."

"What possible reason could you have?"

"Eleisha."

I flinched. I had no response to Wade's actions. My instinct had been to leave the body on Maggie's floor and let the police try to figure out what happened after we left the country. Maybe Wade was right to bury the evidence? It also occurred to me that Wade himself would certainly be picked up for questioning . . . and I had not thought of that before. So was he working to save himself or me?

Looking up at his face . . . I believed he was protecting me.

But no one asked for his help. No one asked him to hang around and clean up my mess. And it must have hurt to see Dominick like that. Nevertheless, he'd done it, and now he was standing up to Philip—not an easy feat.

"If you've been at the house burying Dominick all this time," I asked, "how did you find us just now?"

He hesitated. "How much does golden boy know?"

That struck me as half humorous, half dangerous. "His name is Philip, and I wish he knew you a lot better than he does."

Philip's eyes softened, some of the cruelty fading. "This won't work, little one. He has to die. You know that."

"No, he doesn't. Just sit down on the couch, both of you." I was desperate. "Wade, let him read your past, what Dom used to be like. Show him how, like you showed me."

Both of them jumped slightly, stunned speechless. I looked to Wade. "Burying Dominick means nothing.

No one asked you to do that. But do this for me. Please, do this thing for me."

Without a word, he walked to the couch. I almost sagged in relief.

But instead, I whirled back around. "Philip, it's easy. You don't have to touch him. Just sit down and look inside his head."

"No," he said harshly. "You kill him, or I will."

"Just look at his thoughts!"

"Why?"

"Because if you do, I won't care what happens next. If you do this for me, I'll let you tear his throat out and not blame or hate you."

He tensed, staring down at me uncertainly. I'd just offered him the one thing he wanted.

This was a bet, a gambit on my part. If some higher power had let me choose any two companions in the world, I must admit my choices would have been Edward and Maggie. But they were gone. Mourning or missing them didn't help. Somehow I thought if Philip became psychically involved with Wade—and vice versa—the two of them might be okay together, not friends exactly, but not enemies.

Besides, Philip needed a glimpse of humanity. He had long since stopped thinking of mortals as sentient beings, viewing them as little more than toys in his personal playground.

"You ask too much," he said quietly, "more than you know."

"I won't enter your thoughts," Wade said. "And if your ability works like Eleisha's, you'll be able to block me after the first second or two anyway."

"Don't speak to me until asked." Philip wouldn't even look at him. "You should have been dead five minutes ago."

This was getting us nowhere. What was Philip so afraid of? I'd known him only three days—an intense three days. He didn't strike me as the type to back away from something new. Last night I'd actually used my psychic ability as a weapon against Dominick. Until experimenting with Wade, a mental attack would never have occurred to me. This new gift could be useful. But for some reason, instinctive perhaps, I hadn't told Philip the extent of my growing telepathy, or even mentioned it to him. Why?

"Do this one thing for me," I repeated. "Please."

"Afterward, when I kill him, you won't hate me? Once we see Julian, you'll forget all this and come to France?"

"Yes."

How did Wade feel, hearing his life discussed as a bargaining chip? His face was unreadable.

Philip walked slowly to the couch and sat down, looking disgusted and uncomfortable. "What do I do?"

"Look at me," Wade answered. "Imagine your eyes are fingers pushing inside my head, searching for pictures."

They stopped speaking. With rapt interest, I watched Philip's face. Could he do it?

Expecting both their expressions to go blank, I was stunned when Wade began crying. Philip, of course, had no tear ducts, but a sobbing choke escaped his mouth. Is this what Wade and I had done while lost down histories past? Did we feel each experience in our forgotten bodies?

Their faces both shifted into faint smiles. What were they seeing now? Perhaps I was wrong to observe this private exchange. Wade had unselfishly given up the core of his most hidden self simply because I asked him to.

Telling myself every few moments to get up and leave them alone, I stood there for over an hour, gauging every flicker, every twitch, wondering what memory had passed by.

A Japanese vase overflowing with freshly cut red and yellow flowers sat on the table behind them. Wade's near-white hair contrasted sharply against the bright tones, and Philip's blended perfectly. Bizarre pair, these two men. One ruled by unrealistic concepts of right and wrong, the other by incomprehensible physical drives. Maggie would have laughed at them.

Without warning, Wade grabbed Philip's wrist and looked away.

"No more. It hurts."

Instead of jerking his hand back, Philip sat with chattering teeth. I went over and crouched by his leg. "Do you see now? You won't hurt him?"

"Such an existence," he whispered. "Spending every day in the same building. Typing on computers . . . walking in the sunlight. I'd forgotten what the sun looks like."

"That felt different than melding with Eleisha," Wade said, still trying to get his breath. "I kept showing you darker emotions, uglier scenes."

Philip carefully drew his wrist away. "A sad life. Alone, like us." He gazed down at me. "But we have to run now. No more truce with Julian."

I blinked, confused. "You said he'd let me go."

"Not now," Philip answered. "If he finds us now, we are all lost . . . and your pet."

Too much. Too fast. I thought to solve Philip's fear, his hatred. How could things be worse? "What are you saying?"

"A nightmare from the past, something long over. When I sought you out, wondered about the company of my own kind again, I had doubts. Would my gift affect you? Would you even want me? Could I hunt with someone else? But not this, never this."

"Never what?"

He looked so sad, defeated. I hated it. Philip feared no one, not even Dominick. Why was he doing this?

"Can you see inside of me?" he said. "Read my thoughts?"

"I don't know. Can't you just tell me what's wrong?"

He turned to Wade, almost politely. "I have to show Eleisha something private. Will you go into the bedroom for a while?"

Wade opened his mouth as if to argue and then closed it. Keeping secrets from him seemed pointless. He knew so much already. But his manner with Philip had changed drastically since an hour ago. Finally, he nodded. "Call out when you're finished."

"Yes."

I remember noticing that Wade was wearing a thick canvas jacket—probably something he'd bought on his shopping excursion—and he hadn't taken it off. Since the room was warm, I thought this odd, but events were moving so quickly, I never bothered asking about it.

The bedroom door clicked shut behind him.

Philip pulled me up to the couch, and I turned all my attention to him. Not waiting for words, I slipped inside his eyes, finding access almost too easy.

chapter 22

Philip

"I can't! Why can't I do it?"

Julian's anguished voice echoed off cold library walls. The winter of 1825 proved harsh, although Philip seldom worried about things like weather. He didn't need fire or warmth, only blood. At first the idea of spending December in Harfleur with his master, Angelo, and his undead brothers pleased Philip. But Julian's growing discontent dampened this visit, making him wish he'd remained in Gascony with Maggie.

"Why do you bother?" he asked, growing bored. "It's only a candlestick."

Julian often sat for hours at a time at their aged oak table, trying to move various items with his mind. "Because John developed his psychic powers within months of being turned," he answered, "by receiving thoughts from Master Angelo. That is how our mental powers develop, through contact with our makers and with other vampires . . . but I have nothing. Angelo has tried with me, but even after all this time, I have no power."

"Ridiculous," Philip answered, shaking his head. "Your gift is strong."

"Against mortals, not against other vampires."

This made no sense to Philip. Why would any of them need a defense against each other? Julian's gift for inducing fear was overwhelming. Philip thought it much more useful than telepathy.

"I never developed psychic powers either," he said.

"You're different. You cannot even remember your mortal life."

"I don't care."

"You don't care, Philip? Not a bit of psychic power in you, and you truly don't care?"

"Why should I? I'm pleased with my gift."

"Only because you're vain, shallow, and conceited. Get out and leave me alone."

Philip knew they all thought him simple because he was the youngest and had no passion for their histories or studies or dusty old books. Blood mattered. And Julian entertained the greatest gift of them all. Why should he pine so pitifully over this psychic ability of John's? Fear was a better weapon than telepathy or telekinesis—at least for hunting.

Master Angelo had chosen the three of them because they were so different from each other. "My sons," he called them. "Feed and explore and live forever."

Wasn't that enough? Shouldn't that be enough for anyone?

This library was on the main floor of Angelo's stone fortress. An empty hearth stood in the back wall, but shelves of faded, leather- or clothbound books lined the other three. A large oak table stood near the hearth, surrounded by four chairs. Philip never sat in his chair, as he'd never liked this room and he hated sitting for more than a few moments.

Julian focused his brooding gaze on the candle again, so Philip turned and walked away.

He moved up the corridor, slipped through a narrow doorway, and went downstairs to find John reading a book in the wine cellar. Three fat candles illuminated the casks and bottles stretching back into darkness beyond their light's reach.

"Isn't anyone going hunting tonight?" Philip said. "It's snowing. We should be outside chasing carolers."

John looked up through a lock of uncombed, sandy-blond hair. He was a large man with dark blue eyes and ever-present stubble on his strong jaw. "Why don't you take Julian? He's not been out for a week."

"He's still staring at that candlestick. Can't you talk to him?"

"Master Angelo tried last night. Don't worry. It's just a phase. If you had half a brain in that pretty head, you'd want more power, too."

"Well, thank God I don't," Philip said. "Tell me what I'm thinking right now."

John concentrated briefly and then threw the book at him. "You're thinking I'm a stuffy old porcupine for sitting in this chair reading when I should be outside running in the snow with you."

"Too right."

Since he had no memories of mortal life, Philip didn't understand concepts like social tension between the

French, Welsh, and Scottish. John McCrugger had simply always been there, a permanent fixture, good-natured, oversized, and unwashed.

"You're so simple, Philip," he said. "Such a purist. No wonder Angelo loves you."

"Love is for mortals and sheep, not Angelo. Get off that chair and come outside."

Philip tried to duck right, but John caught the back of his neck and shoved his body against the ground, pushing his face into the cold, crisp snow. Philip was faster on his feet, but once John got a grip, the game was over.

"Give up. You're done for," the Scotsman said, laughing. "Or I'll grind that pretty face blue."

Philip arched his back and tried unsuccessfully to break away. "All right, I give."

"You won't kick me?"

"No."

After one last shove, John took his hand away. Philip, of course, twisted around instantly and kicked up hard enough to snap his companion's jaw. "Can't you tell when I'm lying?"

John roared and lunged for him again, but he was off and running for the nearest tree. These were good times. It seemed strange that both his brothers and his master tended to change once they were alone with him, dropping all that intellectual nonsense and living like real hunters, wild and strong. John most of all . . . Julian least of all.

"Climb up and get me!" Philip called from a low branch, knowing John was no climber.

"You can't stay up there forever. Might as well come down now and let me break that foot."

"I think not." Philip's mind switched focus so quickly he often frustrated people. "Let's go into town. I'm hungry."

"How could you possibly be hungry? You fed last night."

Philip dropped to the ground. "I'll race you."

"No, if you really want to go that far, we should saddle the horses."

"All right, but my horse is faster than yours."

Wrestling match forgotten, they were soon flying through the icy air down the road toward Harfleur proper. Angelo's winter home stood four miles away from the city, giving him easy access without being too close. The muscles of Philip's horse felt solid yet fluid beneath his knees. He liked his bay mare, Kayli. The trip from Gascony would have been lonely without her. He didn't function well without company.

"Slow down," John called.

Reining Kayli down to a walk, Philip swiveled his head back. "What's wrong?"

"Nothing, it's still early and a crisp night. I thought we might talk awhile."

"Talk?"

Their horses fell into step along the snow-packed road. "I was just watching you ride," John said. "Strange how you remember things like riding and where to grow the best grapes, how to speak both French and English, yet you don't recall anything of your mortal life."

Philip shifted in his saddle, bored already. "That's old hat."

"You couldn't even speak at first, not at all. Frightened Angelo pale. You were like a newborn babe. Did you know I met you once, before he turned you?"

"You did?" Philip was suddenly interested. "What was I like?"

"Different than you are now. Almost timid. The idea of filling your father's shoes as marquis seemed a death sentence. When Angelo offered you a way out, you jumped on it."

"Angelo asked me?"

"Of course he did. It was Julian's idea. Angelo wanted three sons, you know."

Philip did know. In fact, he knew more than his brothers suspected. Not that they would have minded; they simply viewed him as mentally deficient. John had been turned in 1801, Julian in 1818, both emerging into the undead world exactly as Angelo wanted them.

But Philip woke up in darkness, unable to communicate, yet terrified to be alone for fear that without someone else in the room to prove his existence, he might disappear. Then Angelo showed him how to hunt, and he found purpose. Language came back to him slowly, and the memory of a face, ivory with brown eyes and chocolate hair.

"Why did you turn Edward?" Philip asked suddenly.

"To see if I could," John answered. "And because he's the right type."

"Did Angelo mind?"

"No."

"Then why was he so angry when I turned Maggie?"

"Because you were too young and incapable of teaching her. And you might have damaged yourself. You aren't like the rest of us, you know." John's broad face clouded slightly. "Promise not to laugh if I tell you something?"

"I'd never laugh, just kick you in the face."

"No . . . listen. I've been having dreams lately."

"Dreams? Have you told Angelo?"

"No, but they might not be dreams, more like premonitions. Something dark hides on the edge of my vision. I can almost see it, but not quite."

The switch in topics disturbed Philip. John shouldn't be discussing this with him. He knew nothing of dreams or visions. And anyway, this psychic nonsense bored him beyond words. They ought to race again.

"Something is coming," John said with his eyes fixed on empty space. "I don't know what, and I can't stop it. But it is coming."

Too much. Philip kneed Kayli into motion. She leapt forward, kicking up small clods of loose snow. A second later, he heard John coming up behind, and he smiled into the wind.

At the Wayside Inn, Philip reveled in the scent of pipe smoke along with the pleasant aroma of warmth and life. A human smorgasbord to choose from. After they had stabled their horses, John's dark mood passed away, leaving his usual good-natured self in its wake.

Indoor hunting was best for winter nights. Inns

like the Wayside teemed with customers who sought
out company, wine, and hot food. Round barmaids
with reddened cheeks maneuvered trays of cups and
tin plates among sweat-scented bodies and laughing
faces.

"This is a fine tavern," John commented. "See the
woodwork on that door?" He leaned back in content-
ment. "I like the scents and the wine and the way everyone tolerates each other because there's nowhere else to
go in this weather."

Philip nodded. "Good hunting."

"Oh, will you look around?" John said. "Listen with
your mind. Most of these people haven't two francs to
their name, and everyone's still excited about
Christmas."

"What is that?"

"You don't remember?"

"No."

"It's a celebration, a religious holiday. Perhaps your
family didn't practice such things. I wouldn't be surprised. Your father is the coldest man I've ever met."

"My father?"

"He's a bastard. I saw your shoulder once. Those
burns. You panicked a few nights after being turned. I
tried to hold you down and your shirt ripped. Angelo
thinks you're such a mystery, but I told him to use his
mind. You don't remember anything because it's too
black."

"Do you think I care? None of that matters. Let us
hunt now. We have forever to talk."

"Can you feel anything? Anything at all?"

The din around them grew louder. Philip leaned forward. "I feel like hunting."

A bit of light left John's eyes. He nodded with a sad smile. "Of course. Who have you picked out this time?"

"Those two whores by the bar. See them? I want the one in the green dress. She's been staring at me."

"How strange," John whispered in a cynical tone, "that she should be staring at you. I've often wondered how someone with your face can think only of blood."

"What would you do if you had my face?"

"Do you really want to know?"

"Yes."

"Well, for one, I wouldn't have joined with Angelo. I'd have lived on as a mortal searching the world for that one perfect love, who adored me for myself, yet thought herself lucky that my soul and mind were housed in such a form."

"Sickening. You would not."

"Oh, yes, I would."

"I'm sorry I asked you."

Philip used his beauty at every opportunity, and then despised those who succumbed to it. Fools. If women were taken in by long, red-brown hair, a tall form, and ivory skin, that was their weakness—part of the game.

"Here they come," he said.

The woman in green looked about twenty-four, with dull brown hair and too much rouge. Her companion was a dark blonde in cheap blue velvet. Philip knew a lot about prostitutes. Many of them were alcoholics. Most of them had several children they couldn't afford to feed, and nearly all of them hated men no matter how much they smiled. He liked them because they were easy to draw off alone.

"Buy us a drink?" the blonde asked.

"Depends," John answered. "How much will it cost me?"

"No need to worry about that yet." She flashed him an almost genuine smile and sat down. John wasn't handsome, but Philip always marveled at the number of women who fell into comfortable conversation with the oversized Scotsman. This was John's gift. In his presence, all worries faded and vanished. He put everyone's mind at ease.

Philip, on the other hand, was no master with words, and used his foot to push a chair out for the woman in green.

"You asking me to sit down?" she said.

"If you like."

She had eyes like glass and a false laugh, but not many wrinkles from wear and no visible scars. "What's a fine gentleman like you doing here?"

"Getting out of the cold. Our horses were tired, so we decided to stop."

"Travelers?"

"Yes, on our way to Nantes."

"Staying the night?"

"Looks like we'll have to."

This was an old game, one she'd played a thousand times. "I have a warm place where you can sleep. Won't cost you much."

"Will you wait outside for a moment?" He pushed a small pouch into her hand. "I need to speak with my friend."

Surprised at her own good fortune, landing a generous young man so easily, she nodded and stepped out the door. Philip waited a bit, then went out after her. Being seen leaving with her might cause him problems later. Her companion wasn't a concern since she'd be dead within the hour as well. He had been ordered to play by Angelo's rules when it came to hunting.

"My name is Camille," the woman said when he came out.

"Where do you live?"

She led him down ice-covered streets, past dingy buildings to the oldest part of Harfleur. "I have only one room," she said. "But there's a stove and coal."

Her home was small, on the ground floor, but Philip cared nothing for aesthetics. She lit a candle and the dark room came alive with flickering shadows across dirty walls. "Do you want a drink, sir?"

"No."

"What's in Nantes?"

"Business."

He didn't want to talk. Words were pointless. She took off her cloak and dropped it on a chair. Walking past the candle, he grasped her neck with one hand and jerked open the front of her dress with the other.

"Careful," she whispered, not startled by his actions. "Don't rip it."

Her mouth moved up to his, and he kissed her. Although never admitting the fact to John or Julian, he liked affection from some of his victims. It felt good to put his lips against warm flesh and let the hunger build, feel the blood with his tongue just below their skin's surface, knowing he had only to take it.

Her hands pulled off his cloak and tugged at his clothes, while she made small, gasping sounds. Candlelight danced across his cheek. He stopped long enough to take his shirt off and pin her down onto the bed, pushing the dress below her shoulders to expose large, white breasts that tasted good in his mouth.

Sometimes he took them quickly, killing swiftly before they even knew death had arrived. Sometimes he took longer, letting them flail and beg in a useless attempt to invoke his pity. How they died changed the pictures that flowed into him along with their blood. It all depended on his mood.

Events from tonight had driven his mind into forced motion. Julian's growing dissatisfaction and John's visions filled his thoughts with unease. He wanted to forget.

Camille writhed beneath him, trying to raise her heavy skirts. He moved up, crushing her breasts with his chest, to kiss her mouth again. Slowly, inch by inch, his lips brushed down her cheek with feather breaths to her jawline, to her throat. He bit down gently on the top layers, not puncturing deeply, just enough to taste. She stiffened slightly.

"Sir, don't do that. I know you paid me well, but—"

He struck hard, like lightning, not for the jugular, but slashing a wound big enough to drink through. She screamed, pushing at his chest. Oblivious, he ignored her voice. Women screamed in the night all the time. Nobody cared.

Images of lying beneath many men entered his head.

"Don't." She was sobbing now. "Please."

He felt nothing beyond the need to forget, and so he bit deep enough to absorb her life force completely. Pictures of inns and wine and flushed faces passed by him. A kind man named Pierre who was already married. A pale girl named Katrina who came from the east, but who shared clothes and food and remembered how to laugh. The birth of a child who died. Being beaten with a riding crop. Smothering an old man who slept and taking his purse.

Camille's arms ceased flailing. Her heart stopped beating. Philip raised his head to look at her, flesh torn and shredded, black-red liquid seeping down her collarbone, eyes locked on the filthy ceiling. She had helped him to forget, at least for a little while.

Getting up, he used her chipped washbasin to rinse himself clean, and then put his shirt back on. Would John be finished by now? Perhaps not. He always spent more time wining and dining his victims than Philip could even comprehend. Whatever did they talk about?

Leaving Camille's body on the bed where it lay, he picked up his cloak and stepped outside into the sharp air. The temperature had dropped, but Philip knew it would keep going down until dawn, part of their inverted world. Mortals felt the temperature rise all day. Undeads felt it drop all night. Master Angelo taught him that as a defense mechanism. "Never forget the passing time, my son. Watch your sky and feel your air." Good advice. Angelo knew many things.

Philip quickly moved down the empty streets, back to the Wayside Inn. Although the hour neared two o'clock, a mass of people still milled around inside, eating, drinking, talking—a few playing at cards. No sign of John. Philip moved around the back of the building, looking for too-large footprints in the snow. Then he changed his mind abruptly. No sense disturbing his brother's kill. He was just about to turn and go back inside the inn to wait when a slight shuffling sound caught his attention. A small, faded toolshed sat directly behind the Wayside's back door. Someone was in there.

Boredom and mild curiosity rather than any real interest drove him to walk over and peer inside. What he saw caught him by surprise.

Heat from the inn leaked inside, keeping the temperature above freezing. John's enormous hands were gently resting the dark-blond prostitute on a tattered blanket. In a deep sleep, her chest rose and fell lightly. Her neck was undamaged, but two small red punctures glowed out against her white shoulder. John drew a dagger and connected the punctures, making the wound appear as a jagged cut. Then he covered her with the wool cloak she'd been wearing earlier.

"What are you doing?" Philip asked.

John's head whipped up, all traces of joviality or good nature absent. "Get out."

"But she's still—"

"Get out!"

Philip stumbled back out in the snow, bewildered.

This didn't make sense. Why was John shouting at him? He stood in the snow for ten minutes, until the shed door opened and his brother ducked beneath the arch to step through.

"Is she dead?"

"Yes." The anger had left John's voice. "Let's get the horses."

"Can I see her?"

"No, it's growing late. We have to get back."

For an answer, Philip moved quickly around him and made a grab for the latch. His feet left the ground as John picked him up and threw him backward.

"Philip, I'm not playing with you! You get up and get your horse, now."

"We can't leave her alive. She saw both of us. We'll never be able to come to this part of the city again."

"Trust me now," John said in what looked like despair. "Let us go home."

Neither one spoke for the first half of their ride back through the trees. Doubts swirled in Philip's mind. He hated them. What could he call these unwanted thoughts? Concern. Yes, that's it. He was concerned.

"Why did you leave that woman alive?" he asked finally, breaking the tense silence. "She will remember us."

"No, she won't."

"Of course she will."

"Angelo warned me about hunting with you," John said quietly. "Try to remember that you aren't like me. Master wants you to grow and develop at your own pace with no preconceptions of what you should be. Do you understand?"

"No."

"I can do things you can't. Believe me, that woman won't know us if we go back to town. She won't remember anything."

Philip pulled up his horse. "Oh, it's a trick? One of your little psychic tricks? You made her forget?"

"Yes."

"Well, why didn't you tell me?" Relief and annoyance replaced concern. "You've ruined the whole ride home for nothing. We could have raced or chased down some peasants."

John laughed and kicked his horse into motion. "Still plenty of room for that," he called. "I let you win last time."

Unpleasant thoughts forgotten, Philip urged Kayli to bolt, leaping forward across the snow.

"Julian?"

A few nights later, Philip searched the upper west tower for companionship. Master Angelo had gone out on business, and John was cloistered with a book again. This tower hadn't been cleaned in years, and he felt uncomfortable here in this dead, cheerless place filled with ancient ghosts. Not that ghosts bothered him, but the outdoors beckoned, fresh air and wind rushing through the trees.

Dust flew up into his mouth as he called out. Julian's company didn't appeal to him any more than this tower did, but talking to someone else, anyone else, was preferable to being alone. Loneliness hurt more than hunger, and he was no good at entertaining himself. Angelo tried to teach him a game of solitary cards once, but he couldn't sit still or focus long enough to learn.

"Julian?"

"Who's there?" a dull voice called from somewhere ahead.

"It's me. Where are you?"

"Philip?"

"Yes, of course. Which room are you in?"

A tall form dressed in black stepped into view down the hallway. "Down here. Are you alone?"

"Quite alone. I'm so bored even you sound like good company right now."

"Come ahead then."

He followed Julian into a small, alcove-styled room with an open window that faced Harfleur. Lights and smoke from city fires glowed in the distance. Julian looked terrible—and he smelled stale. His skin was sallow with dark circles under his eyes. His hair was lank and uncombed, and he was wearing a cloak that had not been brushed out for weeks.

"Shouldn't we light a candle?" Philip asked.

"No," Julian said. "You're a vampire. You can see in the dark."

"I suppose."

"Why did you come here?"

"Looking for you. Come out hunting?"

"Not tonight."

Philip rolled his eyes and dropped into a dusty wooden chair.

"What's a bastard?" he asked after a few moments.

"Someone without a legitimate father." Julian was

looking out the window, but his profile was clear, and his expression lost its melancholy cast. He sounded mildly interested. "Why would you ask me that?"

"John said my father is a bastard, but he must have meant something else then."

"Oh." The corner of Julian's mouth curved up. "It can also be used to call someone heartless or cruel. Your father did treat you badly, but only because you disappointed him. He wanted you to be strong. Take his place."

"Is your father a bastard?"

"Mine? No. Mine is . . . an unusual man. I wish your memory hadn't erased him. He taught you to ride when you were six."

"Truly?"

"Yes, you were afraid of horses, and my father understands fear. We probably should have switched places. You loved it at Cliffbracken, and I always felt stifled."

"I can't imagine being afraid of horses."

"No, you've changed. Tragic, really. Your father would worship you now." He paused and frowned. "You're certainly full of words tonight. I haven't seen you this coherent since before Angelo turned you."

"I have things on my mind."

"What mind?" Julian snorted coldly.

"John and I rode into town a few nights ago, and he . . ."

Julian turned away from the window. "He what?"

"He used one of his mind tricks to make a whore forget him, forget he had fed upon her, and he left her alive."

Julian fell still, gazing at Philip through the darkness. "Has he or Angelo ever done that to you? Tried to enter your mind? Tried to make you obey? Or tried to make you forget something?"

"What?" This turn in the conversation startled Philip. "No. Of course not."

"How would you know," Julian whispered, his dark eyes glittering, "if they'd already made you forget?" He stepped closer. "We have no defense at all. Do you understand what that means? They could make us think anything, do anything . . . and even make us forget . . . and as we have no such power, we could do nothing to stop them."

Philip fidgeted in his chair. "What is wrong with you these past nights?"

"We have no defense against them . . . against any of them."

"Stop saying that!" Philip snapped.

Julian fell silent, turning back and staring out the window into space.

"Oh, please, Julian," Philip begged. "Can't we do something, anything—riding, hunting? We could even practice fencing if you like. One more moment in this house and I'll die."

"No," his undead brother whispered. "You won't die."

A few nights later, Julian vanished, and Philip had no idea where he'd gone.

Several weeks passed, and then one night, Philip came home an hour before dawn to find his master and John in the library, deep in whispered conference.

"Telling secrets?" Philip asked, smiling. "About me?"

Angelo Travare, Earl of Scurloc, rested in a stone chair. He was a slender Norman creature who told stories of crusades and knights with swords, his flesh long since grown so preternaturally pale he scarcely passed as human. Dim candlelight exposed deep lines of strain now marring his milky forehead.

Two thick pieces of parchment lay on the oak table before him.

"Sit down, son," Angelo said.

"What's wrong?" Philip asked.

"Our time this winter is over. You must return to Gascony."

"But it's not even January yet. We have months to go."

"How many vampires do you know?"

"How many? You, John, Julian, Maggie, and John's servant, Edward. What does it matter?"

"Do you ever wonder if there are others like yourself, beyond your circle?"

"No."

"There are, Philip. Nearly thirty others in Europe alone."

"Like us?"

"Just like us," Angelo said. "But tonight, we've learned that three of them are dead." He pointed down to the parchment letters.

"Dead?" Philip repeated. "We can't die. We're immortal."

"Of course we can. I've explained this. 'Undead' does not mean your body can't be destroyed. Fire, sunlight, and decapitation will end your existence. Now, listen to me carefully. Do you know why Maggie has no psychic powers?"

Philip frowned without answering.

"Because you were not able to teach her," Angelo said.

John leaned forward in his chair, nodding, dark blond hair falling across his eyes. "And neither does my Edward because I chose not to teach him yet, and he has no contact with others of our kind."

Their manner annoyed Philip, speaking to him in short, slowly spoken words. "I'm not simple! I'm not a half-wit, but I don't care about psychic powers." He motioned to the parchments. "And what does any of that have to do with us? A few vampires we've never met have flown off to the great beyond. Why do you care?"

"Because they were murdered," Angelo said flatly. "Decapitated by Julian."

"By Jul—some kind of fight?"

Angelo always had seemed ancient to him, but tonight was the first time his master looked old and fragile.

"No, Philip, not a fight. Julian has left us. He has become an enemy to his own kind and is destroying vampires who possess psychic power."

"What? Who told you that?"

"It is the truth. His gift has turned back in upon itself, and he now fears what he does not possess . . . to a degree that has sickened his mind." Angelo paused as if gauging his next words. "Psychic ability isn't truly a gift like the one great power we each use against mortals. It is learned, developed. And as John did with his Edward, I have chosen to postpone your training until you have existed longer, learned more of yourself and our world. But I cannot explain Julian's lack of ability. I have sometimes thought his gift to be so strong it has kept him from developing other powers."

"Have you told him that?"

"Of course." Angelo almost smiled. "Long ago."

"And he still fears you?"

Angelo did not answer.

Rubbing his hands, John peered up at Philip through tired eyes. "It's important that you don't become involved in this. I don't think you're simple or a half-wit, but you could be hurt if you stay. Go home to Gascony and wait with Maggie until this thing is over."

"What will you do?"

"I leave tonight. I'll go to Amiens and get Edward first. He and I will go back to Edinburgh. Master Angelo has a few affairs to tie up here, and then he'll leave in a week or so for his summer home in Venice."

"Why are you splitting up? Wouldn't we all be stronger as a group?"

"No," Master Angelo said. "I am hopeful that Julian may come to his senses, and giving him so much ground to cover makes his current task more difficult, if he means us harm at all. Killing strangers is one thing. Killing those in our circle is another."

"How many of the other vampires are psychic?"

John's gaze dropped. "All of them besides you, Julian, Maggie, and my Edward."

"All of them?" Philip's eyes widened. "Then what does he possibly hope to gain?"

"Nothing. He is simply afraid . . . to the point of madness."

This made no sense. Philip experienced a moment of intense unhappiness and hated the emotion. "All right, John. You go. I'll stay here with Master until he's ready to leave for Venice."

Angelo leaned back in his chair. "I have no need of protection, my son. My hands can snap Julian like a matchstick."

"No matter. I'm staying anyway, until you're ready to leave."

With no more words to say, John moved for the stairs, looking back at them once.

Eight nights later, Philip and Angelo packed a few scant belongings and prepared for their separate journeys. The short time they had spent alone together pleased them both. The old master forgot his books and cerebral conversation, preferring to spend spare time outside hunting with Philip. But the house had now been secured, carriage horses stabled inside Harfleur, and bank accounts transferred to Venice.

It was time to leave.

Philip jogged with snow-covered boots into the library. "Horses are saddled. You ready?"

Angelo gazed around. "Yes, but I will miss this place . . . and you."

"Don't be so maudlin. Julian will forget this by summer, and we'll all meet in London, or maybe Paris."

They walked outside into the night air. Dark trees lined the path to the barn, allowing bits of light from the moon to glimmer through. Philip seldom formed attachments to places, but this path had always held a certain charm with its hidden black spaces—but still so wide that he could drive Kayli into full gallop two steps out of the stable door. Wanting to lock this night in his memory, he stared at each tree they walked past. Because of this, he stopped short when movement caught his eye.

"Angelo, there's something—"

Before he could finish speaking, a shadow stepped out from the base of a tree, and moonlight glinted in his eyes. He heard the sweeping arc rather than seeing anything. Then Angelo's body toppled to the ground, his separated head landing with a soft thud in the snow. The whole picture took a few seconds to sink in.

Then the pain hit.

Searing, scorching, hysterical faces exploded inside his eyes. Turks, ragged peasants, pale children, sobbing women, all danced and clawed at his brain while he writhed helplessly, scratching at his own temples to get them out—men with long surcoats, crosses in one hand and swords in the other, crying fanatical words while rushing to battle, horses and fire and a lady called Elizabeth who always waited, a dark-skinned vampire with no name biting his shoulder, hating him, making him pay for all eternity by stealing his dream of heaven. The visions and agony went on and on, a parade of lost souls seeking retribution. Finally the waves began fading. The sounds hushed.

"You're all right. It's over." Julian knelt beside him, a sword in one hand, blood smeared all over the other.

Twisting up to all fours, Philip stared at his master's

body as it began to turn gray and crack. This couldn't be happening. "You killed him."

"I had to," Julian rasped. "Don't you see? We are meant to be alone, not to live in twisted families like mortals. Our kind has become diseased, feeding upon each other's powers until some of us began to throw off the balance . . . growing stronger than others, creating a threat. I'm putting the balance back. Soon we will be pure again, equal . . . safe."

The words sounded far away, at the end of a long corridor. Philip climbed to his feet in shock, not understanding or absorbing Julian's words. "What will John say? This will make him sad!"

"No, it won't. He's already dead." Still kneeling, Julian pressed the sword into the snow and leaned on the hilt with his hands. "Angelo must have known. He must have felt it."

"What?"

"Four nights ago, I took his head right in front of his servant."

"Edward? Where is he now?"

"Long gone. He's not one of them."

This was a night of new emotions. Acute pain and sorrow faded as something infinitely worse crept up Philip's spine. Julian's black eyes bored into him, emanating fear, making him back away.

"You may not remember," Julian whispered, "but we've been friends since childhood. That existence is over. You are an immortal hunter, forever alone. Do you understand? Alone."

"No. Maggie's mine."

"You stay away from her, or I will send her after. I'm not being cruel, only strong. You will thank me later. And it's not so harsh as it sounds. We can speak to each other, sometimes even hunt together. But never can we live together, never feed off each other's gifts. If even one of us gets this disease, the whole nightmare might begin again. Purity is what matters now—your first priority, more than me, more than Maggie, more than hunting. Do you understand?"

Terror filled Philip until fear was all he could see. What would he do? Existing by himself was worse than death. Perhaps this was a vision, the dream on the edge of John's sleep that he never quite saw, the bad thing he saw coming and couldn't stop. Julian's voice echoed through the darkness.

"Alone. Do you understand? Alone . . ."

chapter 23

"Alone."

I pulled out to see him mouthing the word almost silently, amber eyes lost in a fog of memories.

"Philip, wake up."

He blinked and looked down at me. Without thinking, I laid my face against his knee in a gesture of comfort, like a mortal, like a woman.

"It's all right," I said. "Long past now."

Julian had hurt him, filled his world with lies.

"I think he went on killing . . . all of them, Leisha," he whispered, "all but Edward, Maggie, and me."

"Did you send Maggie away?"

"No, I just didn't go home. Julian never had to chase her off. Then she left for America on her own in 1841, about two years after you."

"So she waited sixteen years for you to come back to Gascony?"

"We saw each other . . . sometimes. Like that first night you saw me at Cliffbracken, we'd all been out hunting together. I was happy. But after a few nights together, Julian broke us up."

How many had Julian murdered? Angelo said, "Nearly thirty in Europe alone." But how? Julian had been turned less than a year before Philip. If we grow more powerful with age, then how could he destroy such ancient beings?

I flashed the question mentally at Philip. He didn't seem to realize no words had been spoken and nodded at me.

"I wondered that, too. He told me later that they couldn't feel him coming. Maybe because he doesn't have psychic powers? But the same technique worked every time. He'd track his target down, hide behind a tree—like with Angelo—or a door or a building and just wait. Nobody ever felt him, and nobody ever saw him coming."

I stood up, trying to get my head around all this. "But I lived with Edward for seventy years."

"Yes, and Julian didn't know what to do at first. He feared what might happen."

"He never said anything."

"How could he? To stop the situation by force meant traveling to New York. That meant seeing his father. And if he wrote to order you away and Edward refused, this would be . . . The shame was not worth risking for Julian."

"We didn't even know psychic ability was possible."

Philip's brows knitted. "That's true. Perhaps he didn't want you to know. He kept watch on you for years, waiting to see what would happen. But nothing ever did, and in the end, you left on your own, proving Julian's point that we were all meant to live alone . . . He didn't consider William a true vampire."

"You're missing the point. Edward and I developed no psychic powers from living together. It never even occurred to us."

"I know. Angelo said such power must be taught . . . like Wade has done for you. Perhaps we all have the power buried, waiting to wake."

"All except Julian."

Yes, all except Julian. That was the crux. He feared what he did not possess, enough to murder his own kind.

Philip stood up, towering over me. "Leisha?"

"Mmmmm?" He pulled me out of concentration.

"Do you remember a few weeks ago, when Maggie called me and told me you were living with her?"

"Yes, I remember."

"It hurt, and I hadn't felt anything for a long time."

"You missed her?"

"No, it wasn't that. But she spoke of fireplaces and the three of you talking together. It didn't seem fair when I had to stay by myself. It made me think of John and Angelo—things pushed to the back of my head for so many years."

"And you like having company now?"

"Yes, but look at us! Julian was right. Only a few nights together, and it's started."

I turned to him angrily. "Listen to yourself! He's been rationalizing his own fear, his own weakness, for so long you've started believing it. Telepathy isn't a disease. It's more like a muscle. The more you use it, the stronger it grows. If not for Wade . . . Oh, he's still in the bedroom."

"Oh."

Philip jumped up and crossed the room. "I am sorry, Wade. We're finished." He spoke like someone who'd known Wade for years.

When they came back to the couch together, I noticed similar lines of sadness below their eyes, on their foreheads. What a team the three of us made. Almost everyone we'd ever cared about was dead or gone, taken away in this unstoppable conflict, which started with the single action of Edward Claymore jumping off his own front porch.

Why couldn't we mourn? Wade had tear ducts. Why didn't he cry for Dominick? Philip rarely mentioned Maggie unless he had to. And me? I couldn't think about William, couldn't let the image of his face enter my consciousness or I might dry up and crumble. What a team.

A fruit basket sat cheerfully on an oak writing desk against the wall. I picked it up and peeled back the plastic cover. "Wade, you should eat some of this. Do you like apples? Maybe these grapes?"

He nodded tiredly, and I flashed inside his mind, *I'm sorry about Dominick.*

No answer came, but he took some grapes and a banana from me.

"We should go," Philip said. "I called Julian hours ago, but he did not tell me his location."

"Couldn't we just keep all this a secret?" I asked. "Why does he have to know?"

"He'll know," Philip answered softly.

I wasn't so sure, but those stories of Julian stepping out from nowhere frightened me enough. I kept fantasizing his dark visage popping up behind the couch, a broadsword arcing in his grasp.

Wade's hands were shaking, maybe delayed shock from everything he'd gone through tonight. Helping him peel the banana, I asked, "Do you still have the Prius?"

"Yes."

"Good, we'll let Philip drive. One ride with him and nothing will ever scare you again."

We all laughed briefly, but the laughter was forced. Taking the fruit basket seemed a good idea. It would be easy for me to forget that mortals had to eat every day. Wade seldom spoke up about things like hunger or sleep.

He'd have to come with us, at least for now, at least until we figured something else out. He was just so vulnerable, so unprepared for what lay ahead. Even his growing tolerance, perhaps acceptance, of Philip might fade away after witnessing the first hunt. Running all night, sleeping all day. What kind of life was that for a man like Wade?

But nothing could be done about it now.

"Help me take those blankets off the windows," Philip said. "We won't need them anymore, and the maids might wonder why we put them up."

"Okay," I answered uncertainly.

How could he worry about things like blankets over hotel windows and then kill cops on busy streets? Sometimes he was too weird—even for me.

The next few seconds caught me completely off

guard. Thinking about Philip's inconsistencies took my mind from our immediate problems. I reached out for the hanging blanket nearest the west wall, and a pale hand snaked from behind it, grasping my wrist like a vice.

"Having a party?" a voice as cold as ocean depths echoed from behind the drape. "Without me?"

Julian.

I almost screamed, but didn't. He stepped out, still holding me—dressed in black, looking identical to the image imprinted on my memory: broad, pale features set off by cold eyes. All I could feel was fear. Uncontrollable, sickening waves of fear washed down my throat, making my teeth click rapidly together.

From the corner of my eye, I saw Philip turn and stop. "Did you climb all the way up the side of this building just to impress me?" His voice was light and flippant. He had good control.

"Of course not," my maker answered. "I took the stairs to the roof and climbed down one floor. Did I impress you?"

"As always. It's good to see you."

Even through my haze of fear, I could hear that their casual banter was wrong—it didn't fit. And from the corner of my eye, I could see Philip's face, guarded but terrified, no matter how calm he sounded.

His gift didn't work against Julian. Strange how the one person Philip feared in this world had been the reason for my existence, always there, but distant, hiding in the shadows, the one person William truly remembered.

Had Julian ever felt my gift? Did he know what his pretty creation could do?

Reaching up with my free hand, I touched his fingers softly. "Master, your grip is too tight."

I focused on emanating an image of myself—small, fragile, hardly worth the bother of a creature like Julian, far beneath him in every respect. A peasant, and yet somehow one of his own. How could he think of hurting me? Harmless and defenseless, I needed protection and the strength of someone like him.

His susceptibility to suggestion surprised me. Philip had played along when we first met, even allowed himself to be affected, but he always knew the game. He always knew exactly what I was.

But Julian let go instantly, actually steadying me to make sure I wouldn't fall.

"My father is dead?" he asked, his words sounding more like a statement than a question.

Some of my terror began to fade, and I bowed my head for a moment, as if not worthy of looking him in the face. Then carefully, I raised my eyes.

"Yes, my lord."

"And where is his murderer?"

"Dead. Philip killed him."

A flicker of relief passed across his pale features. His work here was done. The senile abortion he called father no longer haunted him. Revenge had been exacted, and Philip and I were no threat because we had been beaten into states of eternal fear. Things must have looked quite rosy.

He didn't seem to sense or suspect a thing about our

growing telepathy. Maybe Philip gave him too much credit?

My hope began to rise.

Maybe if we just behaved correctly, fed his ego, and walked three steps behind him, we'd get out of this without a fight. I had no pride left, not when it came to Julian.

But then he turned to Wade, who'd been standing silently in the corner, just watching, breathing quickly. Even wearing his canvas jacket, he looked so slender, almost fragile, his white-blond hair hanging forward over his eyes. After that first intense scan of my memories a few nights ago, Wade knew my maker well.

My heart sank again.

"Who is this?" Julian asked. "Did Philip bring dinner?"

I wanted to scream, to claw his eyes out. What had I been thinking? Hoping we could flatter our way out of this? Julian would never let Wade out of the building.

Of all the ways I thought to die, defending a mortal wasn't one of them. Then again . . . I did possess one weapon, and I still might be able to use it here.

But it was difficult not to think of days long past. The sight of Julian brought back memories long forgotten, interfering with my gift. I remembered serving my first banquet at Cliffbracken, when he sat at the lavish dining table . . . back when the house was still alive. He had seemed so large, and I had felt so small.

Not anymore.

Not unless I wanted him to see me that way.

I pushed the memories away . . . pushed my fear

away, and then moved between him and Wade, focusing hard on emanating my gift.

Concentrate. Get him on his knees.

"Master, please." I reached out again and used the tips of my fingers to touch the back of his hand. "He is not worthy of you. Come. Let me find you a lovely woman." I took a step toward the door, pitching my voice to an even softer tone. "I've dreamed of hunting with you, of learning from you. Let Philip have this one." I took another step toward the door.

Julian's mouth opened slightly as he stepped after me. His eyes seemed puzzled and pleased at the same time as I could see him mulling over the sweet portrait my words painted of him as the teacher, me as his grateful student, working to please him, to find him better prey.

Philip hadn't moved in several moments, and he was watching silently, allowing me to take over.

"Come into the city with me," I whispered to Julian.

He took another step.

Then, suddenly, he glanced over at Wade, and his eyes changed. He shook his head as if to clear it and looked back at me in shock . . . and then rage. His large hand flashed out and gripped my wrist, jerking me up against him.

"What are you doing?" he snarled. "You would try that on me?"

He whipped his free hand back to hit me, and I braced myself.

"Julian, don't!" Philip shouted.

The blow never landed—but not because of Philip's

angry shout. Instead, the room exploded in a deafening sound, and I fell back against the floor, looking around wildly to see what happened.

Another explosion sounded, hurting my ears.

Julian's chest was bleeding from two gaping holes as he stumbled backward. Wade was holding his Beretta out in both hands, beads of sweat trickling down his narrow face.

He fired again, catching Julian in the shoulder.

I'd forgotten about the Beretta.

"His throat!" Philip yelled. "Aim for his throat!"

I twisted over to sit in a crouch, uncertain what to do. Wade fired again, but Julian dropped low, and the bullet missed him completely.

But his pale face was so shocked I wondered how he had the presence of mind to even act.

Philip bolted across the room, his loose flannel shirt billowing behind him. He grabbed Julian by the shoulder and leg, lifting him into the air and throwing him at the window. Julian's body crashed against the drapes.

Glass snapped and crackled.

Let him fall through. Please, let him fall through.

Dropping twelve floors to the pavement might not destroy his body, but he'd be out of working order for a while.

But in despair, I saw his hand catch the drape. He managed to steady himself, pain and confusion twisting his features as he stared back in shock—as if unable to believe Philip would attack him to defend me.

Philip actually snarled at him.

I realized this was a new situation for Julian. Fearing

a psychic combat he could not win, he'd always hidden himself away, striking only unaware victims. Physical battles with an equal were almost unknown . . . and he was wounded, bleeding.

But Philip was strong. He charged forward again and swung hard with his right fist, catching Julian across the jaw. The crack echoed as Julian's head snapped back.

Wade moved past me, looking for a clear shot.

"Don't!" I called. "You might hit Philip."

We needed Philip whole.

"Stay behind me," Wade spat back, still holding the gun with both hands.

Philip reached down to try and get another grip, but this time, Julian swept out with his leg, knocking Philip off his feet. Julian lunged up to stand behind the couch, his face a mask of hatred, and then his eyes grew more focused, emanating his gift.

The fear hit me like a wall.

I started gagging.

Wade didn't even get off one shot. He fell to his knees, dropping the gun. His mouth was open in terror but no sounds came.

Philip cried out from fear, and he tried struggling up to crawl. Julian kicked him in the chest so hard his body flew against a wooden chair, smashing it to pieces. When he hit the floor, his shoulder popped out of its socket and his arm lay at an odd angle.

Julian ignored him and strode directly to Wade. The waves of fear washed over and over me, but despair flooded in as well when Julian grabbed Wade's hair with one hand and the Beretta with the other. He smashed the butt of the gun against Wade's cheek-bone.

"You like this gun?" Julian asked. His chest and shoulder were still bleeding, soaking his black shirt. He pressed the barrel to Wade's temple. "Do you like it now?"

He wasn't even going to feed. He was just going to shoot Wade in the head.

And Philip was down, his body broken, his mind lost in fear.

"Master, no," I started begging. I hated begging.

I had to do something.

In desperation, more from instinct than intent, I pushed my own thoughts into his mind with all the force I had once used on Dominick. Only this time, I didn't fire ugly images.

Stop!

He froze, his dark eyes wild.

Let go of him!

He dropped Wade first, then the gun, and his mouth formed a horrified O shape. He half turned and staggered toward me. I felt him trying to force me out of his mind. He focused his gift on me at the same time, trying to bury me in terror.

I gasped aloud, fighting for my hold, feeling him push me out, knowing if he did, we were all dead.

I closed my eyes, blocking out the sight of him, but this time, I sent images . . . memories I'd seen inside of Philip.

Angelo's face. His smile. The sword arcing, slicing off his head.

All Julian's resistance failed as he cried out. I could

feel what he felt in this moment, and he had never felt anything like it. I kept my eyes closed and pushed harder inside of his mind.

Show me.

I was inside his memories, inside his existence, and he could not keep me out, nor could he stop the flow I had started by forcing him to see Angelo. He began to remember it all. I saw so many faces, so many of my kind as Julian butchered them . . . a red-haired vampire turning in surprise as the blade swept in . . . a dark-skinned girl, little more than a child. I wanted to weep, but could not.

Instead, I gripped his thoughts more tightly with my own. I altered them, warped them, creating images of the ghosts of his victims. I built a nightmare in his mind as they crept toward him with bloody lines across their throats. He could not escape as they clutched at him . . . grabbing him, nailing him to a cross, and raising it.

Angelo picked up a torch and set the cross on fire.

Julian screamed and fell to the carpet.

I crawled over to him, with my mouth to his ear.

"Is this what you fear, Master? One of us taking over your thoughts, your body?" I pressed my mouth closer, tasting the stale flesh of his temple. "Then fear me. I could make this much worse, and I could make you relive it over and over again." I paused, watching his face twitch in horror, ashamed how much I enjoyed the sight.

"We want to be left alone," I whispered. "That's all. But if you ever come near me or Philip or Wade again, I will trap you in your own hell. Do you understand?"

I released some of my control, letting him have partial function of his body again. He did not respond, but turned his head to stare at me. I was a stranger to him—as if he could not believe his little servant girl could conjure images ugly enough to make him writhe and force them into his brain. He didn't know me. His mouth was still locked in the O shape.

"I will let you up if you swear to leave, if you swear to never come near us again," I said.

The fear and disbelief in his eyes grew.

"Do you swear?" I demanded.

"Yes," he finally hissed, finding his voice.

"Remember what I can do!"

But then the sound of crashing glass broke the last of my connection, my hold on him. Wind swept through the room, and I looked up to see Philip standing over us with a chair leg in his right hand. His left shoulder was still dislocated. The hotel window behind him had been smashed.

He'd broken the window?

He dropped the chair leg. Then he grabbed Julian, pulled him up and threw him backward. Julian was still dazed from the horror show I had sent into his head and from the shock of having lost control of himself. He nearly fell through the broken window, but managed to grab one side, cutting his hand, as he fought wildly to pull himself back inside. Philip strode toward him with a savage expression I never wanted to see again.

"Philip, no!" I called. "You don't need to—"

But Philip didn't even hear me. He kicked Julian square in the chest, and I watched as my maker's arms flailed and his eyes widened in his pale face before he fell from view . . . twelve stories down toward the pavement.

Then he was gone.

"Why did you do that?" I shouted at Philip. "I had him! You didn't need to . . ." I trailed off as Philip turned, anger draining from his face.

He came back quickly and dropped to his knees, grabbing my hands, examining my fingers and arms. "Did he hurt you?"

I didn't know how to answer.

Wade moaned and sirens blared outside. It had only been moments since the first shots exploded in the room, but hotel security must be on its way up—and someone had called the police.

"We have to go now," Philip said, walking to Wade and leaning over to pick him up.

"I can walk," Wade mumbled. His cheek was cut and turning purple.

They both started for the door, but I couldn't help running to the window first and looking down.

The pavement below was empty.

chapter 24

Five nights later I was on the streets by myself. I wanted to be out alone, away from Philip and Wade.

I'd thought recovering from our shared horror of fighting Julian would be difficult . . . but so far, we'd barely even talked about it.

Wade had snapped Philip's shoulder back into its socket, and that was the last time any of us mentioned what happened that night.

Without even examining our options, the three of us moved into Maggie's. Simple, mechanical, civilized, unspeakably calm, we set about putting our immediate environment into neat order. I quickly pulled all of my money from Portland and put it into a private account.

Philip took over Maggie's room, but he didn't alter the feminine decor even though he didn't like it.

Wade settled into the stark upstairs second bedroom—sleeping on blankets on the floor. But he'd only bought two new changes of clothes.

I slept in the cellar because it felt safe.

Philip did not arrange for new bank accounts in America, nor would he mention moving back to Paris. Wade avoided the topic or his job or Dominick's death or any future plans beyond the next five minutes. They both seemed to be waiting for me. But what did I want?

Neither of them had asked me what I did to Julian . . . but I had a feeling Philip figured out I'd attacked him telepathically.

Of course none of us knew what happened to him after he fell.

Philip kept looking over his shoulder, as if waiting to see a sword arcing out of the darkness. But I didn't. I believed I'd ended this conflict forever. I could hit Julian with the one thing he truly feared, yet I would leave him alone if he left me alone.

He'd stay away.

But . . . where did that leave me?

Every aspect of my undead existence revolved around William or Julian in one form or another. Now, sweet William was gone. I accepted that reality with mixed emotions.

I was free.

But free to do what?

To go on killing and feeding and plying my gift in one long, endless stretch of time? Is that all there was? Perhaps Edward had been the only sane one after all.

Certain doubts—concepts—had been plaguing me for several nights. I couldn't stop thinking about the memories Philip had shown me.

Nearly thirty vampires in Europe alone.

Did that mean there were other vampires in places

like Asia, Australia, or South America? If so, had Julian hunted them down, too? Philip didn't know, and the topic upset him. He'd spent most of that time of terror in hiding.

But even if all the vampires had lived in Europe, how did they manage to hide and feed without depopulating entire areas? The best-case scenario meant fifteen hundred and sixty deaths a year if each vampire made only one kill a week. That's nearly sixteen thousand deaths over a ten-year period and didn't take hunters like Philip into account. How could this be?

An idea, a possibility, began forming in my mind over the past few nights. I don't know how it occurred to me, or when it began, but I needed to be alone to try it. So I hit the streets without Philip and headed down to Pike Place Market.

Even after closing, the market teemed with life. Hookers, bums, guys playing guitars on street corners, their cases left open for donations, and teenage kids looking for something to do all milled around in a kaleidoscope of colors and scents.

Wearing a white cotton dress, my hair in a French braid, I looked clean and bright, like a girl from a Bloomingdale's hatbox. Maggie had taught me more than she'd realized, but I could never rely on a gift like hers. My own was too deeply ingrained.

Falling into character, I left the busy area and stood outside an alley, arms crossed, back to the wall. Ten minutes later, a tall man in his mid-thirties walked by. Obviously in a hurry, he still stopped when I made eye contact.

"You all right?" he asked.

People in Seattle rarely speak to strangers on the street, at least not without a good reason.

"I got on the wrong bus," I answered. "It took me here."

"Where are you supposed to be?"

"Greenwood."

My voice pitched high but soft, as if I didn't want to talk to him but didn't know what else to do. Casting out tentatively, I felt no malice or violence, only haste. He sighed in frustration, wishing he'd taken a different route and left my pretty, frightened plight for some-body else to handle.

"I've got to be in Lake Forest Park in an hour," he said, "but I can take a detour and drop you. Who lives in Greenwood?"

"My sister."

"Come on, then."

Not moving, I stared out in indecision. Jumping in right away with him would have looked unusual. But his frustration mounted.

"Look, there won't be another bus this time of night. You either stay here or come on."

Obviously the prospect of staying in an alley wouldn't appeal to any young mortal girl. I stepped out and followed him, half jogging to keep up. Three blocks away, he unlocked the passenger door of a newer Ford pickup and reached out for my hand.

"Watch your dress getting in."

His manner affected me somehow. On a normal hunt I'd never have chosen a victim like this. Though slightly condescending, he had no motives besides taking me somewhere safe. Even in a rush, he'd stopped to help one person in this crowded city.

He hopped in and slammed the driver's door. The street was fairly dark and quiet. Reaching out, I stopped his hand from sliding a key into the ignition, and I focused my thoughts, touching the edge of his own.

"Wait, not yet."

He turned at my words, seeing me through a downy white mist. I pressed a suggestion into his mind.

You're so tired. You need sleep.

"What are you . . . ?" he mumbled.

Sleep.

His eyelids grew heavy, and his head lolled back against the seat. His body went limp except for his chest, which continued to rise and fall.

I scooted across the seat and moved up for his throat.

He looked so peaceful, so helpless, that I stopped.

Changing my mind, I lifted his wrist instead. No tearing or ripping this time. Using my eyeteeth, I punctured the large blue vein above the callused curve of his palm. Carefully, keeping the holes as small as possible, I drew down on his wrist, drinking blood and absorbing life force while his heart beat quickly. My mind filled with visions of a farm in Nebraska and a hard-faced mother who never laughed, a soft-eyed sister who dreamed of being a dancer, and a stocky chestnut horse named Buck . . . his memories, his past treasures.

Once I had taken enough, I pulled out and used my fingernail to connect the little holes on his wrist, making the wound into a jagged cut—messy, but he was not bleeding badly.

My focus turned to his thoughts again, taking him back to the moment he'd rounded the corner and seen me up against the wall. I erased the memory.

No frightened girl had waited for him, only an empty street. But in his haste he'd stumbled and cut his wrist on a broken bottle. The pain didn't bother him at first, but then it grew worse. He got in the truck and felt dizzy. He must have passed out.

Opening the passenger door and pressing the lock button down, I let go of his altered memories and hopped down into the street, leaving him to sleep peacefully a little longer.

Numb shock faded as I ran through the night. Then euphoria began to rise inside of me. This was it. Their secret.

I didn't mourn for all the lives needlessly lost in my ignorant past, but instead, I rejoiced for those saved in my future. I didn't have to kill. I never had to kill.

This was the way of the vampires who existed before my generation. They were not murderers, not slavering hunters who wiped out whole villages, merely survivors who used what gifts they had, like everyone else.

Where had they come from? Where did I come from? Perhaps Philip was right and we came from black spirits who roamed the void before some great god created the earth. Perhaps not. There was no one left to teach me. Perhaps I'd find out one day.

None of that mattered. I didn't have to kill anymore. We were a new breed, Philip and I, like our predecessors. Would Philip care? Would he evolve? I couldn't wait to bring him outside and show him what I'd discovered.

I waved down a taxi. This state of limbo had to end. The undeclared war was over. Nobody really won, but it was over just the same, and it was time to go on. I kept mulling over the same thought all the way home.

We don't have to kill.

After tipping the driver, I jumped out of the cab and was about to run toward Maggie's house when I noticed the small door on the mailbox was half ajar. We hadn't paid any bills since moving in, and even though I was desperate to get inside and talk to Philip about tonight's revelation, I also didn't want the water or power shut off, so I jogged over to get the mail.

But inside, I found an ivory envelope . . . and to my shock, it was addressed to me, here, at Maggie's. I studied it for a few seconds. The blue script was lovely, nothing like Julian's blocky handwriting. Seeing no return address, I ripped the envelope open and pulled out a small note on matching ivory paper. It read:

> *You are not alone. There are others like you. Respond to the Elizabeth Bathory Underground. P.O. Box 27750, San Francisco, CA 94973.*

I just stood there, frozen, for a long time. What did it mean? The Elizabeth Bathory Underground? Was it some sort of trick? Was Julian trying to lure me off alone somehow?

No, Julian was a blunt instrument. This wasn't his style. I shook my head and closed my eyes briefly.

You are not alone.

After all my questions, all of my burning need to learn more about my own kind, I didn't even want to look at this note. In this moment, it was an unwanted intrusion.

And it was too much, too much to deal with right now.

Deliberately, I put the note back inside the envelope and folded it into thirds. Then I slipped it into the pocket of my dress. I wasn't going to show this to either Philip or Wade tonight—maybe tomorrow.

Tonight, we had other things to discuss.

I went up the steps to Maggie's front door and walked in to find Wade and Philip sitting on the living room floor by the fire facing each other in telepathic connection.

Lost in my own private dilemma these past few nights, I may have been blind to their growing relationship. Originally, simple tolerance would have pleased me. But thinking about it, they had both been starved for companionship, for long talks with friends who actually listened. Attaching themselves to me had probably been easier for them at first. But my distance lately might have driven them closer to each other, both surprised to find a willing ear or mind.

I was well aware that before anything else, the three of us had to make some decisions about the future. We could not put it off any longer.

I walked over and sat on the carpet beside them. Warmth from the fire soaked into my skin. I reached out and touched Wade's hand with the tips of my fingers.

"Wade?"

He instantly dropped mental communication and looked at me. This too was becoming easier for them, to slip in and out of psychic contact without losing themselves in the memories.

"Yes?" he asked.

Philip turned his head and frowned when he saw my white dress. "Have you been hunting without me?"

Wade's narrow expression grew expectant, even impatient, as if he preferred to go on practicing mental interaction with Philip . . . or maybe he just didn't want to talk yet.

"What is it?" he asked.

They both sat there, looking at me, but now that I had their attention, my courage began to fail. Open confrontation was not one of my strengths.

But I couldn't walk away.

"What . . . what do you plan to do now?"

He blinked and shook his head in puzzlement, but his brown eyes were anxious, even frightened.

"I mean tomorrow," I rushed on, "and the tomorrow after that? Do you just go on like this . . . your job lost, your degree wasted, sitting around in this house we haven't actually moved into?"

Philip flinched. He looked away, into the flames.

"Eleisha, don't," he said.

I ignored him, and kept talking to Wade. "You buried your best friend, and you didn't even report him missing. Or have you forgotten?"

"No, I haven't forgotten," he whispered.

"Maybe you want to become one of us? Forget the

past and get lost in a safe little world feeding off the living? Is that what you want?" I held out my thin, white arm. "Like this forever?"

He turned away. "No, not that, but—"

"I don't want him to go away," Philip broke in. "Leisha, don't make him go away."

"Should he stay here in some shadowed half-life with us?"

He flattened his hands on the floor, and his eyes narrowed. "If you try to make him leave, I'll turn him."

"That worked well with Maggie, didn't it?" I said harshly.

They both stared at me, and I could feel the tension building.

"There's nothing left for me to go home to!" Wade suddenly shouted. "Can't you see that?"

"I don't want you to go home!" I shouted back. "I just want you to live! Get a job here. Get an apartment. Make some friends. Use your gift . . . like with that child in Kirkland. You can be a part of us and live with your own kind, too." I paused and lowered my voice, moving closer to him. "That's what you really want anyway. Otherwise you would have bought more clothes . . . maybe a bed for your room here."

He froze, just sitting there for a moment, and then dropped his head. I'm not certain, but he may have been silently crying. I knew he was torn between our world and his own. He'd be wasted as one of us, and miserable, probably jumping to his own death before the century turned.

"It's all right," I whispered. "As long we all keep trying to move forward, we'll be okay."

Philip's panicked eyes clicked back and forth between us.

"Can you lend me some money to get started?" Wade whispered. "I don't think I have enough left in savings."

"Anything you want," I answered.

Maybe he really would be okay.

Philip kept his hands flattened on the floor. "I don't understand . . . Is he leaving?"

I turned my attention from Wade and looked at Philip. His red-brown hair hung forward over his shoulders.

"Yes, but not far," I said.

"What about us?" he asked, almost like a child. "What do we do?"

I didn't know how to answer.

Bringing Wade out of limbo might be difficult, but Philip was worse. I needed a future, a plan . . . and he'd spent an existence from one hunt to the next.

I knew I didn't want to go to France anymore, or Finland. Maybe he didn't either.

"If we stay here, Philip, we have to make this place ours. All of Maggie's things go into boxes and get stored in the attic."

He pulled back, poised on his knees, and I could see his mind rolling over my words as if they'd never occurred to him. "Would you want that?" he asked. "To make a home here . . . in this house?"

"It's a start."

I knew he was terrified of being alone again. After so many years in isolation, he didn't want to go back. After so many years of being wrapped up in William, I didn't want to live alone. We were weak, perhaps, but this was the truth.

"We'll get boxes tomorrow night," he said, nodding. "And then go shopping for furniture at IKEA."

Relief flooded through me. This was a small step for both of us, but it was something. Then I remembered the reason I'd come running home to get him. Another element of our world had shifted tonight. We didn't have to kill anymore . . . and I needed to show him how.

"We have to go out," I said.

"Now? You just got back."

"Yes." I turned to Wade. "Can you order a pizza and hang here for a while?"

He frowned, probably thinking we were going hunting—which was half true. But what could he say? He knew what we were. I'd tell him everything I'd discovered tonight later.

"All right," he answered.

So Wade stayed behind while Philip and I ran down the front steps and headed two miles away from the house.

"Steal us a car," I said.

"You want me to?"

"Yeah, some old, heavy thing with great big tires and a cassette player."

My mood infectious, he glanced around and spotted a '71 Ranchero sporting a chipped paint job. "That one."

Moments later, as we roared down the street, I plugged in a Blue Oyster Cult tape and watched him smile.

"How come we need to go hunting right now?" he asked.

"Because there's something . . . I want to show you."

Maybe we'd all be okay.

AVAILABLE NOW

HUNTING MEMORIES

The second book in the "exhilarating"* new vampire series from

Barb Hendee

Eleisha Clevon has begun a correspondence with fellow vampire Rose de Spenser. Both reluctant predators, they venture outside only when the hunger becomes unbearable, trying not to draw attention to themselves— and feel guilty when ending human lives.

But Eleisha has learned a way to draw blood from her victims without killing them. She wants to share this knowledge with like-minded vampires and create a haven where they can exist together—and forge a united front against Julian Ashton, a vampire who has been hunting down and destroying his own kind...

*SF Revu

Available wherever books are sold or at penguin.com

AVAILABLE NOW IN HARDCOVER

IN SHADE AND SHADOW

A Novel of the Noble Dead

by Barb & J.C. Hendee

After her adventures with Magiere and Leesil, Wynn Hygeorht has returned to the Guild of Sagecraft, bearing texts supposedly penned by vampires from the time of the Forgotten History and the Great War. Seized by the Guild's scholars and sent out for copying without Wynn's consent, several pages disappear—and the two sages charged with conveying these pages are murdered. Suspicious of the Guild, separated from the only friends she fully trusts, and convinced the Noble Dead are responsible for the killings, Wynn embarks on a quest to uncover the secrets of the texts.

Available wherever books are sold or at penguin.com

National Bestselling Authors
Barb & J.C. Hendee
The Noble Dead Saga

DHAMPIR

A con artist who poses as a vampire slayer learns that she is, in fact, a true slayer—and half-vampire herself. And her actions have attracted the unwanted attention of a trio of powerful vampires seeking her blood.

SISTER OF THE DEAD

Magiere the dhampir and her partner, the half-elf Leesil, are on a journey to uncover the secrets of their mysterious pasts. But first their expertise as vampire hunters is required on behalf of a small village being tormented by a creature of unlimited and unimaginable power.

THIEF OF LIVES

Magiere and Leesil are called out of their self-imposed retirement when vampires besiege the capital city of Bela.

Available wherever books are sold or at penguin.com

Also Available from
National Bestselling Authors
Barb & J.C. Hendee
The Noble Dead Saga

TRAITOR TO THE BLOOD

The saga continues as Magiere and Leesil
embark on a quest to uncover the secrets of their
mysterious origins—and for those responsible for
orchestrating the events that brought them together.

REBEL FAY

Magiere and Leesil were brought together by the
Fay to forge an alliance that might have the power
to stand against the forces of dark magics. But as
they uncover the truth, they discover just how
close the enemy has always been...

CHILD OF A DEAD GOD

For years, Magiere and Leesil have sought a long
forgotten artifact, though its purpose has been
shrouded in mystery. All Magiere knows is that she
must keep the orb from falling into the hands of a
murdering Noble Dead, her half-brother Welstiel.
And now, dreams of a castle locked in ice lead her
south, on a journey that has become nothing less
than an obsession.

**Available wherever books are sold or at
penguin.com**

THE ULTIMATE IN
SCIENCE FICTION AND FANTASY!

From magical tales of distant worlds to stories of
technological advances beyond the grasp of man, Penguin has
everything you need to stretch your imagination to its limits.

penguin.com

ACE
Get the latest information on favorites like
William Gibson, T.A. Barron, Brian Jacques,
Ursula K. Le Guin, Sharon Shinn, Charlaine Harris,
Patricia Briggs, and Marjorie M. Liu,
as well as updates on the best new authors.

ROC
Escape with Jim Butcher, Harry Turtledove, Anne Bishop,
S.M. Stirling, Simon R. Green, E.E. Knight, Kat Richardson,
Rachel Caine, and many others—plus news on the
latest and hottest in science fiction and fantasy.

DAW
Patrick Rothfuss, Mercedes Lackey, Kristen Britain,
Tanya Huff, Tad Williams, C.J. Cherryh, and many more—
DAW has something to satisfy the cravings of any
science fiction and fantasy lover.
Also visit dawbooks.com.

*Get the best of science fiction and fantasy
at your fingertips!*